07.08
BG

A TIME FOR VIOLENCE

An accused murderer, Bart Wagner has come to Texas to hunt down the only witness who can prove he killed in self-defense. He soon discovers that his witness is the occupant of a freshly-dug grave. He also discovers the witness' widow—the beautiful, iron-willed Catherine who seems mysteriously involved with the men who killed her seventy-five-year-old husband.

Bart agrees to help the determined Catherine defend her ranch against Xenophon Jones and his gang. When the outlaws try to drive her off her property by setting fire to her buildings, Bart finds himself involved in something more than clearing his own name . . .

Noel M(iller) Loomis was born in Oklahoma Territory and retained all his life a strong Southwestern heritage. One of his grandfathers made the California Gold Rush in 1849 and another was in the Cherokee Strip land rush in 1893. He grew up in Oklahoma, New Mexico, Texas, and Wyoming, areas in the American West that would figure prominently in his Western stories. His parents operated an itinerant printing and newspaper business and, as a boy, he learned to set lead type by hand. Although he began contributing Western fiction to the magazine market in the late 1930s, it was with publication of his first novel, *Rim of the Caprock* (1952), that he truly came to prominence. This novel is set in Texas, the location of two other notable literary endeavors, *Tejas Country* (1953) and *The Twilighters* (1955). These novels evoke the harsh, even savage violence of an untamed land in a graphic manner that eschewed sharply the romanticism of fiction so characteristic of an earlier period in the literary history of the Western story. In these novels, as well as *West to the Sun* (1955), *Short Cut to Red River* (1958), and *Cheyenne War Cry* (1959), Loomis very precisely sets forth a precise time and place in frontier history and proceeds to capture the ambiance of the period in descriptions, in attitudes responding to the events of the day, and laconic dialogue that etches vivid characters set against these historical backgrounds. In the second edition of *Twentieth Century Western Writers* (1991), the observation is made that Loomis's work was "far ahead of its time. No other Western writer of the 1950s depicts so honestly the nature of the land and its people, and renders them so alive. Avoiding comment, he concentrates on the atmosphere of time and place. One experiences with him the smell of Indian camps and frontier trading posts, the breathtaking vision of the Caprock, the sudden terror of a surprise attack. Loomis, in his swift character sketches, his striking descriptions, his lithe effective style, brings that world to life before our eyes. In the field he chose, he has yet to be surpassed."

A TIME FOR VIOLENCE

Noel M. Loomis

GUNSMOKE

First published in the UK by Collins

This hardback edition 2007
by BBC Audiobooks Ltd
by arrangement with
Golden West Literary Agency

ISBN 13: 978 1 405 68116 2

British Library Cataloguing in Publication Data available.

Printed and bound in Great Britain by
Antony Rowe Ltd., Chippenham, Wiltshire

To CONNIE KAY NOEL LILJENBERG

for the thoughtful look in her eyes
at the age of seven days

PREFACE

TO THOSE familiar with Texas Panhandle history, it will be evident that J. Evetts Haley's *Charles Goodnight* offers much of the material for the substance of this novel; Haley's book is already a classic.

I myself was raised in the Panhandle and on the Llano Estacado, Goodnight's stomping ground. I had my first experience with higher learning at old Clarendon College, a good Methodist school, not far from the ranch where Goodnight died, and where I learned to play a fair hand of stud poker. On a memorable fall day, too, I was chased off the football field at Canyon, Texas (a few miles from where Goodnight had gone into the Palo Duro Canyon forty-five years earlier), by loyal students of West Texas State Normal College who said, with some justification, that I was making too much noise for a freshman. And now that old Clarendon College has been burned (a disaster in which I was not involved), and the records, presumably, not immediately accessible, perhaps I am safe in claiming a minute portion of credit for an assist against the magnificent efforts of Dutch Studer & Co. in a 20–20 tie that Thanksgiving Day.

Charles Goodnight died eight years after I was enrolled at Clarendon, so the telling of this story is like a walk on familiar ground. This is not a story of Charles Goodnight, although it is based on a true incident in the establishment of legal processes in Texas' Thirty-fifth Judicial District in the Panhandle. Goodnight engineered that coup, even to the chuckwagons; a shoot-out, however, did not take place, for the outlaws backed down.

Temple Houston was well known in Texas, and later went to Woodward, Oklahoma, where, a few years ago, died a man named Temple Houston Chapman, son of Amos, who was with Billy Dixon at Buffalo Wallow.

Judge Frank Willis, whose son, Newton P. Willis, used to come into my father's newspaper office, and whose grandson, with whom I went to school in Canadian, Texas, now practices law in New York City, will be recognized by old-timers. Frank Willis was a picturesque and powerful factor in the final civilization of the Panhandle, but his story is yet to be told.

"Cap" Arrington, as I knew him, was a slight man with a very tall hat and a very white beard, who used to spin tales with my father while I fed a 10 x 15 job press just across the counter. He had been, in 1879, the first Ranger and the first law in the Panhandle. It was a preposterously huge territory for one man, but even the most brazen outlaw did not welcome the news that Arrington was on his trail.

The principal characters in this book, of course, are fictional, although many are the documented names of men who carried on the trade of outlawry almost in the manner of a business.

For further facts, I recommend *Charles Goodnight*.

Noel M. Loomis

Descanso, California,
The Land of Tranquillity

CHAPTER I

IT WAS June, and below the Caprock there was still a running stream. The "silver waters of the Quintafue were bubbling along over a bed of golden sand," as they had done in 1841 when the ill-fated Texan-Santa Fé Pioneers had stumbled into the valley from the east. Even then it had been a place of violence, for five of those men had been massacred by the deadly Kiowas.

Before that time, and after it, the *comancheros* had come from New Mexico to cross the arid plains with impunity, to trade bread and Taos lightning and Dupont and Galena perhaps less violently to the Kiowas and to the several tribes of Comanches for stolen horses and cows and sometimes white captives—women and children—whom they took back for the ransom money, or sold to another tribe if the trader could make more money that way.

A few years later, in 1874, had come the Walk-a-Heaps—the infantry of Miles and Hazen, and the cavalry under Mackenzie, and the Buffalo Soldiers—the Negro cavalry of Grierson and Davidson. For a few months, the Panhandle had been criss-crossed with Army trails. The plains and the breaks had resounded with gunfire from Captain Baldwin's fantastic Wagon Train Charge, Billy Dixon's incredible stand at Buffalo Wallow, Mackenzie's slaughter of two thousand Cheyenne horses to break the back of Indian resistance, and the heroic but tragic fight of the Quahadis in Blanco Canyon and their subsequent retreat northwest in the face of a paralyzing sleet storm. For those few months, fire had blazed and powder smoke had spread its acrid cloud of violence upon the High Plains. Kiowas, Comanches, Cheyennes, and Arapahoes had run before an avenging army, had turned at times to fight, but in the end had surrendered to keep from starving.

The buffalo hunters had swarmed over the land like locusts, taking hides and tongues, leaving tens of thousands of maggot-infested carcasses. After them had come the bone-pickers, and their work was not quite finished by 1883, and perhaps the bones of the dead Pioneers who had suffered from the violence of a re-public's growing pains were still to be tossed into a wagon and hauled East to be ground up for fertilizer.

All through history it had been a land of violence, and that violence, Bart Wagner knew, as he sat his black horse above the Quintafue, was not over. Perhaps, indeed, it was only the begin-ning, for now, six years after the first Texan had settled on the High Plains, the nearest court still was two hundred miles away, and outlawry, they had told him at Fort Union, was practically a business in the Panhandle. Many of the outlaws were well known on sight, and made no effort to hide, for, with the court so far away, there were no warrants out for them, and therefore they feared nothing but being caught in the act.

That situation would have to end, Bart foresaw, and he moved uneasily in his saddle. Once again there would be violence; once again the prairies would reverberate with the thunder of gunfire, and the acrid clouds of powder smoke would roll over the grama grass, and men would fall and men would die. And perhaps that time was not far off.

Bart, motionless for a moment, studied the valley of the Quin-tafue below him, noting an unearthly quality that he could not immediately place. But he shook his head. Probably it was weariness and hunger and the pain of the bullet that was heavy in his left arm. And he reminded himself that, as of that moment, the outlaws were pretty well in control of the land, and if he should run into them down there along the stream, he could not expect them to have much sympathy for an ex-lawman. At least it had been so in Tascosa, and the bullet in his aching arm was a grim reminder of it and of the old man who had helped to put it there. But first there was the need to find a place where he could rest up for a few days. Then he would move on—find the old man, and see if he could get back to El Paso alive.

He turned awkwardly in the saddle, hampered by his left arm, which was slung in a bandanna, and scanned the Llano behind him. It did not seem reasonable that the outlaws of Tascosa would follow him, but the Caprock was a bad place to be cornered. Then he scanned the valley again and tried to figure out what it was that gave that eerie atmosphere. Far below, three men were fogging it up the creek, but, as he watched, they turned off and rode at a walk toward a sod ranch house. He watched for a moment as they rode to the back door, and a woman opened the door. It was too far for him to hear voices, but he saw nothing unusual in their actions. In a swift glance he followed the creek north to where it turned east beyond a hill. A little farther north, the Prairie Dog Town Fork of Red River flowed east; somewhere out of sight, it would receive the Quintafue.

Somewhere to the east, perhaps beyond the first low hills of the breaks, was Charles Goodnight's famous JA ranch and his headquarters; Bart expected to end up there before long.

He looked back to the ranch house. The three men had not alighted, and he wondered if the woman had not asked them to. She might even have held a rifle in her arms without its being visible to him, but he dismissed the idea. The Panhandle was wild, but not to the point that a woman met visitors at the door with a rifle.

His empty stomach growled, and he kicked the black toward the path that led down the precipitous canyon wall. He eased his left arm in the sling, and held it in against his side to avoid hitting it on the rocks that occasionally jutted into the path. His arm had come to ache considerable since he had left Tascosa, and he gritted his teeth as he dodged an overhanging cedar-tree root.

Both he and the black needed rest and food. The black had had only a few hours of poor grazing since they had left Fort Union, two hundred and fifty miles west—and nothing since they had left Tascosa, fifty miles northwest.

He rode easily and depended on the black to find its own footing, while he scanned the bottom of the canyon. He saw the three men wheel their horses and ride back to the corral, and he guessed the meeting had been peaceful enough. He scanned the valley again: steers grazing in the beargrass, a dog sleeping in the shade of a cottonwood tree near the ranch house. He was almost at the bottom, and saw that black-and-white-barred chickens were scattered around the corral. Then the three men, with wild yells, rode at a hard gallop toward the creek, and Bart frowned. He glanced back again at the ranch house and saw smoke coming up from a shed. The woman was running clumsily in her long dress, with a heavy bucket in one hand. She scooped up a bucketful of water from the creek, and ran to the shed.

The black stepped out on level ground; it smelled the water and wanted to go, but Bart turned it toward the burning shed and dug his heels into its flanks. The black jumped over a green-and-purple tumbleweed and lined out toward the shed. Smoke was rolling up in clouds, and red flames burst out from the roof.

He slid the black to a stop, leaped off at the same time, and ran to meet the woman. She was struggling with the heavy wooden pail, forced to use both hands to carry it, and trying at the same time to avoid tripping on her dress, which brushed the hard-packed earth. She must not have anticipated the fire, for she had not taken time to put on her sunbonnet. She was pretty, and wore two glossy black braids, one at each shoulder, but her brown eyes were brimming with tears of helplessness and futility.

She let him take the water without a word, and ran at once back toward the house—probably to get another pail.

He ran to the fire. The roof of the shed was burning fiercely, and he did not waste the water on the flames. A dozen sacks of shelled corn were stacked on the rough flooring, and the top sacks were beginning to smoke from the heat above. He went as close as he could and drenched the sacks. He could not go in long enough to move even one sack, for the dry cottonwood rafters burned hot. By that time the brush on top had burned out, and the fire had settled down to blue, almost smokeless flames as the bigger pieces of cottonwood, dry and cracked, burned with startling rapidity.

He dropped the bucket and seized a fence post from a pile at the other end of the shed. He went as close as he could to the fire, and used the post to knock away the brush so the fire would not carry. He ran back to the creek for more water, and she met him there with a brass kettle. They drenched the sacks of corn. Then he got the post and began to knock the blazing roof-skeleton apart. His bad arm was painful and somewhat clumsy, but, by the time the fire reached the place where he had knocked away the brush, he had it under control. He stopped, breathing hard, and looked at her, dusty and panting. Soot had settled under her eyes, and she looked forlorn but somehow still proud.

"Was it set on purpose?" he asked.

She nodded.

He pulled off the top sack of corn. The sacking was scorched, and fell apart as he lifted it. He felt a shattering blow of pain in his left arm, and dropped it suddenly.

He glanced down at his hand, where blood dropped from the ends of his fingers. The woman saw the blood, and her eyes widened. "Leave your rig under the cottonwood in front of the house," she said, looking up. "You need some attention."

He nodded as he pulled the bandanna sling back into place. He mounted the black slowly, almost too tired to get into the saddle, and rode around the house while she walked to the back door with the empty pail and the brass kettle.

It came to him, on that slow walk around the house, that the unearthly quality of the scene was created by the fact that nothing moved in that ranch yard. The dog did not raise its head when he approached. The chickens, scattered over the yard, did not walk or scratch, but lay on their sides, motionless. He turned to look back. In spite of the excitement of the fire, a horse lay on its side in the pole corral, also motionless. A medium-size wagon stood near the corral—a Conestoga-type wagon such as a family might have used to come cross-country.

His eyes narrowed as he took in the entire scene. He was not old, but it was difficult to tell his age. His skin was weathered like a saddle skirt, and he had two straight, vertical marks at each side of his mouth, and a fine web of lines at the corner of each eye— the kind of face that had looked into many blazing suns, into one man's share of bone-chilling blue northers, into countless days of searing hot winds; across the square end of his chin was a short, bristly strip of black whiskers. And as he turned back to the front, he realized also that nobody was engaged in any sort of ranch work: the woman was the only person he had seen.

The ranch house, he noticed, had been well constructed, and had not rain-washed much but looked to have been plastered when it needed it. He rode around to the front and noted the Quarter Circle JB Connected, burned into the rough-hewed cottonwood planks with a running iron, then observed a small black ribbon fastened under the brand with a square nail, and noted that the latch string was not out. He pulled up his horse. There was real glass in the windows—which jibed with the presence of the woman. That had puzzled him at first, because there were not many women in the Panhandle except on the big ranches, but now he was satisfied—because the cost of freighting glass down from Dodge was so high that no rancher would do it unless a woman insisted.

He sat for a moment, getting his bearings. A hundred and fifty feet east of him was the big cottonwood, with an enormous spread of branches. The dog he had seen from above was under the tree —and now that he looked more closely, he realized that the dog was dead.

He made out a mound of earth to one side of the cottonwood, in a small clump of willow saplings. A few wilted—but not dried-up—beargrass blooms were on top of the mound, and he knew the grave was only a few hours old.

He heard the dry scrape of the opening door, and turned to look into a rifle muzzle. He sat still and quiet, so as not to alarm her, for she was undoubtedly wrought up. He watched the rifle—an old buffalo Sharps, weighing maybe sixteen pounds—and already it had sagged until it was in no position to be fired.

"I told you to leave your rig under the tree," she said.

He frowned, glanced at the grave and back at the rifle, and finally at the woman in the open doorway. He said, "I know Mobeetie is outlaw country—but isn't that old Sharps pretty heavy for you?"

She answered impersonally. "Never mind how heavy it is. I can hold it dead center, and the slug plows a furrow deep enough to plant potatoes."

He tried a brief smile. "Right glad to hear you say that, ma'am. I come from a potato country myself."

She ignored him. "A body never knows who is friend and who is enemy."

He said, "I just helped you, ma'am."

"That's why I haven't pulled the trigger—yet," she said.

"Your husband gone for supplies?" he asked.

She indicated the grave with her head. "I buried him yesterday," she said.

He looked at the shovel still standing against the cottonwood tree. "Man-killin' job, ma'am, in this hard ground."

She took a deep breath that did not hurt her appearance at all, and he knew she probably was still exhausted from the digging. He turned to the headboard under the wilted beargrass blooms and asked, "Mind if I look?"

"Help yourself." But she kept the rifle pointed at him.

He rode over to the cottonwood and got down easily, keeping his slung arm clear. He dropped the black's reins on the ground and walked stiffly to the grave. The clods on top had already dried out to the color of the gray-brown earth.

He lifted a limp stalk of beargrass blooms from the board and read the inscription burned in with a bridle-bit ring: "Ben Lewis, murdered June 18, 1883. RIP." A brand, the same as that on the front door, was burned under the inscription. He noted the word "murdered" and its implication of unchangeable accusation. He replaced the wilted stalk and walked slowly back toward the house. "I'm sorry, ma'am."

A sudden thought seemed to come to her. "Are you a Texas Ranger?" she asked hopefully.

He said regretfully, "No, ma'am. It's too late anyway for a Ranger to help you, isn't it?"

She said, "He could keep them from coming back."

He nodded slightly. That explained a lot of things: the dead dog; the horse in the corral, still unmoving; the chickens that did not scratch and did not cluck. He looked back at the woman and said, "It might be I could give you a lift, ma'am."

"Which side are you on?" she demanded.

He laughed easily, trying to reassure her. "I'm not on any side, as far as I know. Right now I'm plumb by myself like a skunk in the middle of a Fourth of July barbecue." He had hoped for a smile, but it didn't come. "I stopped by to see if I could maybe wangle a meal," he said, and refrained from reminding her that he had helped her put out the fire on the shed.

She stared at his slung arm. "Since you're on the scout, you're probably an outlaw, all right—but you better come in. You helped me, and I can feed you. And maybe your arm needs some attention."

"Thank you, ma'am."

"You can drop off your saddle and let the black graze if it won't go too far."

"He's a home-lovin' critter, ma'am." He went to the horse, flipped loose the cinch strap, took the heavy saddle with all its trappings by the horn with his right hand, and lifted it off in one powerful sweep. The black shied a little and moved its hind quarters away but kept its head in place. He turned the saddle and dropped it on its side, rifle boot up; he did not touch the

.44-40 Winchester in the boot. He pulled the blanket from inside the saddle and snapped it free of twigs it had picked up from the ground, then laid it across the saddle. He went to the black, unfastened the throat latch, pulled the headband over the black's ears with his one good arm, and heard the bit strike the horse's teeth. He threw the bridle over his left shoulder and slapped the black on the rump. "Stay close now." He dropped the bridle across the saddle and went back to the house, leaving his rifle in the boot.

"You're welcome to eat," she said, acknowledging his needs, "but I'll have no foolishness." She looked pointedly at the .44's in his holsters. "If you make any move toward your guns, I'll shoot without warning."

Amused, he said, "That old Sharps won't swing very fast, will it?"

She ignored the question. "If you're one of Xenophon Jones's outfit," she said, "I know you won't shoot me. They just want to run me off."

"Why?"

She seemed to hesitate a moment, and her answer, when it came, was evasive. "He needs this ranch to hold his stolen stock."

He thought there were some complications to the idea of running a person off his place and then taking it over, but he did not mention them. "I've heard a little about Xenophon Jones," he observed.

She said with obvious feeling, "Because the courts are so far away, he carries on his outlawry like a business. Everybody knows him and knows what he is, but he doesn't hide. He comes and goes as he pleases, even in the towns."

"And the law—"

"What law?" she demanded. "Captain Arrington is the only lawman in the Panhandle."

"Some counties are organized," he said. "They must have sheriffs."

"What good is a sheriff? He'd spend all his time taking prisoners to Henrietta."

Bart said after a pause, "I'm not a Jones man or any other outlaw. I was a lawman in El Paso and killed four brothers in a gun-fight. I got a clean bill from the coroner, but some don't recognize that, and there is still talk against me, and the only way I can clear it up is to find an old man who sided the brothers. I heard he is in the Panhandle, and I came to look for him."

"What was his name?" she asked.

"Nobody seemed to know—and he skipped out. I think he had different names."

"You aren't telling me any of them," she observed.

"I'm not telling anybody until I get the lay of the land. I don't want to scare him out."

"What if you find him?"

He said grimly, "I'll make him confess."

She seemed to consider his words for a moment. "All right." She moved aside for him to enter. "You can wash in the kitchen."

He went to the bench. "There's no water in the bucket, ma'am. Like for me to fill it?"

She was still holding the big rifle. "There's a barrel out the back door."

He went out, and noted the barrel was almost empty; then she had not left the house since she had buried her husband. He dipped the bucket in, got it two-thirds full, and went back into the kitchen. He took a tin dipper from a nail and had a long drink. The water was about the temperature of secondhand dish-water, but it was wet. "Mighty dry up on the Yarner," he said, filling the dipper again.

"It's always dry up there." At last she set the rifle in a corner near the hot-water reservoir, and put more wood in the stove.

He emptied the dipper and hung it back on the nail. He poured water into the tin washbasin, dipped a fresh bar of square-cut yellow soap into it, and turned it over and over in his one hand, rounding off the corners and working up a lather; then, still one-handed, he washed his face and rinsed off the soap and reached for the towel. It felt good to be rid of the trail dust for a change.

She was dropping a second piece of cedar into the stove. She put the lid in place and pulled the brass kettle to the front of the stove. "You get along all right with one hand," she noted without turning.

He grinned. "I do better two-handed."

She did not look at him. "Is it a bullet?" she asked.

He nodded. "Small caliber. Probably a .31. It was a hideout gun."

She glanced at him at last. "He must have been stingy with his powder, or it would have gone on through."

He was drying with his one hand. "It went through the edge of a door first."

"I hope there wasn't any paint on the door," she said, picking up a big fork. "That is poison in a bullet hole."

He looked at her again. She was not the greenhorn he had taken her for. He noted how her hair at the back of the neck, escaping from the braids, grew in curls the size of a half-dollar and lay tight against her skin, which had been turned by the sun to a sort of golden brown, especially in protected spots like the hollow of her neck. Maybe the fact that she was young and very pretty had fooled him.

"You been out here long?" he asked, hanging the towel on its wooden peg.

"Four years," she said, and then, seeming to read his mind, added: "My folks have been moving west for six generations. The women don't know what it's like to live civilized. We've always been on the frontier."

"Why didn't you marry a city man?"

"City men don't come to places where my family has always lived," she said, fishing a large chunk of meat out of an iron stew-kettle and putting it on a thick white plate. She reached up to the warmer and got a loaf of homemade bread, cut off three thick slices. "Sit down," she said, "and get started." She moved toward the rough table. "I can hear your stomach growling from over here."

He smiled softly. It was the first sign of friendliness about her. He picked up the washpan with its dirty water, stepped outside about ten feet, and flung the water away. He turned back quickly, feeling her eyes on him, and saw her face through the crack along the hinged edge of the door. He took his time about going in.

He heard the heavy crockery dish thump on the homemade table, and went inside. He looked for the rifle, and saw it had been moved from its previous corner to a spot near the door, where she could get it without reaching over the little pile of wood at the end of the stove.

"It's antelope," she said, indicating the meat. "Quick-killed."

He nodded, his mouth full of bread. She had cut the meat into pieces he could handle with a fork. He ate three or four mouthfuls before he sat back to draw a breath. Food had never tasted that good.

"Mighty fine light-bread," he said.

"Nobody ever told me that before," she said slowly. Her pleasure was almost pathetic.

She added quickly, "You were hungry."

He paused between bites, a piece of meat on his fork. "There's nothing but grass between here and Fort Union," he said, and added thoughtfully, "At that, there's some bare spots."

"Didn't you have something in your warbag—parched corn or something?"

"Didn't have a warbag," he said, his mouth full, and added, "If you hadn't been so busy lugging that buffalo cannon around, you'd have noticed a thing like that."

Her eyes darted to the corner of the room, and he bent over his food. "It's by the kitchen door," he said, inclining his head toward the rifle.

She stared at him for a moment, but he could not read her thoughts. She seemed about to say something vehement, but then her long-pent-up feelings broke through her reserve, and she suddenly put both hands to her face and began to sob.

He was taken aback. He thought her crying would stop in a moment, but to his dismay the sobs grew louder and most anguished, and tears dropped from her fingers to the floor. He got up hurriedly, not bothering to push his chair back but dismounting from it as he would have done from a horse. He went around the table and patted her clumsily on the shoulder. "It's all right now, ma'am," he said.

Unexpectedly he found her weeping on his chest, and put his good hand on her shoulder. He liked the solid feel of her. "Tell me about it," he said.

Her tears lessened gradually, but his shirt and his buckskin vest showed damp spots. She backed away, wiping her face on the corner of her apron. Her eyes were wet with tears.

He went to the stove and poured two big cups of coffee and took them to the table. "It will do you good to talk," he said reassuringly.

She sat down, then looked up as he hesitated. "There's sugar on the shelf," she said.

He carried the crock to the table. "Tell me the whole story," he said. "Maybe I can help."

"The whole story," she repeated, staring at the table. "Do you know what it's like to need to talk?" She looked up without seeing him. "For four years," she said slowly, "I needed to talk—not all the time—just once in a while. Once a month—once a year, even." She paused. "For four years I did not get to talk to a woman."

"Mrs. Goodnight was over on the JA, wasn't she?"

She looked at the table. "Ben didn't like women for company on the ranch."

After a moment he suggested, "Your husband was too busy to listen, maybe."

She stared at the front door. "Ben was a good husband. But he was older than me, and he could never see the need for things I was hungry for."

Bart realized he did not need to ask her any more questions.

"We moved up here from Denison in 1879," she said, calling up the thoughts in her memory. "It was a new country, and Ben said the opportunities were wonderful. But with no courts, no judge, no law, the outlaws got a hold and spread out all over the Panhandle. Mr. Goodnight said not long ago there were four to six hundred outlaws."

"Billy the Kid is gone," he said.

"He was only one. French John is still up along the Canadian, and some say he has three hundred men. Pierre Martín and Xenophon Jones and Archeveque and Goodanuff and a dozen smaller gangs are all over the plains."

"With headquarters at Tascosa?" he asked.

She nodded slowly, looking at him. "That's what the LJ thinks. Tom Harding says if the ranchers would organize a posse and clean out Tascosa, the Panhandle would be a different place."

He blew on his coffee and tasted it, but it was still too hot.

"Two months ago," she went on, "Xenophon Jones and half a dozen men came onto our place looking for a spring where they could camp."

"You own this land?" he asked.

"Ben—my husband—bought it from the state."

"Good."

"Ben had put up a fence around the spring because there is a bog just below it, but Jones cut the wire and took his horses right into the spring. He and Ben fussed about it, but Jones did whatever he wanted to do."

"Then your husband finally got tired of it, and went up there to run them off, but they killed him," Bart suggested.

She stared at him for a moment, and Bart had a feeling he had guessed only partly right, and he waited to hear the rest. Then her eyes filled again with tears. "They brought his body to the back door. And they said I had a week to get off the land."

"You didn't go," he observed, still feeling that this was not all of the story of the killing.

She shook her head. "I don't aim to," she said firmly. "I helped to build up this land. It doesn't look like much that we've done, but it's been a lot of work. I followed Ben's plow and cut up the sod to make this house. I helped load it on the wagon, and I helped build up the walls. I cut poles for the corrals, and I dug the postholes." She paused.

"That's all hard work, ma'am—mostly man's work," he said, looking at his coffee.

"It *was* hard, but I didn't mind. I liked working on the land

—building my own house. The only thing I mind is leaving it. It's my land," she said with an unexpected flash of spirit. "I helped build it—and I'm going to stay."

"You have no children?"

"None."

"Then I take it you've been happy here."

"No!" she said with astonishing vehemence. "I was never happy here. I hated it for a long time. I hated it until yesterday afternoon —when I buried Ben."

"That changed your mind?" he asked softly.

"That's exactly what happened. When I got through shoveling in the dirt, I realized that I had left my family of my own free will. At the time I left, I might have thought Ben had enough money to make up for the difference between him and me." She looked at him challengingly, but he did not comment. "But whatever I thought, and however I felt after we came out here, I did my best. I was the best wife I knew how to be."

"Was Ben satisfied?"

She stared at the table. "He never said—yes or no."

"But now you're too proud to go back to your folks, and you've found out also that the land itself means something to you."

She took a deep breath. "A lot more than I thought before." She was silent for a moment. "I'm only sorry I had to wait till Ben died to see it."

He tried to reassure her. "It was just a question of time." He finished his coffee. "What happened to the horse out there in the corral?"

"That was Ben's riding horse. They shot it," she said starkly.

"The dog too?"

"Yes."

He frowned. "And the chickens too?"

She stared at him, and for the first time he saw hardness in her eyes. "They galloped their horses back and forth, yelling and shooting the chickens' heads off, and every time one hit a chicken somewhere else except the head, he had to buy the rest a drink." She asked abruptly, "Do you want a job, mister?"

The suddenness of it caught him off guard. "I hadn't thought about that. I figured I might stay around a day or two—"

"I can't live inside the house forever," she said. "But the minute I go outside to take care of the work, they will burn the place while I'm gone. They've already burned half the shed." Bart realized they could still smell the smoldering wood. He looked at her, wondering. Then he rubbed the whiskers on his chin. "I wasn't—"

"I won't be able to pay you much until the fall roundup," she said hurriedly. "I don't think Ben has much in the bank—though he never showed me the book. I've got a few dollars I made out of eggs, and I can keep you in tobacco until fall—and I'll pay— I'll pay my debts."

"You've got stock?" he asked, thinking of the work that might have to be done.

"Eighteen hundred head," she said promptly, "with two hundred and ten three-year-olds that will bring prime prices in the fall."

He thought about it. "I'd like to help you out, but I've got to find the old man I'm looking for. When I find him, I've got to go back to clear myself in El Paso. If I don't find him, I'll have to keep moving."

She stared at him. "Then you won't—" Her voice faltered, and it touched him, because he knew that she had thought for a moment that her problems were solved.

"I'll make you a deal." He got up wearily. All through that conversation, his arm had throbbed painfully, and was beginning to reach an intensity he would find hard to bear. She had promised help from the beginning, but had taken time to feed him and tell her story, and he had waited. Now he was ready to bargain to get her help, for he could not stand the pain much longer. "I've got to get the lead out of my arm. You do that for me, and I'll stay around a couple of weeks or so and give you a hand."

He saw her thinking it over, and knew she was wondering what would happen at the end of the two weeks, but he did not offer any further suggestion.

She asked finally, plaintively, "Are you sure you—"

"Unless I can prove those brothers were after me, and that I had to defend myself, I'm technically an outlaw in the state of New Mexico, and whenever I stop, somebody will come along and feel free to take a shot at me, because they figure the law is not going to be too severe on a man who kills an outlaw."

She frowned in concern. "But you—"

"I tried it once, and it turned out very bad. As long as there is a doubt in the minds of men, violence breeds violence, and it never dies."

She studied him, and then said earnestly, "It seems to me that on the frontier there is a time for violence, and that, when it comes, somebody has to have a strong hand. And I do not see why that should lead to more violence."

But he shook his head. "That's just the way it is."

"And that's why you had to leave New Mexico?"

"Without even a saddlebag," he said. "And that's why I've ridden straight through from Fort Union, stopping just long enough to graze the black."

"It must be a good horse," she said after a pause.

"The best."

She looked straight at him. "And the rider?"

"Considering what he's been through," he said, "he's pretty lucky."

She stood up. "I'm sure," she said confidently, "it's more than luck."

CHAPTER II

SHE PUT another kettle on the stove, and he filled it with water and went outside to get some wood. Coming back in, he neglected to duck, and knocked his hat off against the top door frame.

"I told Ben he made those doors too short," she remarked, reaching up to open the damper.

"It's all right if you remember," he said, picking up his hat. "Was Ben—a little man?"

"No, he was medium." She glanced at Bart. "Half a head shorter than you, though."

He let the wood roll off his good arm. "He probably never figured I'd be walking through them," he said lightly.

She answered soberly. "Nobody ever knew what Ben figured."

He let that pass. "You reckon I could wear some of his work clothes?"

She looked at him, the full length of him. She stared curiously, for the first time, at his white, beaded buckskin vest and his striped California pants. "You left *somewhere* in a hurry. That's plain to be seen."

He glanced down at his incongruous clothes. "After I fought the Yagers, I figured I had played my luck pretty far, so I turned in my badge and went to Socorro and opened up a monte game," he said.

"And you fleeced a poor greenhorn out of his money, and—"

"No, ma'am," he said patiently. "I was trying to make an honest living, but word got around that Bart Wagner was in town—and it happened just as I had always known it would: the one brother I hadn't killed in El Paso showed up, and I had to finish the job."

He thought he saw a touch of fear in her eyes as she said slowly, "So you're Bart Wagner."

He smiled. "I hope it doesn't give *you* notions, ma'am."

She stared at him for a moment, and then shook her head and turned away. "I'll get you the clothes," she said slowly. "Overhauls and shirt. Ben didn't wear a vest."

"Suits me fine."

She brought out some clean clothes. "You *can* do ranch work, can't you?"

"I worked for the Shoebar and the Matadors after I got out of the Fourth Cavalry," he said.

She motioned. "You can change clothes behind that curtain. Leave your shirt off and I'll take a look at your arm."

Bart went behind the curtain into a sort of pantry. He saw that the "overhauls" were made out of denim, fastened together with copper rivets, but had no bib—"levis," they called them some places. Clumsily and somewhat painfully he removed his clothes and put on the levis. They were all right for him in the waist, but six inches short at the bottom. He came out, and she looked at him as curiously and impersonally as she might have looked over a colt she was thinking about buying. "You don't show much fat," she said.

"Haven't had time to accumulate any lately," he told her.

She nodded absently. "Get your arm on the table."

She had laid out some old and well-worn copies of the St. Louis *Republican*, that seemed to have been read a good many times, and put a towel over them. He started to untie the bandanna from around his neck with one hand, but she pushed his hand away and did it herself—quickly and efficiently.

He gritted his teeth when he sat down and tried to lift his arm onto the table.

Watching his face, she nodded. "I *thought* it would be stiff."

"It wasn't hurting much," he said. "At first."

"Keep it up there now." She looked at the three kettles on the stove. "There should be plenty of hot water. I'll put some wet cloths on it, and you can rest a little. How high does it hurt?"

"Up to the shoulder."

She untied the white handkerchief he had around his arm just above the elbow. "It doesn't look very good," she said after a moment of examination. "It's black and blue all the way—but that's to be expected. When did it happen?"

"Yesterday afternoon."

"In Fort Union?" she demanded.

"No, ma'am. Tascosa."

She nodded briefly. "You'll be all right if we get it out."

He liked her air of competence and the gentle touch of her fingers as she felt for the bullet. It had lodged in the triceps muscle underneath, and he stiffened when she touched the spot where it rested.

"I'm sorry," she said. She watched the black blood oozing out. "It's all right. We won't have any trouble getting at it. May pain a little, though." She wrapped a hot cloth around it. "Let it loosen up—and you the same. It'll hurt less."

He agreed. "That hot water feels good."

She wrung out another cloth in the steaming kettle, and replaced the first one.

"I can see you know what you're doing, ma'am," he said, "but haven't you forgotten one thing?"

She looked at him and said cheerfully, "Oh, I'll use crochet hooks to get it out. I've done it before—when the Kiowas raided Holt's Corner. My father had two bullets and an arrowhead, and I got plenty of practice. My grandmother showed me how."

"How about your mother?"

Her face tightened. "She was killed and scalped in the same raid." She changed the cloth. "Grandmother's eyes weren't good enough to do it herself, but she told me how."

"It's a long time since you've had any practice," he noted.

"I've taken two bullets out of Ben."

He wondered why Ben had made a habit of getting in the way of hot lead, but he did not say so. Instead, he sighed. "I take it Ben was a teetotaler."

She looked up quickly. "I *did* forget." She went behind the curtain and came back with a quart bottle of Cedar Valley. "Will that be enough?"

The bottle was three-fourths full. "This will do nicely," he said, "and it will leave some for next time."

He took three big swallows out of the bottle, and set it on the table in front of him as she brought the crochet hooks. She took a lid off the stove and held the hooks in the open fire until they were red hot, then took them out, let them cool, and laid them on the towel. By that time the water in one kettle was boiling. Hastily he turned up the bottle and took two more swallows. He hoped it would work fast.

It did. In a couple of minutes he felt his blood begin to warm, and then his lips started to turn numb. He took another big drink.

"You say when you're ready," she told him.

He took another drink to speed it up. The whisky went through him in seconds. He looked at her. All he could see for a moment was a tight black curl, the size of a half-dollar, lying flat against golden-brown skin. Then her brown eyes came into his focus. "All right," he said.

"Lie on your stomach across the table, arms at your sides." She was very businesslike. "Get your arm over the towel. You can grip the edge of the table when it hurts. All ready?"

He wanted nothing as much as to go to sleep, but he said thickly, "Ready."

He felt the first hook jab through the damaged flesh. It did not hurt a great deal, for she was following the path of the bullet. He heard the hook scrape on the lead, and knew she had found it.

He was numb all over by that time, and for a moment he thought his arm was not attached to him. Then she pushed in the other hook and started working it around the bullet, and it was as if she had stuck the needle three inches into his heel.

He grunted hard, and his head jerked up, and he was grateful for the edge of the table beneath his fingers.

"Hurt much?" she asked, and pushed the second hook past the bullet on the opposite side.

His back was bowed up. "No, ma'am," he mumbled finally. "It feels good. But get it out—"

He felt a hard pull at his arm, and knew she had the bullet between the hooks and was pulling it backward, creating a giant, almost unbearable ache. Then it hit new flesh, and the blood rushed to his head, and he lay on the table, limp.

She did not falter. It felt as if there was an enormous corkscrew in his flesh, pulled by a span of mules, and he fainted.

When he came to, she was mopping up blood. The bullet, distorted some by going through the door, was on the table in front of him.

She said, "I doused the hole with whisky while you were out."

He mumbled, "I was drunk enough already," and lay quietly while she put on a few more hot cloths, then wrapped his arm gently but firmly in clean white strips of sheet.

Finally she was through, and he got off the table and sank gratefully into the homemade chair. He was wet with sweat, and almost too weak to sit up. "Thank you, ma'am," he said. The pain had almost killed the effect of the whisky, and he reached for the bottle. As he did so, he glanced at her across the table. Her face was white. Her hand went to her forehead and she swayed toward the table. She put out both hands blindly and half fell against the table, and Bart, forgetting his own weakness, jumped up to catch her.

She leaned heavily against him, and it took all his strength to hold her up.

"I'm sorry," she whispered. "It's always worse when it's over."

She straightened up slowly, shook her head a little, and moved away.

The weakness and fatigue of the last few days, the lack of sleep, and the somnolent effect of the whisky, finally caught up with Bart Wagner also, and he said, "I'm afraid I can't stay on my feet much longer." He stumbled, then lay down on the rough boards by the back door. "I'll watch this one," he said, and went to sleep.

He awoke to the smell of fresh coffee. He started up, and found himself lying on a buffalo robe, with a comfort over him. It was daylight; he got up and stretched.

Her voice came to him. "It's nearly noon," she said. "You've slept the clock around and then some."

His arm was sore, but otherwise he felt like a spring colt. He asked, "No trouble during the night?"

"No trouble." For a second he thought she sounded almost regretful. "I suppose they saw you ride up, and knew you stayed."

"That won't last long," he predicted. "Meantime, we'd better go ahead with the work. Have you seen my horse this morning?"

"He came up to the house, and I gave him a handful of oats."

He smiled. "The black is a grateful cuss. He'll never forget you."

They finished the light-bread and antelope meat, and he buckled on his gun belt and went out to catch up the horse. His arm was sore but not stiff; the girl had known what she was doing.

He rode up-canyon, following the creek to the spring. The cows looked good, but the fence was down all around the spring, and he found a heifer bogged down in the mud. He got a rope around her horns and worked her out, with the help of the black. He finished his ride around the pasture, and went back and checked supplies in the half of the shed that still had a roof. There were not many supplies on hand. Whatever Ben might have done, he had not believed in laying in supplies—or maybe he had not had the money. Yet he must have had *some* money, for his stock was shorthorn blood—not the best, certainly, but ahead of longhorns for beef purposes

Bart returned to the house, unsaddled the black and hobbled it.

She was at the door. "You didn't hobble him yesterday," she pointed out.

He chuckled. "Yesterday he was tired."

"How does it look in the upper pasture?" she asked over coffee.

"Grass is fine, but the fence needs rebuilding around the spring."

"Did you see any unbranded calves?"

He looked at her curiously. "Not one."

"There should have been. Ben said there were twenty-one he hadn't burned yet."

"They're gone now," he told her.

"Why would anybody take a calf?" she asked. "They aren't worth much on the market."

Bart said soberly, "A cow will follow her own calf."

She was puzzled for a moment. "You think—"

"The main fence was down in one spot. I put it back up to stop drifting. Cattle had been driven through there—or led, if you want to put it that way."

She looked harassed, but went ahead. "What else?"

"You need salt mighty bad. The cattle are chewing up the fence posts—and I didn't see any salt in the shed."

"Ben had some money in his pocket when he was killed." She looked at him steadily, sizing him up, then said, "Tomorrow you can take the wagon into Clarendon to get supplies."

He got a big drink of water from the bucket. "You will be alone again as soon as I pull out," he noted.

She looked up from the stove. "I'm not afraid to stay alone. I have the Sharps. Besides," she added softly, "there's somebody on my side now. You'll be back in three days, and they will know that, because you're taking the wagon."

He hung up the dipper. "You've been throwing that rifle around a lot in the last few hours. Ever shot a man?"

"No," she admitted, stirring something in a deep tin pan.

"I thought not." He glanced at the water bucket. "First thing I better do is rustle up some water from the creek. Your barrel outside is mighty near empty."

"There's a sled out by the corral," she told him.

"Another thing," he said curiously. "I know the places out here are far apart, but it seems strange there haven't been any neighbors in to see how you're getting along."

She stopped stirring for a moment. "I haven't left the place," she said slowly, "and nobody knows, because I haven't had a chance to tell anybody."

"There haven't been any callers," he noted. "A man might think, with all the shooting and hoorahing—"

She said, with her eyes on the floor, "I guess Ben wasn't much of a hand to encourage callers."

He considered that for a moment, then asked, "Who's your closest neighbor?"

"There's the Half Moon, north and east, but there's no woman there—only an older girl who takes care of a houseful of young'uns. And east of them is the LJ. Their ranch house is eighteen miles on the road to Clarendon."

"Do the LJ's know about this trouble?" he insisted.

She shook her head and resumed stirring.

He brought in water on the sled, and on his way up to look at the spring again, got a shot at a yearling doe and brought her down clean with his rifle. He dressed out the carcass and saved the hams and loin and forequarters, and hauled them in on the skin. She set about at once to cook the meat, boiling it all in the kettles, for deermeat would hardly keep overnight in the early spring, let alone late June.

At supper they had pie with some kind of creamy filling. "Mighty good," he said after his second piece. "Is this what you were stirring all afternoon?"

Her immediate pleasure was apparent—and, he thought, a little childish and somehow pathetic. He guessed that among Ben Lewis's unattractive characteristics, he had not been one to waste words in idle compliments. He thought about it as he took his time over his second cup of coffee. Finally he said, "Mrs. Lewis—"

She looked up from across the table. "I'd as soon you wouldn't call me that."

"I have to call you something, ma'am."

"My name is Catherine," she said.

He nodded. "Nice name." But he wondered if Ben had ever called her by it.

"What did you start to say?" she asked.

"Um—"

He looked at her dark eyes. How could he tell her what came to his mind: that she was pretty and pleasant and eager to please —and ripe for anybody who might come along and tell her sweet things. He didn't know anything about her relationship with her late husband, but he was sure of one thing: in spite of her competence in frontier matters, she was a child as far as men were concerned. She had the body and mind of a woman but the experience of a young girl, and apparently Ben had taken her out of circulation before she had had a chance to get acquainted with any young fellows. That of course was not unusual in a country like that. A man always needed a woman's help to run a ranch, and sometimes he would marry any girl strong enough to carry a bucket of water. But Bart could not tell her those things. "I forgot to notice," he said, "whether there is any extra barbwire around."

"There are half a dozen rolls back of the corral," she told him, watching his eyes as if she had some knowledge of his thoughts.

He nodded. "We don't have to worry about that, then."

He got up, feeling pretty good. He had used his arm considerable that day to keep it limbered up and also to find out how bad the wound was. It had bled from time to time, but not too much, and he guessed it would be well within a week.

He took his gun belt from the peg near the door and buckled it on.

She spoke from across the table. "You trust me now, don't you?"

He looked at her, half amused. "I reckon I do," he said.

"What would you do if I made a move toward the rifle?"

"That's idle speculation," he said. "You've had all kinds of opportunity but you haven't taken it. Anyway, there's no reason for you to aim the Sharps at me again. I have no wish to harm you."

"You might be one of the outlaws—maybe some other band besides Xenophon Jones's."

He put on his hat, and it struck him that the civilizing influence of a woman was soon felt, for that was the first time in years that he had taken off his hat to eat. "If I were an outlaw," he said, "I would not have wasted all this time."

"You don't *look* like an outlaw, anyway," she observed.

"I reckon that's a compliment."

"It was intended to be."

"Thank you, ma'am."

She looked at him inscrutably across the kerosene lamp, and he knew what she was thinking—what any healthy young woman or young man in their position would think: that they were alone for the night, and a long way from nowhere. It began to look as if Ben Lewis had neglected more than one phase of his married life. He turned away. He had thought the same thing, but he put it out of his mind. "How far is it to Clarendon?" he asked.

"Twenty-two miles."

"I'll be up early. It might be I can make it there and back in two days."

"You needn't hurry," she said. "I'll know you're coming—and that's a lot."

He glanced again at her eyes. If there was anything he could be sure of, about her, it was that she had not had much chance in her lifetime to feel sure of anybody, and it was like such a girl to trust the first decent-acting man who came along. He took the tag of his Bull Durham sack, that hung from his upper left vest pocket, and pulled out the sack, occupying his hands as he tried to figure what to do next. He made a trough of a cigarette paper, and started to tap tobacco into it. Then something rubbed against the door—like a shoulder.

Both his hands flashed in the yellow lamplight, and long before the fluttering cigarette paper had reached the level of his belt, he had drawn both .44's, swung on his heel, and faced the door. Then he backed up softly.

"Open the door," he told her under his breath, "and stay behind it."

She looked at him, her eyes big. Then she went around the table on her toes, making no sound, while he watched the door and waited for it to move. She crossed in front of him and stopped behind the door, near the Sharps, and looked questioningly at him.

Without moving his eyes from the door, he nodded.

She grasped the peg that served as a door-handle, and quickly and smoothly pulled it toward her.

Bart stared for an instant. The muzzle of the black turned toward him, and the horse's upper lip raised to show its teeth, and then closed again.

Bart laughed. His body eased its tension. Relaxed, he dropped the six-shooters into their holsters. "You got a piece of cornbread?"

"Left over from yesterday," she said dubiously.

"Just right." He gave it to the black, then pushed the animal's head away from the opening and closed the door. "This time of night," he explained, "he likes a bite of something to eat—anything —before he lies down for a while. Good thing he didn't know what a chance he was taking."

Catherine smiled briefly, moved to the table, and sat back. She reached for her cup of coffee but did not lift it. Her hand was trembling.

"That scared me," she said, and clasped her hands tightly together and looked at Bart, who still stood by the closed door. She said, "My efforts to defend myself must have looked pretty futile to you."

He looked at her intently. "Another reason I'll never be able to settle down unless I get a clear bill," he said.

"I don't understand."

"There are men in the Southwest who know that about me, and there'll always be somebody wanting to try me out if there's any excuse at all."

"There's always somebody to try out anyone," she said, unclasping her hands and lifting her cup steadily.

"It's different for me. I've lived a violent life—"

"It's different for anybody," she said. "Even for a peaceful man in a town back East there comes a time when he has to use his strength to assert himself and to keep from being thought a coward, or to protect himself from people who would take advantage of him. In a country like this, that is especially true, but a man like you is better equipped than most to take care of himself."

"It brings problems," he said.

She smiled faintly. "A mouse has problems too," she reminded him.

The discussion had become involved. He turned toward the door, aware that she would have kept him up all night just to talk—if nothing else.

"I put two comforts and a blanket on the floor for you," she said, pointing, "and you can have the buffalo robe."

"Thank you, ma'am." He scooped them up in his arms and started out, but again forgot to duck, and again knocked his hat off. He stopped to pick it up, and put the bedclothes on the floor for a moment, avoiding her dark eyes. He picked them up again and went out. "Goodnight, Catherine," he said as he stepped into the darkness.

"Goodnight," she said.

He started off, went a few steps and stopped, listened for her to bar the door. But she did not do it for a moment, and he went on a few steps. Then he swung around and saw a shadow cross the window, and heard the click of the iron bolt. He went on to the shed. The night seemed unusually warm. He went to the end of the shed where the roof had not burned, and found a place to spread his blanket between bales of sweet-smelling hay. He put the robe down, and the first quilt. Then he pulled off his boots and set them at the foot of his blanket; he rolled up his gun belt, with one holster on top, and set it near his shoulder. He settled down, pulled the other quilt over him, and went to sleep.

CHAPTER III

IT WAS still dark when he awoke. He moved to a sitting position in one easy motion, sat there for a moment, and listened. He heard nothing. He got out from under the quilt and put on his boots and hat, then his gun belt.

He sat for a moment, waking up slowly—a luxury he could not always afford. He reached in his vest pocket, but the tobacco sack was missing, and he remembered he had dropped it on the floor. But why hadn't he picked it up? He'd *never* gone off and left his Bull Durham behind.

But he had this time. He looked toward the house, saw a light in the kitchen window. He went up and knocked.

"Bart Wagner," he said, and added in a low voice, "Catherine."

She swung open the door and handed him the sack of tobacco. "I saved it for you."

"Thank you." He began to make a cigarette, his eyes on his work.

"The coffee's hot," she said.

He glanced at her. "You been up all night?"

"I kept it on the stove."

He hung up his hat and sat down. "I'll warm up over a cup," he said. "I ought to get out there and harness up, but—"

"Coffee will do you good," she said, pouring it into a tin cup. "As soon as you get harnessed, I'll have pancakes."

"Sounds good."

"There's no butter, but I saved some bear fat."

He looked up. "Do bears bother the calves?"

"They never have, as far as I know."

He finished the coffee, lifted a lid on the stove, and dropped the cigarette stub in. "Those four mules grazing behind the shed yesterday afternoon—they had harness marks."

"They're the ones."

"Hard to catch up?"

"Drive them toward the corral this time of morning."

He went out and found the mules grazing. He pushed them toward the open corral. They went in, and he threw them a few forkfuls of hay. He went back to the shed, lit the lantern, and looked over the harness. It was patched but it might hold. He bridled two of the mules and took them to the shed, harnessed them, and went to the wagon. He had picked the biggest animals for wheel positions, and he backed them in place. He harnessed the other two and hitched them to a doubletree fastened to the end of the wagon tongue. He set the brake on the wagon and went inside. "I hope they'll stand," he said, hanging up his hat.

"I think they will," she answered.

The warm fragrance of cooking pancakes made his stomach growl again. He poured himself a cup of coffee, got the sugar, and sat down. She gave him a stack of nine cakes as big as the plate, and he poured bear oil over them. "Mighty good cakes," he said five minutes later.

"I'm glad you think so."

He reached for his hat. "Shall I charge the stuff in Clarendon?"

"I have the money." She brought a roll of somewhat worn bills of small denominations out of her apron pocket, and carefully counted out ninety dollars. "You may not need that much," she said hopefully.

He looked at her list of food. "It doesn't take much to run up a bill. You got any left?"

"About fifty dollars."

He nodded. "You're a gambler—trusting me with this much of your money."

"I'm not worried," she said. "Anyway, I still have the three-year-olds—and there are always posts to be cut. The JA will take all the posts I can deliver."

"Why haven't the outlaws taken your three's?" he asked.

"So far," she said, "they've done most of their stealing from the big ranches—I suppose because they figure the big people won't miss them. It's only when they find unbranded stuff that they steal from the smaller spreads."

"That won't last long," he commented. "Even the big ranchers find out their stuff is missing sooner or later. And when they do, they get real mad."

"That's tomorrow," she observed. "An outlaw doesn't worry about tomorrow."

He stood quietly while she picked up the money from the table and put it in his big hand. Then suddenly and unexpectedly she looked up at him, and he saw fear and uncertainty in her face. "I don't even know where you came from," she said.

He smiled, but made no attempt to move his hand. "It's pretty late for that," he said.

"Maybe it is, but—you could give me some assurance that I'll see the goods. That's nearly all the money I have."

He recognized her sudden panic and sympathized with it. "I've partly told you, but to be exact, I was deputy marshal in El Paso a few years ago," he said soberly. "Worked with John Selman's badge, matter of fact. Got in a gunfight with the Yager brothers in the Elephant Saloon. An old guy flashed a mirror in my eyes and they opened fire." He paused. "I killed three, but one got away."

Wide-eyed, she watched him.

"The fourth one drygulched me in Socorro two weeks ago. I had been avoiding him, but he took it wrong. He thought I was afraid of him."

"I'm sure you weren't," she said.

"I had to kill him—but he had a lot of friends around Socorro. It would have been worth my life to stay in that town."

"So you left—in a hurry."

He looked at her. "Not exactly in a hurry—but not slow, either. I stopped at Fort Union, and I figured to settle there. But the sheriff at Socorro had got the governor after me. They put me in jail and took my money. So I escaped and headed east."

Her eyes were cloudy. "You killed—four men?"

"That's the way it adds up."

"You should have gone back to Socorro to stand trial."

He shook his head. "The Yagers had too many friends. They would hang me in thirty days."

"But law—"

He smiled. "As you said, there comes a time when you have to take things in your own hands. I figured this was such a time—so I left."

She said slowly, "You killed four men. What did you gain?"

"Nothing for myself. But I got rid of four troublemakers who had their sights set on being tough hombres. They would have gone along and maybe killed some innocent men before they got stopped. Likewise, it showed other would-be badmen in El Paso that the law meant business. It was a step toward bringing law and order."

"But those four—"

"Those four," he told her, "were looking for trouble. They had no respect for law, and so the law had to do what it was made to do. Most lawmen try to avoid that, but they can't always." He drew a deep breath. "The idea behind the badge is that when the law has to, it can use a strong arm. There is a time for that as well as a time for talk. Mostly a man can talk his way out of trouble, but once in a while things come up and he has to step down hard. That's the way it was when I killed the Yagers. They were all four set to draw down on me, and they had this old man flash the mirror in my eyes. Nobody knew who the old man was, either." He looked up. "But the whole thing was a trap, and shooting was the only chance to come out alive."

"Isn't it on your conscience—the killing of those four men?"

"No. It was done and done legally. My only problem is to find the man who put the light in my eyes and make him tell about it in court, so there can be no question even in the mind of the public as to what the Yagers were up to." He looked down at her. "I can tell you one thing more: the Xenophon Jones outfit sure won't let their consciences worry them about killing your husband." He studied her thoughtfully. "By the way, how did Ben know it was Jones?" he asked.

"He seemed to have known him somewhere before."

That was something to think about. Had Ben Lewis maybe been an outlaw himself, and had he, Bart Wagner, stumbled into the middle of an outlaw feud?

She was saying, "Do your best with the money, Bart."

He nodded, and put the money in his lower right vest pocket. "I'll do my best."

"Oh—and I want you to find out how much a granite gravestone will cost."

"In Clarendon?"

"There's a blacksmith that takes orders for them."

He got the list out of his upper right vest pocket, and a stub of a pencil with it. "You'd better write it down so I won't forget."

She wrote easily, and handed the list back to him, with the pencil.

He said curiously, "You're mighty conscientious about Ben."

She looked at the floor. "He was my husband. I wasn't able to give him a Christian burial, but I want to get a gravestone when I can afford it."

He nodded. "I'll ask." He poured a last half-cup of coffee. "By the way, that dead horse in the corral—I figured I'd tie the carcass on behind the wagon and drag it up the road a piece. It's beginning to smell."

"I wish you would."

The coffee was scalding hot. "And the dog? I'll throw it in the wagon." He blew on the coffee. "The buzzards will take care of the chickens if the coyotes haven't."

She showed an unexpected flash of anger. "They killed them because I liked them."

He looked at her skeptically. "How did Xenophon Jones know you liked the chickens?"

She said, "I told you Ben had known him before—and when Jones first came here, looking for a hideout, he ran across my husband in Clarendon—and Jones came out to stay on the ranch for a couple of weeks."

He looked at her speculatively. "There's more here than you've told me," he said.

"No!" She stood straight and proud. "Jones tried to make love to me, but I would not allow it. He swore he'd get even. That's all."

"And the chickens? Where do they come in?"

She rubbed the knuckles of one hand against her lips. "They are the only things I ever had of my own." She stared at the stove. "I liked the chickens because it was so lonely here. I liked their clucking; it was like friends' talking—the only friends I knew in the world. They woke up in the morning and started crowing with the sun, and I woke up and lay in bed and listened, and it was good to start the day. But Ben would open his eyes and say, 'Confound those chickens!' and then he would get up, eat breakfast, and leave for the whole day without a word—sometimes gone all night. Never a word. Nothing here but me and the chickens. Never any company. The chickens would scratch under the cottonwood tree and cluck to themselves, and in the afternoon when it was so terribly lonely, they were almost like people—friendly people, talking to me all day long." She looked at him. "Does that sound childish, Bart?"

He patted her shoulder. "It sounds all right to me." He looked at the door. "And Jones killed them all."

"He and his men."

"Right nice feller—this Jones."

He started out, but once again forgot to lower his head, and the upper edge of the door frame knocked his hat almost off his head. "Ma'am," he said, straightening his hat, "if I was going to work for you very long—which I'm not—I'd sure saw out another foot at the top of that door."

She smiled through misty eyes. "Or learn to bend down," she said. "That would be the easiest."

He looked at her. "It's easy if you're only five-foot-three." He went through, keeping his head down. The sky in the east was still black. "So long, Catherine."

She came to the open doorway with a package wrapped in newspapers. "Here's your lunch," she said. "So long."

He left the two carcasses out in the open, dragging them as far from the road as he could among the mesquite bushes. The coyotes and buzzards would take care of them before long.

He pushed the mules steadily until noon. He knew then that he was on LJ range, for though he had not passed a fence, he saw very few cattle that did not bear the LJ brand—big, flowing letters shaped like handwritten capitals. It was a nice brand, but the four loops must have made the flies bad at branding time. One thing he noticed: they were all of good blood—a lot of short-horn blood and some Durham. He had seen that cross also on Goodnight's ranch.

He stopped a little before noon to let the mules graze and to eat a couple of Catherine's sandwiches. He had tossed a bale of hay into the wagon, but the grass was good, and the mules did not need the hay.

In the early afternoon he harnessed up again and continued to follow the winding trail among the mesquite bushes.

In midafternoon he saw what looked like the headquarters of a good-sized spread, and presently he came to a big archway. Down there the canyon was several miles wide and somewhat like a rolling prairie, and it looked a little foolish for a big gateway to be standing out in the middle of nowhere, but he saw the LJ brand burned into a cottonwood log across the top, and he knew he ought to drive in and let Catherine's neighbors know what had happened to Ben Lewis. With only four or five miles left to Clarendon, he had plenty of time.

He turned in through the archway and followed the road over

a mile to where it dipped into a flat meadow along the creek. Without warning he rounded a turn and came out of the mesquite and saw the LJ spread before him: a big ranch house that covered a considerable amount of sod, barns, and corrals all over. Three freight wagons stood in the yard, and all were newly painted in blue and red—army wagons.

The LJ had a different air from the JB: horses pawed in the corrals; smoke rose from the kitchen chimney; two dogs chased a wild animal into a draw, barking furiously—but there were no chickens around; he noticed that.

The contrast with the JB was discouraging. All that activity on the LJ made the deadly quiet at the JB seem to be the indication of imminent dissolution.

He drove up in front, and a big-hatted man with remittance-man sideburns walked out from the front of the ranch house to meet him. Bart pulled up the mules and set the brake.

The big man's eyes flicked over the brands on the mules. "Your outfit?" he asked.

Bart recognized the question as an invitation to trouble. He said easily, still holding the reins: "Not mine. Ben Lewis's—or, rather, his widow's."

The sideburned man looked at him sharply. "His widow?"

Bart said, "He was killed by outlaws two days ago."

The man nodded. It did not seem to astonish him. "Too bad. You helping Catherine out?"

"For a while."

The man seemed to make up his mind. "Get down, then. We've got coffee on."

Bart tied the reins around the foot-iron and climbed over the side.

"Name's Harding," said the man. "Tom Harding. I own the LJ."

"Nice spread." Bart held out his hand. "My name's Bart Wagner."

He saw a flicker of recognition in Harding's eyes as Harding shook hands. "El Paso?"

"At one time," Bart said slowly.

"Aim to be around here a while?"

"Not long," said Bart.

"I'll have one of the boys run your team into the shade while you're here."

"I have to make Clarendon by dark," Bart said.

"No problem." Harding seemed to be warming up to him. "Come on around the back. We've got something going on back here."

Bart followed him around the ranch house and halted in astonishment. Behind the house, a crew of cowhands was squatted around the front of a wagon with the tongue propped up on a doubletree so the outer end was high in the air. A rope ran through the ring at the end of the tongue, and below the ring it was tied around a man's neck. The other end of the rope was held by two husky hands about twenty feet in front of the wagon.

"I saw you coming," Harding said, "and I thought I better meet you. A man never knows but what a Ranger might come up without warning."

A man squatting near the doubletree, drawing idle designs in the dirt with a stick, said, "Haul 'im up again," and the two men on the rope dug in their boot-heels and pulled on the rope until the victim's feet left the ground, and he hung there with about a foot of air below him, and his body twisted with the rope and his face turned blue.

CHAPTER IV

"ALL RIGHT," said the one who had given the order, and they let the fellow down. His hands were tied behind him and his feet were tied together, and he had trouble standing when they let him down, but nobody offered help. He tottered a moment, tried to hold his balance, but fell over, and they let him stay there.

Bart looked around at the crew—fifteen or eighteen hands, all watching and waiting. "Rough treatment," he said to Harding.

"It's too good for him," said Harding grimly. "But most men would rather have a rope burn than a bullet in the ear."

Bart said shrewdly, "They can talk plainer, too."

Harding looked at him. "I figgered you'd guess that."

The one who had given the orders got up, dusted the seat of his pants, and stalked over to them. "He hasn't said a word," he told Harding.

Harding nodded. "Hector, this here is Bart Wagner, helping out on the Quarter Circle JB. Hector Johnson," he told Bart, "foreman of the LJ."

They shook hands. Hector Johnson was big and rawboned and wore a long, sweeping mustache. "Old man Lewis finally broke down and hired a hand, eh?"

"Old Ben is dead," said Harding.

Johnson stared at him a minute, then looked at Bart. One thing was very noticeable: the reaction of these men to the death of Ben Lewis was about that of a man to the news that a coyote had been shot on the Quintafue. "Mrs. Lewis there alone?" Johnson asked.

"For right now," said Bart.

"Let's get back to the hanging," said Harding.

Johnson turned. "Haul him up again!"

The two hands pulled on the rope, hauled the fellow to his feet, and dangled him in the air.

"We won't kill him unless we have to," said Harding.

"I take it you caught him with the goods on," said Bart.

Harding nodded grimly. "He'll talk or we'll find out why. I want him to testify against the others."

"You're going to haul him to Henrietta?"

"Nothing like it."

Johnson gave a sign, and they let the bound man down again.

"We're going to have court in Clarendon," said Harding. "The legislature established a new judicial district."

The rope must have been tight around the man's neck, for he breathed noisily as he lay on the ground. Harding looked at him coldly. "Name of Hicks Gentry. Runs with Xenophon Jones."

A woman's voice came from the house. "Ready for coffee, Papa?"

Harding called, "Bring it out."

Bart looked over the crew. Then a shadow fell across his vest and a throaty girl's voice said, "Coffee, mister?"

Bart looked up and stared. She was some different from Catherine—about the same age or a little older, with her hair fixed up like women in a town like San Antonio or Galveston—piled high on top of her head, with some long curls hanging down the back. She was black-haired also, but her face did not have the smooth brown color that Catherine's had, and he suspected she had put something on her lips. She was slim, and the way her hair was all on top and not on the sides, made her look still more slender. She wore a white blouse and some kind of skirt such as Bart had seen in magazines. Her eyes were dark, and she watched his boldly.

Harding introduced them. "Stella's my only daughter," he said.

She had not taken her eyes from Bart's. "I'm glad you stopped for coffee," she said slowly.

"Yes, ma'am. So am I."

He heard Johnson give the order to haul Gentry up again on the rope, but he watched Stella's slim form as she walked among the men with tin cups and a big graniteware pot of coffee. Bart thought it strange that she did not even glance at Hicks Gentry.

On the ground again, Gentry made unintelligible noises, and the two men on the rope waited. Johnson gave an order, and somebody went up to loosen the rope around his neck.

Harding walked closer, and Bart followed. Harding said, "You ready to talk?"

Gentry said, stretching his neck, "I don't know anything."

"You was with Three-Finger and Indian George."

"I just joined up," he said, somewhat defiantly.

"Where from?"

"Montana."

"And you hadn't burned any calves?"

Gentry shook his head. He was a hard-looking man in a neck-band shirt without a collar, and with a week's growth of beard.

"Hell of it is," said Harding, "he might be right—and there's no use dragging a man into court to testify to something he don't know about."

Gentry tried to sit up.

"Untie him," Harding said suddenly.

They took the rope from Gentry's hands, and he sat up. His neck was bruised and swollen, but he did not look scared. "Maybe about three minutes up there would change your mind," said Harding.

Gentry's jaws tightened. "You can hang me, Harding—but that's murder."

"Question of degree," said Harding. "If I leave you up there long enough, you'll strangle."

"That's—"

Harding slapped him brutally. "You dirty mare-suckin' bastard!" he said, his voice harsh. "You can be defiant but not insolent. Get one thing straight, Gentry: you don't mean a damn to me. You know we make our own laws up here and always have, and I wouldn't hesitate to have you pulled up by the neck and left there all night."

Harding was red in the face and shouting, and Gentry finally had the good sense not to answer.

After that outburst, Harding, breathing heavily and glaring at the man, said nothing for a moment, and then seemed to cool off as fast as he had gotten angry. "You see what it's like up here," he said to Bart. "These outlaws come into a man's own place and defy him. That's what makes me so damn' mad."

Johnson came from his place near the doubletree.

"Where was it, exactly, you found them?" asked Harding.

"Five miles south," said Johnson, "in the chinaberry pasture."

"We were just sitting around a fire," Gentry said truculently, "when you and your hands rode up on us."

Johnson spoke to Bart. "What he didn't say is that they had a couple of running irons in the fire."

"How many in Jones's gang?" asked Harding.

"Maybe twenty, maybe fifty. I don't know. I told you I just joined up."

Harding said harshly, "Listen, Gentry. Go back to Tascosa and tell Xenophon Jones we've got two of his men in jail at Clarendon —Three-Finger and Indian George—and before the month is out we're going to try them in Clarendon for stealin' cows."

Gentry spat. "Hell, everybody knows there ain't no court in the Panhandle."

Harding grabbed him by the front of his shirt and twisted the man back. "There will be a court. Tell Jones that!"

"You won't get by with it!" Gentry said insolently.

Harding controlled his temper. He turned the man loose reluctantly. "That's been talked before," he said with obvious restraint.

"There's more outlaws in the Panhandle than ranchers," Gentry said contemptuously. "They won't stand for it."

"You go back and tell Xenophon Jones we're doing it!" Harding said. "Three-Finger and Indian George will hang—legal."

Gentry picked up his hat. "Do I get my horse?"

"You get no horse. You were riding a stolen horse when you came in—a Frying Pan brand. The horse goes back to the owner. From here, you walk!"

Gentry glowered at him and started off slowly. Then Stella came up. "Cup of coffee?" she asked.

He glared at her for a moment; then his look became more calculating, and he said, "Yes'm."

Harding was talking to Bart. "It's enough to make you grind your teeth, the way the damn' polecats stand up in your own yard and talk back to you even when they're caught red-handed."

Bart nodded. It was noticeable that Stella was not helping matters any, and it was fairly easy to see that that woman would make any kind of trouble just to stir up excitement.

"I'm ashamed of myself," Harding said earnestly, "for hitting a man who doesn't dare hit back. But I won't be insulted in my own yard by a lowdown cow-thief."

"If you've got something on him, why let him go?"

Harding looked at Bart. "What I've got most on Gentry is in the state of Colorado. I was running a trail herd to Cheyenne last summer when I run across him. He was sneakin' unbranded calves out of my trail herd and burnin' the mothers' feet with hot irons to keep them from follerin' the calves. He'd gather up the calves in a big wagon and take them north to sell."

"Didn't you have everything branded when you started?"

"These were dropped on the trail. You can't take time out for branding every morning, with a dozen hands to run 1,500 head."

Johnson lifted the wagon tongue while a man took out the doubletree. He was a strong man, Johnson, and he lifted the tongue from back of the middle.

"You see Gentry now," Harding said, "sizing up my daughter,

· 43 ·

knowing that he's doing it before my face but gambling that I don't do anything about it."

"If you won't," said Bart suddenly, "I'm willing."

Harding glanced at him. "He's your meat."

Bart strode across the hard-packed ground. He took the man by the collar of his bedraggled shirt, and he felt mean about it because, in a way, Stella was as guilty as Gentry, but he also knew the feeling that Harding was going through. He spun Gentry around twice and flung him away. The coffee sprayed over the hard, packed ground, and the cup went clattering as Gentry struggled for his balance. "Get going!" Bart said.

Gentry faced him like a wolf in a trap. "If I had a gun, you wouldn't dare—"

Bart pulled the .44 from his left holster and held it out. "Want to try?"

Gentry glared around the yard, an animal at bay. His eyes passed over Stella, but he didn't see her as a woman at all. He said hoarsely to Bart: "You'd gun me down! You'd never let me get my finger on the trigger!"

"I'll give you first shot," said Bart.

Gentry glared at him, wild-eyed. He looked at the six-shooter, then back at Bart. He backed up a few steps, then turned and started north toward the breaks.

"Mr. Wagner," said Stella after a moment, "you have a lot of courage."

He frowned. "No, ma'am, it's something else. I don't really know how to tell you. You see a polecat in front of you. He's worthless and defiant, and, worst of all, a man who will shoot you in the back the first chance he gets, and you ought to kill him the same as you would a rattlesnake, but something keeps you from it. You'll probably kill him some day anyway, and you might save some lives by doing it now—maybe your own—but as long as we live under the laws we do, his kind gets a fair trial."

She looked up at him, again watching his eyes. "He might be a good shot."

Bart shrugged. "He probably is."

"You see how they act," Harding said, coming up behind him. "They have overrun the Panhandle, and there has to be a showdown. That's why I sent him back to Xenophon Jones. If he won't testify against the others, we can at least serve notice on the outlaws that we are going to have a court."

"You're looking for a showdown?" asked Bart.

"I'd rather have a showdown than string it out for years."

"You might lose fewer men in a showdown, anyway."

"Win or lose, if it's a big enough showdown we'll win, because enough insolence on the part of the outlaws, even if it succeeds in squelching the court, will eventually bring down the Texas Rangers."

" 'Enough insolence' might include some good men getting shot," said Bart. "Even you."

"It's a frontier country," Harding said. "You can't run things from a drawing room or a desk in a big building."

Johnson came up. "You said Ben Lewis was killed?"

"Yes."

Bart could not read the expression of Johnson's face.

"Mrs. Lewis is there alone, then," said Johnson.

Harding said, "I'll send a couple of hands to ride fence and keep an eye on things down there. Maybe Stella could trot over and keep her company for a few days until she gets over the shock. Stella!"

She did not answer.

"Where'd she go?" Harding demanded.

"Back in the house, I think," said Johnson.

"Never mind. I'll speak to her later. Look, Wagner, you want a couple of hands to ride with you into Clarendon?"

"It isn't far," said Bart.

"These are bad hombres," said Harding. "Gentry is not the worst of the lot."

"Who is?" asked Bart.

"Jones has got a couple of hardcases around him. Him and Stud Murphy are two of the fastest-drawing and straightest-shooting hombres in the Panhandle."

"I heard about Murphy," said Bart.

Harding looked at him keenly. "You have a shave with them?"

"I run into their camp south of Tascosa," said Bart. "I had a nice black, and Murphy wanted to trade horses."

"When Murphy wants to trade horses," Harding said, "it's generally a deal—no matter what the trade is like."

"It wasn't this time," Bart said casually, "because I was holding a six-shooter on him."

CHAPTER V

HE LINED out the mules for Clarendon. The sun was still high, and he would have time, perhaps, to do his shopping that evening and get an early start back to the Quarter Circle JB. He was uneasy about Catherine's staying alone there. If men like Gentry were acting as Gentry had acted in Harding's ranch yard, it was only a question of time until some of them would close down on the Quarter Circle JB. No matter what Catherine thought, the fact that they had not taken over her place so far was not due to her work with the Sharps.

He was not an hour past the archway when he saw a rider loping across the prairie to intercept him. He kept the mules moving, but watched until he saw it was a woman riding sidesaddle, and knew it would be Stella.

She waited for him up ahead, very stylishly gotten up in riding skirt, white blouse, broad-brimmed straw hat with a black veil.

"Out riding?" he asked, letting the mules continue their pace.

She came alongside. "It gets lonely on the ranch."

"Big place like that," he said, "ought to keep you busy."

She spoke loudly over the rattle of the empty wagon. "I don't do any of the work." The idea seemed repellent to her. "Papa hires plenty of help—but there's nobody to talk to."

"Must be seventy-five cowhands."

She turned up her nose. "All they can talk is cows!"

"What do you want to talk?"

"Not cows." Without warning she left the saddle and climbed into the wagon-seat. She looked very handsome with her face a little flushed and her hat tipped to one side.

"Mr. Wagner," she said, "I'm bored of the ranch and everything connected with it."

He kept his eyes on the team. "I gathered that," he said dryly.

"I wasn't raised out here, you know."

"Where, then?"

"They sent me to school in Kansas City. I lived there most of my life, but when my mother died I came out here to look after papa." She shook her head. "I'm sick of ranch life. I want to go back to Kansas City."

"Why don't you tell him so?"

"It would break his heart."

He looked at her. "Maybe you just don't dare."

"In Kansas City," she said, "there were parties, and teas, and dances, and the theater."

"They have dances out here," he noted, and turned to be sure the saddle horse was following the wagon.

She closed her eyes in well controlled disgust. "With the smell of cowlots and horse corrals all over the place, and clumsy cowhands tramping on your feet—and a girl is supposed to dance until daylight, one right after the other. You never get a moment with anybody alone."

"Maybe not."

"In this great country of men and cattle," she went on dramatically, "do you think a woman would dare to taste liquor?"

He glanced sidewise at her.

"Liquor in Texas," she said, "is for dumb cowhands, who clamp an arm around you as if they were bulldogging a steer, who grin like apes, and whose breath smells like sour bread dough."

"Ma'am," he said, "I think you've cast an almighty reflection on our whisky."

"I'm serious!" she cried.

"How old are you?" he asked.

"Twenty-four."

"You're old enough to be serious," he admitted. "But your father doesn't know how you feel?"

"No."

"Couldn't you break it to him gently?"

"I've tried," she said. "He always turns it off into the plans he has for me on the ranch."

He watched the road for a moment. "Don't you think you could get to like it?"

"I hate it!" she cried. "It's hot and dirty, and the toilets are outside and filled with flies."

He was a little shocked by her words to a man she did not know, but he didn't let on. Seeing the full extent of her sophistication, he began to realize that it probably was as unpleasant for her as she, in her exaggerated way, was giving him to believe. Obviously she knew a lot more about the world than her father had any idea.

He glanced at her and caught her eyes on him. She was a damned handsome woman, no fooling—and she smelled like fresh roses.

"I know your kind of man," she said. "I knew you the moment I saw you."

"I thought you were attracted to Gentry."

"Don't be a fool! Why do you think I played with Gentry? Because I knew what you would do! I would have bet my soul on it."

After a moment, he said, "What kind of man am I, then?"

"You are many kinds of men in one. You are gallant, and you would help a lady in distress—or a lady being ogled by an oaf. But when it's all over, you won't be here long. You'll be riding through."

"What makes you think so?"

"I can see it in your eyes and your manner. A woman couldn't marry you."

He kept his eyes on the lead mule's ears. "Why not?"

"You'd never be in one place long enough."

He continued to watch the road. "I don't know what kind of man you're used to," he said slowly.

"Mr. Wagner, we might as well understand each other. I am not a country bumpkin. I am used to men like you, who take their women as long as they want them, and then leave them."

"It doesn't sound fair to the women."

"Some like it that way," she said boldly.

He saw her eyes on him, and swallowed hard.

"If you're going toward Kansas City," she said, "I'd go with you."

"Your father would hunt me down with a shotgun."

"Not if we registered as man and wife."

There was no doubt about it: she had had considerable experience. He smelled her perfume again and lifted the hat on his head and settled it back.

"As long as he thinks I'm married, he wouldn't interfere," she insisted.

"If he doesn't think so, he'd put so many buckshot in me that I'd rattle like a dry gourd in August."

She asked, "Are you afraid?"

"No, ma'am," he said. "The thing that bothers me is I might have to shoot him—and I like the old man. He's honest and he has honest feelings."

"Then are you afraid of *me?*" she asked.

He looked full at her and breathed deep of the rose perfume. "You're the most beautiful woman I ever sat beside," he said. "And I learned a long time ago not to be afraid of a woman who takes a drink. Also, I'm not afraid of a woman who would leave me without notice, as you would. We could have a lot of fun while we were together." He turned back to the mules. "The hell of it is," he said, "I've got a lot of fence to put up at the Quarter Circle JB. . . ."

He drove into Clarendon alone, wondering just why it was that he had chosen to stay on the job and put up fence for Catherine Lewis rather than head for Kansas City with a woman like Stella

Harding. He had only two weeks with Catherine anyway. Why hadn't he jumped at Stella's proposal?

He passed half a dozen poor-looking sod huts, and came to a high false front that said, "Trail of Tears Saloon." He remembered that Clarendon was supposed to be a dry town, but there had been a lot of argument over it, and he guessed that right now the wets were having the best of the argument.

Twenty-five or thirty horses were standing along the hitching rails; a buggy was pulled up alongside another wooden front that said simply, "Store." Across the street was another front that said nothing. Two big freight wagons had pulled up in the middle of the dirt street, and the oxen lay alongside the chains.

Bart stopped the mules in front of the store. Two men came out of the saloon, stopped for a moment, and watched him. The sun was at their backs and he could not see them, but he supposed they knew he was a stranger and wondered why he was driving Ben Lewis's wagon.

He tied the reins to the foot-iron and got down and went inside. The store smelled of kerosene and horse tonic and new buggy whips. He pushed his big hat up on his head and rubbed the black whiskers on his chin.

"Somethin', mister?" asked a whiny voice.

"Are you Jonas Myers?"

"That's what they call me."

Bart fished the list out of his vest pocket, saying, "I come for some things for Miz Lewis."

"Ben Lewis?"

Bart looked at him, seeing a small, partly hump-shouldered man with thin brown hair and a wispy brown mustache that was stained on the ends with tobacco juice. "I understand he was a good customer of yours."

"Bought all his stuff here. You workin' fer old Ben?"

"Ben is dead. I'm workin' for Miz Lewis."

"Dead?" Myers did not seem shocked. "What happened to old Ben?"

"Outlaws."

"Too bad." Myers was peering over his glasses at the list. "That says 'coffee'?"

"That's what it says."

"Just got some in from Colorado City. Everything comes from south the last few weeks. Somethin' wrong with the trains out of Kansas City, and no freight comes down from Dodge." He chuckled. "New lawman up there—Bill Tilghman. Hear he's undersheriff. Maybe the freighters don't like to go in Dodge any more account of him."

Bart said impatiently, "Bill Tilghman wouldn't fool with a bunch of drunk freighters hurrahing a town unless they hurt somebody or destroyed property."

Myers stopped as if a six-shooter had been pointed at him. "You know Tilghman?" he asked with respect.

"I know Tilghman. How about that coffee?"

"But Tilghman—he's undersheriff of Ford County."

"He isn't in Dodge at all. He's over in New Mexico building railroads. I saw him last week." He glanced at the list. "Make it ten pounds—and see that you fill the can."

"They'll have to be green unless you can wait till tomorrow."

"We can roast our own."

"Yes. All right." Myers' hands fluttered for a moment; then he turned and went toward a big sack.

"I want to see it before you put the lid on," Bart called. "And I want it shaken down."

"Yes, sir. Always shake it down. Yes sir. Only way to do business. Sell honest measure to honest people."

Bart got sugar, salt, rice, dried apples and peaches, and cornmeal. He got half a dozen blocks of salt and a case of canned tomatoes, haggling over prices and complaining about everything possible, for he knew the storekeeper figured to make at least a hundred per cent. Bart was a little astonished at himself, for never before had he paid attention to the price of anything but a horse.

And when he got all through, he had a fair load of groceries, and there was still some money left.

"Need a bottle of Cedar Valley? Old Ben always liked that brand."

Bart was putting the money back in his vest pocket. "That can wait," he said.

"Want a cigar?" asked Jonas.

Bart licked his lips. "Haven't had a cigar in weeks."

"Big order like this, man is entitled to a cigar."

Bart took it, sniffed it, bit off the end, put it in his mouth and lit it. He puffed a time or two; this was luxury that he had not known for a long time.

"The big places must buy lots more," he observed.

"Too big," said Myers. "They do their own freighting."

Bart finished carrying out the things he had bought. The two men outside had moved in front of another store.

Bart put a foot up on the wheel hub and puffed the cigar. It wasn't a bad smoke at all.

"How can this county afford a judge and all?" he asked Myers, who had followed him out with the last load of groceries.

"Stock Growers' Association—they all got together and assessed every man a few cents on a cow to add to the judge's salary. Only way it could be done. No judge would come out here for the legal salary."

"Does that go for other officials too?"

"Sure. Sheriff, county attorney—even a doctor. They guaranteed Doctor Stocking eighteen hundred a year to settle here and practice —only he ain't here yet. There's so few people in the county they couldn't make any sort of county organization work any other way."

"Who's the leader of the stockmen?"

"Charlie Goodnight."

Bart looked at the sun. It was getting low. He thought he'd roll the wagon out a few miles and camp. That way he'd save livery charges, and get a quick start in the morning. He looked around, savoring the cigar as he did so. There wasn't much in Clarendon —a bakery, from the chimney of which smoke was rising; a small harness shop. From down at the end of the dirt street came the clanging of a blacksmith's anvil. A few pieces of board sidewalk led to a sign saying, "U.S. Post Office." He saw the two men step off one of the pieces of sidewalk and walk toward the blacksmith shop, but it was getting dark and he didn't look at them again.

He glanced toward the saloon. He had a few cents of his own, and one drink wouldn't hurt—it would cut the Panhandle dust. He grinned wryly and went into the saloon. "Cedar Valley," he said.

He fished a quarter out of his lower left vest pocket and laid it down. He got a dime in return, and put it in his pocket. He looped his forefinger around the cigar and puffed on it a couple of times, then took the whisky in his mouth and let it soak into his tissues.

"Another one?" asked the beady-eyed bartender.

"Nope." Bart wiped his mouth on his sleeve.

The bartender looked around. "This one's on the house," he said as he picked up the bottle.

"Nope." Bart backed away. "The house can't afford to buy a free one for a boughten one."

"What do you care?"

"I care a lot," said Bart. "I'm a stranger in town and I don't want to be robbed."

The bartender shrugged and raised his eyebrows.

"It won't work anyway, because I don't get that drunk."

The bartender picked up the bottle again, but Bart shook his head. "Nor do I want to give you an excuse for hitting me over the head and saying I passed out."

"You're a suspicious man," the bartender said, and put the bottle on the backbar.

Bart said, "What about that prohibition clause in the land deeds of Clarendon?"

"The boss doesn't think it will stick. When they get through holding court, all the dries will be through in Donley County."

"How's that?"

"They're going to run the judge and prosecuting attorney and the whole shebang out of town."

"Do you think they can do it?"

The bartender shrugged again. "You're wearin' guns. You know what *they* will do."

Bart frowned. "Who owns the saloon?" he asked.

"Xenophon Jones."

Bart puffed at the cigar. It was really warmed up, and tasted good. "What kind of man was Ben Lewis?" he asked.

"'Was'?" the bartender repeated.

"He was shot two days ago," said Bart.

The bartender looked up at Bart. "It was too good an end."

Bart asked, "What was wrong with him?"

"He was just plain ornery."

Bart went out. Nailed on the wall of the post office was a notice that court would be held. Judge Frank Willis would preside as an official of the Thirty-fifth Judicial District. Temple Houston, son of Sam Houston, would be prosecuting attorney. Court would be held in "the open lot south of the post office." The notice was signed by Tom Harding, acting sheriff.

Bart glanced at the post office. He went inside and found the window closed, and then, having pretty well exhausted the possibilities of Clarendon, he figured it was time to move his wagon and find a place to camp. He walked out of the post office and came face to face with the two men who had been moving around the street.

The bigger one was about his height but much heavier, and wore a full black mustache that hid his mouth. Bart recognized him then in spite of the gathering dusk.

"Wagner," the man said insolently, "I hear you're a horse trader."

"You hear wrong," said Bart.

"I like your black."

This was a baiting, and Bart held his temper. "I haven't got the black with me," he said.

"You've got your hardware, though."

Bart did not answer.

"I aim to beat hell out of you anyway." With a sudden move he brought up his hand and hit the cigar close to Bart's mouth. Bart's teeth were tight on it, and the cigar broke off, and the long portion dropped in the dirt at the edge of the sidewalk.

Bart's hands flashed. He held his six-shooters on the two men and said coldly, "Turn around and walk away slow and don't look back."

Four men were drifting into the street from somewhere. They saw what was going on, and stayed at one side to keep out of range. The clanging anvil had stopped.

Stud Murphy, turning, grinned insolently. "I'm still going to give you a licking, Wagner."

"Keep moving."

A voice from behind said, "Drop them, Wagner."

It was a new voice but not one to argue with. Reluctantly Bart straightened his fingers and let the six-shooters slide into the dirt. He swore inwardly for not watching behind him, but it was too late. Murphy's big fist caught him full on the nose. Bart stumbled back and started swinging.

"Keep your arms down," said the voice behind him.

Bart held his breath. That kind of licking? He dropped his arms slowly, his jaws clamped hard.

Murphy came in on him, slugging him in the face and stomach at will. Bart staggered back, his head rocking from one side to the other. A haymaker caught him on the jaw and laid him flat.

He opened his eyes. A heavy boot had landed on his ribs, and he rolled away.

The voice that had been behind him said, "You better not stomp him, Stud. That damn' preacher Carhart—"

"He has nothin' to say!" But Stud did not proceed with the stomping. He kicked him instead, and Bart rolled in the dust, trying to lessen the force of the boots but knowing better than to get up.

"Xenophon said not to make no trouble before court," the man said.

Stud hesitated. "All right," he said sullenly. He picked up Bart with a huge hand twisted into the front of his vest. He stood him on his feet and hit him on the jaw with both fists. Bart went down again, and heard Murphy say: "Next time you see me, you'll trade!"

When he was sure they had left him, Bart rolled over and got painfully to his feet. He knew he had a couple of broken ribs. He wiped the dirt off his face with his bandanna, and it came away bloody. He stood up, getting his balance. He found his hat and picked it up. He got his .44's, blew the dust out of the barrels, and put them in his holsters. The cylinders would have to be cleaned as soon as possible. He started for the wagon. Then he remembered the cigar, and went back and scratched in the dust until he found the broken piece. It was long enough to light. He put it in his upper left vest pocket and went back to the wagon.

The hump-shouldered storekeeper, Myers, came running out. "I heard Murphy talkin'. You hurt?" he asked.

Bart licked blood from his cut lip. "I feel fine. But one thing is a cinch: that doctor is going to have plenty of work when he gets here." He took hold of the seat-iron and put one foot on the wheel hub. "Know where to buy a gravestone?" he asked.

"Down at the blacksmith shop. Holt, his name is."

Bart turned the team and drove to the end of the street.

Holt was a hairy man, bare to the waist and somewhat hollow-chested. He looked up from welding a tire iron without a word, his eyes watchful.

"How much for a gravestone?" Bart asked.

"Twenty-five dollars."

For an instant Bart hesitated. The voice was the same voice that had been behind him. He took a deep breath and got control of himself. Then he said coldly, "May need one for a friend of mine."

"You want writin' on it?"

"Probably. How long does it take?"

"Three or four months. It comes from Dodge."

"I'll figure out the writing and let you know when I come back to town."

Holt looked at the tire iron and put it back in the fire. Bart went to the wagon and drove out of town. He wondered what Stud Murphy would say when he heard about the gravestone.

CHAPTER VI

IT WAS evening when he pulled into the Quarter Circle JB and up to the back door. He smelled burned wood, looked around and sniffed, saw nothing wrong. The team quieted. He tied the reins and got down as Catherine hurried out of the door.

"Bart!" she said, her eyes wide. "You've been hurt again!"

He said, "It's just a scratch."

"A scratch? Your face is cut up, and I saw you get down, as if you ached all over. Oh, Bart!" She ran to him, warmth in her eyes, her arms outstretched.

He was overwhelmed by her sweetness and her obvious welcome, and he took her in his arms and kissed her on the lips.

"Is it a bullet?" she asked.

"Just a few bruises," he said, shaken.

"I'll have to nurse you again," she said immediately.

He saw that she was as much moved as he was, and he backed away. "This kind of thing can't go on between us," he said. "It wouldn't be decent."

Her eyes were on the ground.

He took a deep breath. "I like you, Catherine—but that is no good excuse for carrying on with a woman like you. Maybe you've been mistreated; maybe you've been starved for love. I don't know. But don't give up to a man's arms unless you know for sure he's going to marry you—and don't take his word for it." He paused. He had kissed women before—many of them—but it had not moved him like this.

She backed away, her eyes on him, inscrutable. "I hope you are not badly hurt," she said.

"It's been a long trip," he said. "I think I could use some coffee before I unload. The mules are in better shape than I am."

"It's hot," she said, and led him inside.

The smell of burned wood was strong, and he saw a board with marks burned in it, and a bridle-ring held in a pair of pincers, at one side. "What happened?" he asked.

Then he saw what she had burned: "Ben Lewis. Mu—"

She poured coffee, avoiding his eyes. "They—Xenophon Jones and his men—rode up and roped the other headboard and dragged it away."

He was aware that she was breathing as hard as he was. "You were in love with him?" he asked.

She looked at him with an unexpected faint crease between her eyes. "Ben had his faults, maybe," she said slowly, "but he did his best—all he knew how—and he was my husband." She picked up the pincers and reached for the red-hot ring.

"I found out about a stone," he told her, blowing on his coffee. "Twenty-five dollars."

She looked at him. "Don't you think I should put one up?"

He put two spoonfuls of sugar in the coffee. "I think you should. He was your husband."

She nodded. "I'll wait until the beef is sold in the fall."

"Time enough."

He gave her the money that was left.

"How about yourself?" she asked.

"I have no need for money."

"Did you get some tobacco?"

He tried the coffee. She made mighty good coffee. "Yes, ma'am, I got a little. I didn't think you'd mind."

"Of course not."

He started making a cigarette.

"Don't you like cigars?" she asked.

He looked up. "Yes."

"Mr. Myers always gave Ben a cigar."

"Well—" He fished the piece out of his upper vest pocket and looked at it. The wrapper was loose and the cigar was about to fall to pieces. He looked at it for a moment, then walked over and dropped it in the stove. Then he started to tap tobacco into a cigarette paper. "Clarendon is changing," he said.

She pressed the red-hot ring against the wood, and a blue curl of smoke shot out. Then suddenly she put the ring back into the ashes at the bottom of the grate, and turned to him. "What happened, Bart?" she asked, unable to hold back any longer. "You must have been in a fight."

He caught the tag in his teeth and closed the sack. "I had known this fellow before. Had the poor luck to run into him again."

She seemed relieved. "I hope it wasn't too bad," she said.

He had stopped at the creek to wash off the dried blood, and now, outside of a couple of cracked ribs, he felt all right, except a little sore where he was bruised. "It didn't amount to much," he said noncommittally.

"I can have dinner in about an hour. I'll put this aside."

He looked speculatively at the board. "I think you better finish the job, ma'am." He didn't want to tell her that Ben Lewis's headboard in the house would make him uncomfortable.

"All right. It won't take long."

He finished the coffee and unloaded the groceries. It would be light for a couple of hours, so he heaved two spools of barbwire onto the wagon, being careful of his side, and drove up to the spring. There was nothing new there, and he placed several lumps of stock salt around. Probably deer and antelope licked as much as cattle, but there was no way of stopping that. He went back and unharnessed the mules and turned them out.

One thing bothered him considerable: Xenophon Jones and his men had killed her chickens, killed the dog, killed her husband, and had ridden up into the yard and roped Ben Lewis's headboard. They had given her notice to move out—but they had not touched *her*—yet. Why? If the outlaws wanted the Quarter Circle JB, why didn't they ride in and manhandle her off the place? It would not make any difference to Xenophon Jones that she was a woman. Unless he or one of his men wanted her *because* she was a woman.

He smelled the delicious, warm fragrance of fresh cornbread out in the yard while he was filling the water barrel. He washed up and went inside.

"One thing sure," he said fifteen minutes later, "you're the best cook this side of Trinidad, Colorado."

She blushed. "Have some more cornbread?"

"I ate fourteen pieces already. I reckon one more won't bust anything." He said a moment later, "I'll go up to the spring in the morning and string wire around the mudhole. You can keep the cattle from dirtying up the creek water and you might save having to pull some out by main strength and awkwardness." He sat back. "In the fall we'll round up the stuff—"

She began to smile. "You've made up your mind to stay!"

He looked at her and shook his head slowly. "No, ma'am, I'm not staying. I misspoke myself."

"Is it because of what happened at Clarendon?" she asked, sounding disappointed.

"No." He picked his hat up from the floor. "But that's a sample of what follows a man who uses violence."

After a moment she asked, "If no man would use violence, who is going to fight the outlaws?"

"I don't know, ma'am."

"In El Paso, you killed for the law, you said."

"That doesn't make any difference." He got up.

She bit her lip. "Where will you go, Bart? To Dodge?"

"Maybe." He hesitated. "Maybe Kansas City. Hard to say."

He slept in the shed again that night, pretty tired and beaten. In the morning he was up early, with the smell of coffee already in his nostrils, and the pungent odor of burning cedar in the quiet air.

She had fried bacon and made more cornbread.

"It's better than last night," he told her.

"I used sugar."

He nodded approvingly.

"I made it best when I had eggs." She looked out of the window and said wistfully, "I hope I can have chickens again. I miss their talk in the early morning."

"You'll have them," he said.

"Chickens are scarce out here. Most of the ranchers don't want chickens or hogs or gardens—nothing but cattle."

"Where did yours come from?"

"A farmer moved here in a covered wagon from Tennessee. His wife had the hen and it took to setting on the way. The wife died of chills before they got here, and the farmer traded the hen and eggs to Mr. Myers. Said he had no more use for them; sold his wagon and went on to California. Mr. Myers was going to kill the hen when I was in to Clarendon—only time I ever was there in three years—and I gave him a dollar for the hen and eggs. Ben had a fit, but I stuck to it—and we had a lot of good eating from the chickens and the eggs."

Her repeated references to the chickens were more touching than her feeling toward Ben, and her next words showed what she was thinking.

"I was at the funeral when they buried Mrs. Harding," she went on, "and I heard her daughter was coming out here. Do you suppose she's there on the ranch now?"

He said, "I saw her day before yesterday. Matter of fact, Harding said he was going to send her over to visit you."

"Me!" Her face underwent a variety of emotions. First it was suffused with pleasure; then for a moment she seemed doubtful;

and at the last, as a woman would, she began to think about the looks of the house. Her eyes darted from stove to washbasin, from one corner to another. "Well, I—"

"Now, look. Don't go to running around as if you were chasing an eight-year-old steer through the chaparral. This woman doesn't care how your house looks."

"But I've never had a woman in this house," she said pathetically.

"How about Mrs. Harding?"

"She was an invalid. I never saw her alive."

"You went to the funeral, though?"

"It's the only outing some of us ever get—a funeral. Anyway, Ben owed Mr. Harding for some corn."

He put on his hat. "If Stella Harding comes to see you, you won't need to worry about your house."

"What do you mean, Bart?"

He grinned. "You'll see."

Again he was up before dawn, but not ahead of Catherine. "I fixed a lunch for you," she said.

He was pleased as he took it. "I'll be back before dark," he said.

He called the black by rattling a handful of shelled corn in a leather *morral*, or nosebag. He went up to the spring with hammer and staples and wire-stretcher. He restrung what wire he could, but where it had been cut he had to put new wire between two posts. He was wrapping an end of the stiff wire around a post when a voice behind him said: "All right, Wagner!"

He whirled and drew both six-shooters with lightning speed. But the man behind him was smiling sardonically, his hands in the clear, away from his sides. He was a good-sized man with cold blue eyes, big hat, and light brown whiskers that covered his chin.

Bart said, still holding his .44's, "You took an awful chance with your life just then."

The man laughed shortly. "I knew Bart Wagner would never shoot a man whose hands were in the clear."

"You might have been wrong about who I was."

"It's my business to be right. I recognized you from the description and also from your work with a gun. I figgered it was you when Murphy told me how you beat him to the draw in Tascosa."

Bart said coldly, "I've seen all I want of Murphy. The next time I draw on him, I'm going to shoot."

"You're a killer—and a killer is always in trouble." The man grinned unpleasantly. He would have been a handsome man if there had not been so much evil in his eyes. "Know me?" he asked.

"I suppose you're Xenophon Jones," said Bart, dropping his pistols back into their holsters.

Jones's voice was harsh and cold, like his eyes. "In Mobeetie they call me the Killer Kid."

"I don't care what they call you in Tascosa or in hell. If you want to impress me, start drawing."

"Tough man," said Jones. "I know there's a price on your head in New Mexico."

"I don't doubt it."

"Sixteen hundred dollars."

Bart paused. "It was twelve when I left."

"It's gone up."

"Like the price on a steer."

Jones was suddenly suspicious because he did not quite understand. "You ain't bigger."

"I'm older," Bart said.

Jones studied him. "The Yagers raised some money to add to the reward."

Bart asked bluntly, "Are you trying to claim it?"

"Not me."

"I killed him in self-defense."

"If you really thought that was a defense," Jones said, "you would not have left Socorro so fast."

Bart put his foot up on a wire. "You know better than that. The whole country is full of Yagers."

"And a hanging by a Yager cousin makes you rot just as fast as a hanging by the law."

Bart picked up the hammer and staples. "You're trespassing on Lewis land," he said.

"Listen, Wagner!" Jones's voice was harsh. "I need help. This court session has got to be scared off."

"Are you afraid of courts?"

Jones shrugged. "The longer we keep the courts out of the Panhandle, the better will be the pickin's."

Bart said, "You can't keep them out forever."

"Why not? We've kept them out this long. It's a thousand miles to Austin, and what do they care down there what happens up here? Do you think the legislature is going to spend money to send an army of Rangers up here to establish court, when court can be held at Weatherford or Henrietta?"

"It's too far."

"What does a man from Clarksville care about that?"

Bart nodded slowly.

"If this first session can be stopped," said Jones, "it will be years before they try it again."

"And you figure to stop it?"

"I'm going to throw the fear of the Lord into anybody who might be qualified as a juror, so they won't dare to convict. They've got two of my men down there, and I don't aim for them to hang."

"Maybe they need it," said Bart.

Jones grinned coldly. "They may—but I need them more."

"I understand they had running irons in the fire. That's illegal in Texas."

"They found no stock," said Jones.

Bart said, "I've got a lot of work to do."

"Hold on," said Jones. "There's something for us to talk over."

"I can't imagine what."

"I've got to burn the Quarter Circle JB."

"It would be cheaper to burn cow chips."

"Old Ben Lewis and the girl have made an issue of it," Jones said, "and I've got to make an example of them. Otherwise all the Panhandle will start acting smart and giving me trouble."

"You killed Ben. Why don't you kill her?"

Jones hesitated. "I'd just as soon—but the Panhandle ranchers would get their backs up and organize for sure. It's one thing to kill a man, but a woman—"

"I never figured that would stop you."

Jones moistened his lips. "I don't like to kill a woman. Maybe that's the Virginia gentleman's blood in me. I've killed them, but I don't like it. I just want to burn the place without hurting her —and I want you to help by keeping her away from that buffalo gun."

"Are you afraid of the gun?"

"She shoots damn' straight," said Jones.

"Why don't you try at night?"

"I have."

"A dark night—"

"It's moonlight every night until court is called—and she sleeps with both ears to the ground. She's awake before we can cross the creek."

"You killed her chickens, didn't you?"

"I thought it would scare her away without any more trouble."

Bart looked at him. "I'll have no part in it," he said.

"I can't let her get by with this," Jones said warningly. "It would break up my own gang."

Bart shrugged.

"I want to get rid of her as painlessly as possible, before it becomes an issue—but she'll have to go."

"I'll still have no part in it."

Jones said coldly, "You want me to turn you in to Captain Arrington?"

"The Texas Rangers are not involved in this," said Bart.

Jones said harshly, "The Rangers do favors for New Mexican sheriffs because they get favors in return—especially in the Panhandle, so far from Texas courts."

"I never scared easy," said Bart.

"All right," said Jones, sounding disgusted, "I'll give you five hundred dollars to keep her out of the picture until my men set fire to the place."

Bart looked at him.

"Then," said Jones, "you keep on moving, like you'll have to do anyway. You might even join up with Goodanuff. He can use a fast gun like yours."

Bart studied the hammer in his hand.

"All right," said Jones, "it's a deal. Some night before court opens at Clarendon we'll hit the house about midnight. You've been sleeping in the shed. When you hear us coming, get in there and take the rifle away from her. As soon as the house is fired, I'll drop five hundred dollars on the old man's grave. All you have to do is pick it up and ride on."

Bart hefted the hammer in his hand.

"You'll need money to keep on the scout," Jones said. "A man like you has got to have money. If Arrington starts after you, you'll have to get out of the country fast."

"How is Arrington going to know I am here?"

"I'll tell him," said Jones, "if you don't do what I said."

Bart could not help thinking, for he had less than a dollar to his name.

"You've always been on the side of the law," said Jones. "And what has it brought you?"

Bart looked up. "What happens to the girl?"

Jones laughed. "Don't worry about her. Murphy and I have been playing monte for two weeks to see who gets her."

"And who does?"

"Murphy gets her first. I get her second. We'll auction off what's left."

Bart controlled himself. "There's more than one reason for not killing her, then."

Jones shrugged. "You don't see one like that every day."

"And you want me to turn her over to you?"

Jones smirked. "I know you, Wagner. You've had all kinds of women, and you know that one is like another one in the dark."

"But this one—"

"Will learn as fast as any. I'll tell you what I'll do. Make it a thousand dollars. If you've got any scruples, that should take care of them. A thousand dollars! You could buy a hundred women with that."

A thousand dollars. What was the point where sentiment went into foolishness? He owed Catherine nothing, to come right down to it.

"I'll do better yet," said Jones. "When Murphy and I get through with her, *you* can have her."

Bart looked at the evilly handsome face and suddenly was filled with revulsion. The frontier was no place for niceties, and yet there were some things—he hit Jones on the jaw and a second time on the nose.

Jones's evil eyes blazed as he came to the attack. Bart gave ground slowly, watching for an opening, but Jones knew how to use his hands. He caught Bart high on the cheekbone and rocked him for a moment. Then Bart charged in with both arms pumping, and drove the man back.

Jones muttered, "You're crazy!" and hit him in the face with a fist that felt like a sledge hammer. It drove Bart back, and one foot stepped in mud just as Jones hit him again. He tried to move, but the mud held his boot, and he went down, floundering, while Jones stood on firm ground and waited.

Bart got out slowly. Jones was holding a six-shooter on him.

"I could kill you," Jones said, "and I wouldn't mind in the least —but I need you."

Bart stared at him.

"Leave the woman out of it," said Jones. "Just keep her from killing my men until we can fire the place."

Bart said, "And then—"

"Don't worry about then. Get rid of the girl, and my men will pick her up."

"And if I run off with her?"

Jones smiled sarcastically. "I'll have men watching. You couldn't get far if you tried."

Bart said, "You can go to hell!"

Jones said, "You're a man who can play the odds. You're smart

· 68 ·

enough to know when you're licked, and here's a chance to get something out of it. I'll still give you a thousand dollars to get that rifle away from her."

Bart did not answer.

"It's a deal, then." Jones said, "Turn around."

A moment later Bart felt his six-shooters being taken from the holsters.

"I'll lay them in the wagon," said Jones. "And remember what I said—a thousand dollars."

Bart turned around slowly, just in time to see Jones mount his horse and gallop over a hill.

Well, a thousand dollars *was* a lot of money.

CHAPTER VII

BART RETURNED to the ranch house before sundown. It was quiet then, and quail were calling up and down the valley. In the bottom of the canyon, the Caprock threw long shadows almost to the other side, and the last few laggard steers had left the grama grass high on the slopes and were making their meandering way down to the creek, while the pleasant smoke of burning cedar rose from the chimney and lay in slowly spreading blue layers in the momentarily quiet air.

Buzzards flapped off the ground ahead of him, taking the air heavily, as if they were gorged, and he saw that the carcasses of the chickens were pretty well cleaned up.

He stopped by the back door. The pail was sitting by the barrel, and he filled it. When he straightened up, he was facing Stella Harding.

"Oh," she said, as if she had not expected to see him. "You are still in the country, Mr. Wagner."

He nodded. "So are you."

Catherine said from the fragrant dimness within the cabin, "Oh,

Bart, Miss Harding—Stella—has come to stay for a few days, just as you said."

"She'll be company," Bart said briefly.

"It will be fun to have a woman to talk to," said Catherine, apparently sensing his disapproval of Stella.

He carried the water into the cabin. "It sure will," he said heartily. "I expect you two will be talking your heads off for a week, so a man won't be able to get a word in edgeways."

"We don't often get a chance," said Catherine, looking at him quizzically.

He smiled at her. "You go right ahead," he said, picking up the soap. "I don't blame you at all."

He started to push his hat back with his forearm, but Stella lifted it off his head almost as soon as he reached for it. "I'll hang it up for you," she said.

Bart glanced at her. She was taller than Catherine and more slender, and perhaps that was why certain womanly features of hers were quite prominent. He noted that she had leaned far over the water bucket to get his hat, and now he watched her as she walked away. Then he saw Catherine look at him, and he bent immediately to his washing.

He ate in silence, with Stella's remarks almost entirely addressed to him. "That's a beautiful horse you have, Mr. Wagner."

He nodded, his mouth full of cornbread.

"I didn't recognize the mark. Is that a New Mexico brand?"

"South Texas," said Bart. "H Flower de Luce."

"You mean Fleur de Lis."

He looked at her. "In Kansas City you can call it anything you want, but in Texas it's Flower de Luce when it's on a horse or a cow."

"Oh, are you from Kansas City, Miss Harding?" Catherine asked. Then her eyes turned briefly toward Bart.

"I won't be from Kansas City any longer than I can help," said Stella, and turned to Bart. "I would like to hear more about brands, Mr. Wagner."

Bart said brusquely, "If you stay in Texas, you'll hear a lot about brands." He got up and left the table. He went outside and walked around to the front and stood there scowling at Ben Lewis's grave and its newly burned headboard.

The front door opened and Catherine called. "Bart, there's pie —apple pie."

He remembered the dried apples. "All right," he said. "I'll be there in a minute."

He went inside and ate his pie in silence. He didn't like those two women together. Stella Harding's game he understood, for he had known women like her. And for that very reason he did not like her around Catherine Lewis, for Catherine was unspoiled.

By the time he had finished his pie, it was almost dark. He went outside in the twilight to have a smoke, but again there was an interruption when Stella Harding came out to stand beside him. "Pretty, isn't it?" she said.

He was looking across the canyon at the wavering layers of gray and red and purple rock, and he answered without thinking, "Yes."

"I mean, pretty damned monotonous," she said in her husky voice.

He turned to stare at her.

"You're not shocked," she said scornfully. "You've heard women say worse than that."

"Not respectable women," he said.

"Women in dance halls?"

He looked at her steadily.

"What's so wonderful about being respectable," she demanded, "when dance-hall women have all the fun?"

"I never figured their life was easy," he answered.

"They make a living at it."

"For most of them," he said, "it's no fun."

"For me," she said pointedly. "it's always fun."

"Stella," he said, frowning, "you're trying to push something on me."

"It isn't something you won't like," she said with assurance.

"That's as may be—but you'll have to let me figure it out however I can." He looked at her curiously. "Why are you so insistent?"

"I know what I want," she said. "I saw my mother become a nervous wreck because all she needed was a man."

"Your father—"

"Was too busy with cows—and mother was too modest to speak her mind and too much puritan to do anything about it with anybody else. And what did it all get her? An early grave." She said bitterly, "I have no intention of going the same way."

He drew a deep breath. "Right now," he said, "I've got a job to do here on the ranch."

"You don't work all night," she told him.

She was insistent beyond anything he'd ever seen in a woman, and he did not answer. Somewhere down the canyon, a hoot owl began to call.

"Are you sweet on that Lewis woman?" she demanded.

Watching the colors in the canyon wall fade into gray, he answered, "It wouldn't be any of your business if I were."

"I'll *make* it my business."

Unruffled, he answered, "You don't need to. I have no designs on her."

She took his arm. Her fingers were strong, and her grasp unnecessarily harsh. "Some day I'll have a ranch a hundred times this big."

He shook her off impatiently. "I'm not the only man in the Panhandle."

She moved in front of him and faced him squarely—a beautiful woman, there in the half-dark. "Bart, I saw you offer your six-shooter to the man they were threatening to hang." Her eyes were almost luminous. "It took a real man to do a thing like that."

He looked down at her. "Other men have the same qualities, even if they are not as flamboyant. What's the matter with Hector Johnson?"

"Why do you mention him?"

"I saw his eyes on you when you brought the coffee."

She said scornfully, "Every cowpuncher's eyes are on me all the time. There isn't a one who wouldn't give a month's pay to climb into my bed."

"Hector Johnson is in love with you," he said.

"Love! A plowhand and a race horse!"

"He's honorable and he's steady."

"I don't want somebody steady. I want somebody who is a man."

The woman knew what she was doing, all right. That extravagant gesture of his in facing down Gentry—which might have been motivated by a subconscious desire to show off before Stella —had had its effect on the woman. And her very persistence, instead of repelling him, seemed more of a challenge than anything else. But he was not ready to make a decision about her; he had other things on the fire.

"Goodnight, ma'am," he said, "and don't walk around in your nightgown tonight. There's rattlesnakes down here."

She said coolly, "I never saw a snake that scared me."

"I believe you—but this time you'd better do as I suggest. If you want me to think about you, give me a chance to make up my own mind."

Her voice changed suddenly. She was almost pleading. "What *do* you think of me, Bart?"

He said, "You're a breath-taking woman, and any man would be honored to have you—but I've got work to do first."

She sighed, but her voice sounded resigned. "Very well, Bart, I'll be patient."

He chuckled. "If you are, I'll wager it's the first time."

He found an ivory toothpick in his lower left vest pocket as they walked back to the cabin. Catherine was sitting in the door, and he wondered how long she had been watching them. "Goodnight," he said. "See you in the morning." He started off, but called back, "I'm not sleeping in the shed tonight. I'm going up by the spring to see if I can get track of a bear."

"We could use the oil," Catherine said, "but be careful, Bart. Goodnight."

He had, he thought, anticipated and prevented any hasty move on Stella's part that might cause them both discomfort. He went to the shed, got his blanket and quilts, and walked up the slope a little way to bed down in the open, just to be sure. No telling what ideas that woman had picked up in Kansas City. And it wasn't a thing to think much about until a man was ready to go through with it.

The next morning he scouted the entire pasture looking for unbranded calves, and found two. He tied a strip of white cloth to their ears to mark them for later, when he would return with a branding iron, and rode to the ranch house with the count of steers and heifers by yearlings and by twos and threes in his head.

Strange horses were under the cottonwood when he reached the ranch house. He left the black among the willows and went to the house. He heard men's voices, opened the door, and went in. Catherine was at the stove, pouring coffee. Stella was standing at the front window, looking out, but she turned as Bart ducked under the door frame.

A big man stood up. He wore a white shirt and dark vest, boots, big hat. He was heavy-shouldered, and his neck sat down between his shoulders. He had a full beard beginning to turn gray, and his eyes were sharp and penetrating. "This your man, Miz Lewis?" he asked.

She said timidly, "That's Bart Wagner, Mr. Goodnight."

Goodnight stuck out a huge hand. "Charlie Goodnight, JA Ranch."

"Pleased to make your acquaintance," said Bart.

"This here—" The cattleman motioned to a black-haired man, not as big as Goodnight but with observant eyes and a calmness of manner that set him apart. "Judge Willis, judge of the Thirty-fifth Judicial District, come to hold court in Clarendon next week."

They shook hands. "I'm pleased," said Bart. "Been hearing about the court, but I never knew whether to believe it or not."

"It's hard to believe up in this country," Goodnight agreed.

Catherine seemed now to have recovered her poise. Bart felt sure she never had had that much company in her life, and he smiled at her as she put coffee before him, but he did not look at Stella, who was watching them.

"That's what we come to talk about," said Goodnight, sitting down. "Miz Lewis, I'm sorry. I didn't know old Ben was dead. Did you see who shot him?"

"No," she said. "He was shot up at the spring, and I don't recollect—"

"How do you know Xenophon Jones did it?" asked Willis in a startlingly deep and musical voice.

"Xenophon Jones said he did it."

"He—or one of his men?"

"He—" She hesitated.

"Can you recall his exact words?"

"He came up when I was feeding my chickens some bread scraps, and he said, 'Old Ben is dead up at the spring, and you'd better get out of here quick if you don't want the same thing.' "

"But he did not actually say who shot your husband?"

"No, sir, I guess he didn't. He just said—"

Willis shook his head. "An implied threat is the most you can make out of it." He was speaking to Goodnight. "You'd better rely on the conviction of Three-Finger and Indian George for branding cattle that didn't belong to them."

Goodnight spoke to Bart. "We came to call a conference, and you might as well take old Ben's place. We're going to have trouble getting a jury. The legislature divided the Panhandle into counties about five or six years ago, but that just means they set the boundaries. Each county was to be formally organized when it got a hundred and fifty property owners. Well, hell," he said, "everybody knows there aren't that many property owners in the whole Panhandle. Nevertheless, we got Wheeler and Donley and Oldham organized, and we got the legislature to set up the Thirty-fifth Judicial District so we wouldn't have to go clear across hellan'gone and back, to go to court. Right now Judge Willis is here to hold court. We've got plenty of evidence against the two men we're holding, but we can't convict them without a jury."

"There should be enough cowhands—"

Judge Willis said in his musical voice, "Jurymen must be property owners, Mr.—Wagner, is it?"

"Mr. Goodnight is a property owner."

"Every rancher in the Panhandle," said Goodnight, "is a property owner—but they are also members of the Panhandle Stock Association, and since the stock association is prosecuting these men, its members cannot serve on a jury."

Bart put down his coffee and began to make a cigarette.

"Here, have a cigar," said Goodnight, reaching for his vest pocket. "Oh, hell, I'm out," he said. "I'm sorry. I've given them all away already."

Bart looked up, and went ahead, tapping on the sack.

"It's a serious problem," said Willis. "I'm willing to stretch every point possible, but we'll have to observe the statutory requirements for jurymen."

"That won't be hard," said Bart.

Goodnight glared at him. "Have you any idea what you're talking about?"

Bart licked the paper and rolled it closed. "I think so. You want jurymen, and you've got to have property owners."

"Well?" said Goodnight.

"The law doesn't say how much property a man has to own, does it, judge?"

"No. It must be real estate, however—not personal property." But Willis began to smile.

"Then take a quarter of land near Clarendon and survey an addition," said Bart. "Deed one lot to every cowhand around the county. The lots won't be worth much but they will be property."

Goodnight's eyes shone. He slapped the table with his big hand. "Fine!" he shouted. "Fine! Why didn't somebody think of that before?"

"A good solution," Willis agreed.

"There must be four or five hundred hands in the county or the surrounding counties in the district," said Goodnight. His massive frame was rocking with energy. "I've got a quarter near Clarendon. I'll get the surveyor up there tomorrow."

"How will you get the names?" asked Willis. "These men have not been voters."

"I'll send out word. I'll prepare a stack of blank deeds and sign them and let my men scatter them through the country. The Shoebars and the Spades and the Matadors and the JA and the LJ will have plenty, for that matter—but I'll give one to anybody employed on a Panhandle ranch."

"You'd better keep a register of the deeds," Willis warned.

"Certainly, judge." Goodnight chuckled. "Anything to be legal."

Bart got a twig and lighted it at the gate, then sat down again, holding the twig downward to get it to burning.

Goodnight was elated. He pounded the table again. "We'll get a conviction that will stand up in any court in Texas."

The pounding of hooves came from near the creek, and Bart went to the window. A man on a gray horse slid off in front of the door. Goodnight was up to meet him. "What are you heatin' up a good horse over?" he demanded.

The man was big and raw-boned and had a sweeping, tawny mustache. Bart recognized Hector Johnson and glanced at Stella. A tiny quirk of scornfulness showed at the corners of her well shaped mouth.

"Harding sent me to find you, Mr. Goodnight, and they told me at the JA you went up this way."

"I did," Goodnight said impatiently. "Yes, I did."

"The outlaws have gotten together," said Hector between breaths. "They hired Piggie Benson to come down here from Tascosa and break up the court."

"How do you know?" asked Goodnight.

"Two of my hands got fired four days ago for fighting. They went up to Tascosa and saw this regular recruiting station where Benson is signing up men—him and Xenophon Jones."

"Your men signed up?"

"No. They're good citizens—no killers—and they came back to warn the boss."

Goodnight's chin stuck out. "How many are they bringing?"

"The talk in Tascosa is fifty."

Goodnight was silent for a moment. Then he said, "It might be less. It might be more."

Judge Willis seemed to find it incredible. "Do you mean to imply they will actually try to intimidate the court?"

"Try!" Goodnight roared. He pounded the table. "Judge, you don't know the Panhandle. There are more outlaws here than honest men, and I say to you on a stack of Bibles, it is my firm belief that they have the gall to intimidate the court if they can. If they cannot intimidate the court, they will intimidate the witnesses."

"Witnesses will be protected."

"And if they cannot intimidate the witnesses—all of whom will be members of the association—they will intimidate the jurymen."

"That is not possible," said Willis. "No court would allow its jurymen to be threatened."

"Judge," Goodnight said impatiently, "you still don't know the character of the country you're dealing with. If you were a cowhand and if you saw fifty or a hundred outlaws standing around the courtroom, you never would bring in a verdict of guilty, because if you had enough sense to lick the bottom of a cake pan you'd know your life wouldn't be worth a plugged Chinese nickel."

"The orderly processes of law—"

Goodnight put both hands on the table and leaned close to Willis's face. "What does that mean to a dead man? These men want to live!" He swung vigorously away from the table. "I tell you, judge, we will never get a conviction under the rifles and six-shooters of Xenophon Jones and his Tascosa outlaws."

Willis began to look worried. "If the situation is as bad as you say, I will not even hold court; it would be a travesty of justice under conditions of implied threat and intimidation."

"You could fight," said Bart.

Willis shook his head. "A pitched battle in a courtroom? Too many innocent people would be killed or injured." He got up. "Charlie, you have just about convinced me you're not ready for civilized law. You'd better forget it until the percentage of outlaws goes down."

"How is it going to be lowered," Goodnight demanded, "when there is no law?"

"I don't know, Charlie."

"Look, judge." Goodnight pounded the table again. "You were appointed by the governor to come here and hold court, weren't you?"

"Yes, but—"

"And the stock association guaranteed you a bonus to make it worth while, didn't it?"

"Certainly, but—"

"If we had things under control the way you think they should be, we wouldn't need a judge," Goodnight said scornfully. "So go on back to Austin and tell the governor to send us a man with some guts!"

Willis seemed unmoved by that outburst, but he studied Goodnight soberly. Finally he said, "All right, Charlie. I'll hold court, but I'm warning you: if this develops into an open gunfight and spectators get killed, it will hurt the Panhandle for a hundred years."

Goodnight slapped him on the shoulder with a blow that rocked him in his chair. "I knew you would if I needled you!" he roared. "How about a drink?"

Willis smiled. "You said something, Charlie."

"Miz Lewis, old Ben have any Cedar Valley left?"

She nodded as she got up.

"Give us a look at the bottle," said Goodnight, "and I'll send you a whole one."

She went behind the curtain.

Goodnight was elated. "Good head on you, Wagner."

Catherine brought the bottle, about half full. She set it on the table and gave them tin cups.

Goodnight poured three big drinks. "Drink up!" he said, and did. He emptied his cup and set it down. "It may not be easy," he said to Willis, "but we'll do it."

Willis set down his cup. "We'd better get on. You've got plenty to do before next Monday."

Goodnight got up. "Thanks, Miz Lewis. I'll see you get a new bottle."

"I won't need it," she said.

"Maybe you want to sell what's left of the case."

"This is the last bottle."

Goodnight looked sharply at her. "I was in Myers's when he bought that case. . . . He must have hit it pretty hard."

She said nothing.

"Nobody else had any?" Goodnight insisted. Perhaps he was trying to find out how close Ben Lewis had been to Xenophon Jones.

"All except Bart—Mr. Wagner here. He had a little out of this bottle."

Goodnight's shaggy eyebrows raised. "Old Ben'd turn over if he knew you was drinkin' his whisky."

Catherine said hastily, "Mr. Wagner had to have something while I took the bullet out of his arm." Then she bit her lip, and Bart felt sorry for her. She had known better than to tell a thing like that, but the unusual amount of company and the prominence of men like Goodnight and Willis, and the sharp-pointed questions of Goodnight, had upset her.

CHAPTER VIII

"A BULLET?" Goodnight asked, and looked at Bart. Bart finished his drink. The eyes of Hector Johnson were on him, suspicious; those of Judge Willis were inquiring; Stella's were excited in their black depths; Catherine's brown eyes were troubled; Goodnight was alert, waiting.

"I picked it up near Tascosa," Bart said, "from one of your outlaws. Matter of fact, I saw him in Clarendon two days ago."

Goodnight's eyes narrowed. "Who?"

"Stud Murphy."

"Did you have a shoot-out with him?"

"No. He wanted my horse, but I persuaded him not to take it; then he shot me as he got up off the ground."

"Where'd you get hit?"

"Left arm."

"All right now?"

Bart nodded.

"Looks all right," said Goodnight. "You swing it good." He turned. "You ready, judge?"

Willis arose. "I must admit I don't like the situation. What you are planning with the sale of lots is legal enough, but you are setting up a situation where you will almost be compelled to use violence in the end. And that does nothing but create a new kind of violence."

"You're wrong, judge. Violence rightly used and not abused gives the law a chance to establish itself. It's the basis of all law, anyway. What would law amount to if you couldn't hang a man or put him in jail?"

Willis went out ahead of him. "I hope you're right."

Bart poured another cup of coffee and followed them out. Catherine went toward the woodpile near the shed.

Bart stood just outside the door, in the shade, and silently watched Goodnight and Willis mount and ride off across the creek. They raised their hands as they looked back, and Bart waved in return. Then he stood for a moment, finishing his cigarette.

The wind rustled down through the canyon and moved the mesquite bushes along the creek. The drooping limbs of the willows whipped back and forth, and the leaves of the cottonwood stirred and fluttered and made a mass of tiny moving lights as the leaves presented different surfaces to the sun, until the tree seemed almost alive.

Bart turned. His coffee would be just right. But Hector Johnson's nasal voice rose from inside the sodhouse. "I say you came here to be close to that gun-hand!"

Stella's voice was low but clear, and filled with contempt. "Hector Johnson, I want no more talk from you. You're a ranch foreman, and that's all, and you never will be anything else. I told you six months ago I didn't want you to bother me any more."

"It's him," said Hector. "It's Wagner! You're stuck on him!"

"Whether I am or not, it's none of your business." Her voice raised sharply. "Now get out of here before I tell my father and have you fired!"

"You heard him admit he was shot in a gunfight," Hector said accusingly.

"He was being a man when it happened. Now *get out!*"

There was no answer. Bart guessed that Hector was accepting

her verdict. Actually, there was nothing else to do, but Bart felt sorry for him, because he had recognized in Hector's voice the acid jealousy of a man inexperienced with women and perhaps almost wholly ignorant of them. Hector had been overwhelmed by Stella's dazzling attraction and probably seduced by her advances, but she had repulsed him, perhaps scornfully, and now he was eaten up with a terrible futility at not being able to possess her.

Bart did not blame him very much. It had happened that way before: that a stranger, coming in, presented a more attractive side than the man already there. It was sad, but—Bart shrugged—women were that way, as far as he knew.

Hector Johnson clumped heavily out the back door and around the side of the house. Bart had not moved. Hector stopped and his eyes widened. "You heard it!" he said accusingly.

Bart dropped his cigarette on the hard ground. "You didn't hold your voice down."

Hector stalked up to him. "I'm going to give you a licking."

"I figgered you were about ready to try."

"You're just going through the country. You won't be here long enough to catch your breath, no matter what. I know your kind: get a woman's confidence, and then pull out in the middle of the night."

"It isn't important," said Bart, but he knew what Hector meant: that a man like Bart Wagner went around making bad women out of good women.

"You can drop your guns," said Hector.

"I can, but I won't."

"You going to fight fair?"

"I don't want to argue with a ninny," Bart said suddenly, impatient with him. "Nobody could take Stella away from anybody, because she wouldn't be loyal to anybody in the first place."

Hector's eyes blazed. "I ought to gun you for saying that."

"Save your lead for men like Xenophon Jones and Piggie Benson."

Hector said, "You're the kind that wrecks homes."

Bart grew tired of the argument and its silliness. He knew that

Hector was confused and frustrated and needed an excuse to work off his futility. So Bart gave it to him. "Do you think," he asked, "that Stella would leave the LJ with a man like me in preference to you?"

That touched Johnson off. He came at Bart with both arms swinging. Bart stepped back, getting the range. Johnson rushed him. Bart met it and pushed him back, then caught him twice in the face as Johnson stumbled away.

Johnson shook his head and came roaring back. He jolted Bart with a hard fist on the chin and another under the heart.

Bart hit him with his left, but it didn't have much power, and it sent a shaft of pain up into his shoulder.

Johnson came on, swinging hard. Bart stepped inside and chopped him twice on the chin with his right, hard. Johnson wavered. Bart hit him again. It sounded like a meat cleaver slicing through a backbone of beef. Johnson rolled on his feet, his arms loose. He straightened up and started toward Bart again, and Bart coldly hit him three more times on the chin with his right, and let him fall in the dirt and lie there. He turned and started into the house.

Stella was at the door, her eyes shining. "You brute," she said huskily.

He did not answer. Catherine was coming in the back door. She glanced at them and sensed something wrong. "Where's Mr. Johnson?" she asked quickly.

Bart dipped up some drinking water. "Outside," he said.

Catherine ran to the door and saw Johnson lying on the ground. He groaned, and she sucked in her breath and whirled. "Bart Wagner, did you—"

He emptied the dipper. "Do you see anybody else around here to suspect?" he asked.

She looked at him, started to say something, but stopped, puzzled.

He offered no clarification. "I'm riding up on the flat," he said.

He caught up the black and crossed the creek and trotted across the slope under the eastern Caprock. It wasn't that there was anything special to do up there; the harness he had used on the mules needed repairing more than anything else, for old Ben (he smiled wryly as he realized he was calling Catherine's dead husband "old Ben" like everybody else) had been a barbed-wire harness repair man, and Bart did not like that at all. Wire did a lot of tricks on harness: it cut the leather, for one thing; sometimes the ends came loose and made a sore on a horse or mule; and of course a piece of wire could not be depended on to hold like a piece of good leather.

But with Hector Johnson picking himself up out of the dirt, Stella Harding hoping to claim the winner, and Catherine Lewis wondering what was going on, Bart figured the best place for him was out of earshot for a while. And too, he was sore and hurt all over from the fights and the broken ribs and the gunshot wound, and he figured it was time to get away and collect himself.

He was not astonished, however, to see a rider come down from the direction of the spring an hour later, out of sight of the house. He continued his ride at a walk, but kept an eye on the rider until he knew it was Stella Harding, riding sidesaddle. Then he stopped the black and leaned on the horn, waiting.

She pulled up, her beautiful face flushed from the ride, her black hair in perfect place under a stiff-brimmed ladies' riding hat worn at a jaunty angle.

"I thought you were here to keep Mrs. Lewis company," he said.

She smiled. "From what I see, you were doing very well at that task."

"I work for her," said Bart. "That's all."

"You two almost emptied the Cedar Valley. Catherine herself said that."

"To get a bullet out of my arm."

She shook her head, smiling. "From the way you chopped down that poor foreman, I saw nothing wrong with your arm."

"The man hasn't had much fighting experience."

"But you have."

He shrugged.

Her eyes shone. "Bart Wagner," she said softly, "everything you do is perfect."

"No. By no means."

"Everything you do is done the way a *man* would do it."

"It's nothing against Johnson that he got beaten. He isn't used to my kind of fighting."

"I'd like to see you in a gunfight," she said breathlessly.

He had to admit that her repeated expressions of admiration were easy to accept—especially because she was such a beautiful woman. The obvious fact that she was also a blood-thirsty woman did not affect that feeling at all. He felt a certain kinship with her, as a matter of fact. She reminded him of a spirited wild horse that had not been properly ridden.

"Have you thought any more about Kansas City?" she asked.

He pulled the black's head up from the grass and started it walking slowly, while she kept pace. "Who would not think about it with such a woman as you?" he asked.

"It would scare some men," she said, her eyes speculative.

"I don't know that it scares me, but I don't belong in a place like Kansas City for any length of time. I am at home in the West, among horses and men. I am used to fighting and shooting." He looked at her thoughtfully. "I don't think that kind of conduct would be popular in Kansas City."

She shook her head. "A man like you would stand out any-where. It isn't the things you do, but the air of confidence those things have given you. You're never uncertain—always sure of yourself."

That wasn't exactly true, but he did not disillusion her.

"You would be a great hit with the ladies," she argued.

"If my guess about *you* is right, I would have to have two or three in reserve."

"I wouldn't share you," she said quickly.

"You wouldn't stay with me, either—only until somebody else came along."

"No man would ever have your strength and power," she said quietly.

He smiled. "But tomorrow you may be tired of strength, and you may want a man you can order around." He turned to look at her. "Tomorrow you might decide a milksop would be more fun."

She kept her eyes on his, promising but reserved and noncommittal. "You're demanding a lot," she said at last.

"I'm not really demanding anything. I'm making some observations. I wouldn't want any promises from you because you wouldn't keep them. You're the kind of woman who will do what you want to do, no matter what you promise or what you might think of at any given time."

"You don't think I can be trusted?" she asked.

He laughed. "You like men too much."

She pointed out, "I'm not attracted to Hector Johnson."

"You might be—some day."

She was scornful. "That hick cowpuncher?"

They rode in silence for a moment. The horses' hooves swished in the crisp grass. A horned toad, out in an open, sunny space near a big beargrass, saw the horses coming, and froze. Bart guided the black around it. Stella's horse, on the other side, snipped off a mouthful of creamy white beargrass blossoms.

He said, "You'd better go back while I think it over."

She smiled slowly, knowingly. "I'll go back—and wait."

"Don't wait too long," he warned. "I may decide that I don't like Kansas City at all."

"You told Catherine you had to keep on the move," she said. "You might as well go east."

She loped her horse back across the valley. She turned in the saddle before she went out of sight beyond a grove of willows, and waved. He waved back briefly, thoughtfully.

He rode on around the bend in the canyon, far out of sight of the house, and considered their words. At the same time he kept an eye on the cattle and their brands, and mentally added up cows and heifers, steers, bulls, calves, yearlings, twos, and threes, and noted their brands. He saw a couple of strays from the LJ and a scarred old Durham bull from the JA. He didn't feel like tangling with the bull just then, but he made a mental note to tell Harding and Goodnight about their stock. Those must have strayed since the calf roundup in the spring.

He found a calf with a swollen front leg and the fang marks of a snake, but the bite was at least a day old from the looks of the leg, and there wasn't much to do at that late date. The calf was bleating a lot, and the cow would not let Bart ride near it until he roped her and tied her to a mesquite, but he thought the calf would recover unless the rattlesnake had been unusually big.

He returned to the house in late afternoon, anticipating the quiet and serenity that he had come to associate with Catherine, and he noted at once that Stella's chestnut horse was not in sight and her sidesaddle not on the corral fence. He unsaddled the black, gave it a slap on the rump, and turned it loose. There was good grazing along the creek.

He looked in the water barrel and saw it was halfway down. He smelled the warm suds of a tub of boiling water, and knew Catherine was washing clothes. He did not go in immediately, but picked up the bucket and went to work to fill the barrel. It took several trips, but he filled it to the brim before he set down the bucket. He did not smell anything cooking, and he was a little early, so he sat on his heels alongside the barrel and rolled a cigarette.

He had hardly gotten it going when the back door opened and Catherine looked out. "Afraid to come in?" she demanded.

He looked up in astonishment. "Not until now," he said slowly.

"There's coffee on," she said, and went back.

He went inside slowly, remembering to duck. His experiences with women had always led to complications, but this one was unexpected. This development obviously was headed for anything but serenity. He sighed as he straightened up.

She had a galvanized tub on top of the stove, and it was filled with clothes and simmering. She started to move it to the back of the stove, but he stepped up and took it by the handles, but turned loose hurriedly when he found out they were hot.

"Here are pads," she said shortly.

He took them, and moved the tub. Then he sat down and blew on his coffee. "I take it something has happened," he said.

"You could hardly expect me to know as well as you," she answered.

"Catherine," he said, "a woman is entitled to act strange sometimes, but I don't like guessing games where I'm supposed to guess what I've done when as far as I know I haven't done anything."

She glared at him. "Don't you see anything different around here?"

He said slowly, thoughtfully, "Stella Harding left this afternoon."

"Why?" she demanded.

"I'm sure I don't know."

"You should."

"Ma'am?" he asked.

"After you fought Hector Johnson, you rode off. Then she followed you—and pretty soon she came back, and then left. You met her, didn't you?" she demanded.

"I sure did."

"But she came back about midafternoon with her nose in the air and said she was leaving immediately." Catherine added plaintively, "I thought she was going to stay several days."

"So did I, ma'am."

"What did you say to her?"

"Nothing in particular."

"You must have insulted her."

He said, "I don't think so, ma'am."

"Think!" Catherine was angry. "Don't you know?"

He sighed. "It's hard for a man to know about a woman, ma'am."

"You must have made improper remarks to her," she said, stirring the clothes with a cut-off broom handle that had turned yellow on the end that she put into the water.

"I'm sure I said nothing that would have offended you, ma'am."

"You—"

"And I'm positive she has a lot thicker hide than you have."

She laid the clothes stick across the edge of the tub. There were tears in her eyes as she turned to face him across the table. "Bart Wagner, you ran off the only woman that's ever been in this house besides me!"

He was on his feet, patting her shoulder. "I'm sorry, Catherine."

She seized the sides of the buckskin vest and buried her face on his chest, sobbing. He stood for a moment, and then, when the worst was over, he pushed her away gently. "I'm right sorry, Catherine. I'll sure try to furnish better entertainment for your company next time."

She looked up. "I know she's pretty and has nice clothes—but is she that much nicer than me, Bart?"

CHAPTER IX

THAT NIGHT he moved back into the shed. After seeing the calf with the swollen leg, he was a little skittery about snakes himself. He watched the moon come up. He saw the light go out in the house, sat up a whole hour longer, smoking. Up-canyon the hoot owl had moved from its roost of the night before, but its lonesome call sounded clear and full on the still night air. Down-canyon a coyote yapped, while up on the rim of the Caprock it sounded like a chorus of them. That was a fooler, he knew. Probably there was only one, for sometimes one could sound like a dozen.

It was a good night for outlaws to ride, he noted, and got into his blanket with his boots on. . . .

He was sound asleep when he heard the pounding of hooves through the earth. He swung into a sitting position, buckled his gun belt around him, and waited.

In the bright moonlight, three men swept across the empty ranch yard near the cottonwood tree and old Ben's grave. Apparently the drumming hooves had awakened Catherine too, for a small-sized clap of thunder went off, and the ranch yard was lighted for an instant by the yellow flame of gunpowder. He stayed where he was.

Two more riders came in from the west, galloping past the shed. He sat in the dark and watched them go. But Catherine must have run from window to window, for in a moment the old Sharps spoke again, and the riders split and went wide around the house. They were not carrying torches; apparently they wanted to start the fire from the inside—perhaps to be sure Catherine would not be burned. Or perhaps the dirt and gravel on the roof made it hard to start a fire from that direction.

The two riders joined the first three at the front of the house, and they all raced back. She met them with lead, and it was apparent she was familiar with their tactics and did not propose to be outguessed.

He set his hammers at half-cock and examined both .44s. There were five cartridges in each cylinder. He put them back in their holsters and stood up alongside a cottonwood post that held up one end of the roof of the shed. He was in the shadows, and he watched the five men come together in a group not fifty feet away, and heard them talk in low voices.

"She fights harder than a damn coyote bitch!" said one.

"She's shootin' straight too—for moonlight. My horse got creased on the right hip."

"I thought Jones said she wouldn't shoot at us no more."

Another growled, "What does Jones care? He ain't here."

"I say we start shootin'."

"Let's try one more run. Maybe that Wagner feller will get her under control."

"He sleeps in the shed, Jones told me. Prob'ly he isn't even awake yet."

"We could damn' sure wake him up."

"Go see if he's back there," said the deepest voice.

"Better call. You go stumblin' around in the dark without saying anything, you might get shot."

One man rode away from the group, and Bart waited. The man started to dismount at the shed, and Bart smelled him.

"Lookin' for me?" asked Bart.

The man jumped and whirled, his hand on his gun butt.

"Don't pull it," Bart said softly.

"Wagner?"

"Yes."

"Aren't you supposed to stop that shootin'?"

"Is that what Jones told you?"

"He said you'd keep us from gettin' hit."

With an easy motion Bart struck a match on his belt buckle and held it in the man's face. The man was swarthy and he wore a straw hat, but he was part *anglo* and he smelled rank like an old billy goat.

"You got a name?" asked Bart.

"Tex-Mex."

"Go on back to your job. Stick to Jones's orders."

"All right."

Tex-Mex rode back and conferred with the outlaws. Bart stayed in the shadow. In a moment the outlaws started a sweep around the house but at a greater distance.

Bart watched them go. Catherine's rifle spoke twice, once from each side, and he noted that she was lugging the big weapon pretty handily. But if she ever realized how easily they could have rushed her, she would have been frightened to death. He walked slowly and carefully up to the back door. "Catherine!" he called.

There was a second of silence, then her voice: "Bart?"

"Yes, ma'am."

She opened the door carefully. It was dark inside, of course, but he could make out the white of her nightgown and he could hear her bare feet padding on the floor.

He closed the door behind him, and heard her push a cartridge into the chamber of the Sharps. He smelled the faint fragrance of her sachet in the dark, above the acrid smell of black powder. Then he heard hooves drumming. "It's company again," she said, and put the rifle barrel through a window.

He went to the opposite side and looked out, his face near the edge. A man had to admire her courage.

The outlaws split again and went around the house on both sides. This time they fired, and he heard bullets smack into the sod walls. One came through the window; glass shattered and sprayed over the floor, but again Catherine's rifle boomed. He waited for a moment, but the outlaws were gathering out by the shed.

Catherine called, "Bart?"

"I'm all right," he said, thinking of the things he could do with a thousand dollars.

"I'm so dry," she said. "I always get this way when they come."

"Natural," he said.

He heard her bare feet on the floor, and then a suppressed scream and a sharp intake of breath.

"You hurt?" he asked. "What's the matter?"

"I—stepped on glass."

He struck a match and looked at her in her white muslin nightgown, her hair in two long black braids down her back. She was smaller without her shoes on.

He noted her tight mouth, and looked at the floor. Her left foot was in a pool of blood.

"We better wrap that up," he said.

He observed her white face, and helped her to a chair. She tucked the nightgown carefully under her legs, and he shook his head when he saw her foot bleeding freely from a cut over two inches long. "Where are the rags?" he asked as the match burned down.

"In the warming oven."

He got up and tossed the match into the stove. He got a rag, found a side of bacon in the pantry, cut a thick strip with his pocket knife, and went back. Her feet were warm and clean-smelling. He put the bacon against the cut and wrapped it tightly in place with the cloth.

She stepped on it gingerly.

"Stay out of that glass until I get it swept up," he ordered, and went to her bed behind the curtain to get her shoes.

Before he reached her, he heard the hooves again. He dropped the shoes in her lap, and ran to the window.

They rode by, shouting: "Come out with your hands up and we won't hurt you!"

Bart looked toward Catherine. In the bright moonlight, she had laid the rifle on the table, and her head was wavering, as if she was about to faint. It would have been easy to put his hand on the rifle and keep her from shooting for a few minutes.

The outlaws started back. Bart waited until they were close. A shot crashed through the top of the window, and Bart noted grimly that they were shooting high enough not to hit her, as Jones had ordered.

He saw the fifth man go by, and took a shot at him. The man yelled.

Bart spoke to Catherine. "All right?"

Her muffled voice answered, "Yes," and he wondered if her head was in her arms.

He waited. They would be gathered by the shed now, trying to find him. He went to the back door and opened it cautiously, in time to see a yellow flicker of light in the direction of the shed. "They're burning the rest of it!" he said, and took two big steps back for the rifle. He sighted along it and took one shot. A horse squealed and rocketed into the night, bucking and trumpeting.

In a moment the shed was blazing high. The roof was sod, but the rafters and supports were wood, and they went up like dry powder. For a few moments the entire ranch yard was lighted up like day.

At the height of the fire he felt again the beating of hooves, and ran to the window. As they went by, he took three pistol shots, and they answered wildly, not aiming at anything. A shot from the rifle sounded at the other window.

He stood for a while, waiting. "I think they've gone for the night," he said.

"I hope so," Catherine said fervently.

They waited another quarter of an hour. Finally Bart found the lamp and struck a match. He lit the lamp and put the chimney on, then looked at Catherine. She was fully dressed.

She saw his questing look, and blushed. Then she swayed into his arms. He flicked the burned-out match onto the stove. "It's pretty early in the morning to be dressing," he said, "but you did the right thing."

At daylight he saw there was nothing left of the shed but charred timbers and smoldering bales of hay. "One thing is sure," he said. "These gents mean business."

He thought she looked pretty pale. "Isn't there any way to stop them?" she asked, setting four big pancakes in front of him.

"We stopped them last night."

"I mean for good."

"Nothing but the courts," he said, reaching for the sorghum.

"Mr. Goodnight seemed to think the court would get started in Clarendon."

"The court has everything in its favor. Once it has sat on a case, it will be only a matter of time until it is firmly established."

"Mr. Goodnight didn't think the outlaws would allow—"

"Not willingly," he said with a smile.

"It sounds as if you have an idea."

"Yes, ma'am." He pushed back from the table and reached for his hat. "I have a real good idea." He stood up. "The outlaws mean business, and it's natural they should. They've had easy pickin's in the Panhandle for a long time. If they get run out of here, there's only Indian Territory, and Judge Parker at Fort Smith is making the Territory pretty warm for them. So they'll be prepared—and I figure we can be prepared too."

She looked at him gratefully. "I'm glad to hear you say that, Bart." She watched him feel in his vest pocket for tobacco. "Where are you going now?" she asked.

"Court opens a week from Monday," he said, "and I think we can get prepared for it just as well as Xenophon Jones and Piggie Benson."

"You'll be gone today?"

"All day," he said.

He saw the doubt form in her eyes. "Bart, are you coming back?"

He grinned down at her. "I'm counting on it."

"You might change your mind."

He said seriously, "That should not mean anything to you, Catherine."

"It does, though. You—you treated me like a woman, not like a child."

He took a deep breath. "Don't have any doubt about that. Remember, there are plenty of men to treat you like a woman. There are a hundred men for every woman in the Panhandle—maybe more."

"They couldn't be like you—Bart."

He watched her eyes. "Maybe not."

"You're sure you mean to come back?"

Suddenly afraid for having won her feeling so completely, he said roughly, "Catherine, don't forget I'm a killer."

It made no impression on her. "I don't care. Anyway, I know about it. Ben told me."

He stared at her. "What did he tell you?"

"He said he saw a man named Wagner shoot three men in El Paso. Ben said it was murder—sheer murder—and he said he tried to help them."

Bart went cold, but asked finally, "How did he help?"

She said slowly, reluctantly but honestly, as if she was resigned to the worst, "Something with a mirror—in somebody's eyes."

He stared at her. "The four of them pulled down on me in front of the Elephant Saloon, as I told you—and then—that old man was Ben?" he asked, incredulous.

She watched his face fearfully. "That's what he said, Bart. He had gone to El Paso for salt, and he met the Yagers and they told him you were a killer, and—"

"Ben told you all this?" he demanded.

"Yes."

He stared at her. "And you were old Ben's wife," he said finally, accusingly.

Her voice was quiet, her eyes asking him to understand. "I had no part in anything like that, Bart."

He was silent for a moment. The old man who had flashed the mirror in his eyes had been seventy-five years old. They had let him go because he claimed it was an accident—and he was cantankerous, irascible, mealy-mouthed—that old man had been Catherine's husband.

"Was it fair?" she asked.

"One against four?"

"Then it wasn't murder!" She seemed almost frantic.

"How could it have been?"

"I never wanted to believe him—but I had no way of proving any different, except I couldn't understand how one man would be taking advantage of four men."

"Why didn't you want to believe him?"

Her eyes were clouded. "He was always looking for things I liked, and then talking them down to me. I think it pleased him to let me like something and take it away from me."

"It must have—but why did you like me at all? You hadn't seen me then."

Her eyes were like stars. "The first time he told it, he was just telling a story to amuse me, and the way he told it, I thought Bart Wagner must have been a very brave man, and I asked him about it. Then when he found out what I thought, he set to work to tear you down again."

He thought about it. "You believe in me now?"

"Of course, Bart," she said simply.

He took a deep breath. "All right, Catherine, I'll be back. I don't know what I'll do when I come back, but I'll be around until Monday anyway."

She looked at him fearfully. "What do you mean, you don't know what you'll do when you come back?"

"I'll tell you Monday."

She nodded slowly.

He had carried in his gun belt that morning, and now he took it from the peg beside the door and buckled it on. So old Ben was little better than an outlaw, and he was an attempted murderer, and a conspirator—and here Bart was, risking his neck for old Ben's widow. It didn't seem to make much sense.

He looked again at her. There was no denying that any association with the man who had helped try to kill him was an unpleasant one.

She watched his eyes, and perhaps she had some knowledge of the thoughts going through his mind, for finally she said apologetically, "Bart, what are we going to do about the dead man?"

CHAPTER X

BART LOOKED at her and frowned. "What dead man?" he asked.

"One of us killed a man last night. He's out there in the yard."

Bart sighed. "I must have gotten him when he passed the window."

"They ought to bury their own," she said indignantly.

"I agree." He unbuckled the gun belt. "You take this."

He got a shovel and went around to the front with her. The man in the straw hat was flat on his face, one arm flung out, the other doubled under him as if he had rolled. A bullet had caught him in the left side just under the heart, and he had not lived very long after falling. His shirt was soaked with blood, though, and blood had dried around his nose and mouth. And in the hot sun he smelled ranker than ever.

Bart said, "We can tote him up on the hill."

Catherine said slowly, "I don't want men buried all over the place. One graveyard is enough."

"You want to bury him down there by Ben?"

"Yes."

"I thought—"

"They weren't so much different," she said. "Ben didn't use a gun, but he could be just as cruel."

He got a pair of bridle reins and looped them under the dead man's arms and pulled him to the cottonwood tree. The man's bootheels left shallow furrows in the dry dirt. Bart took the shovel and began to dig. The ground was hard and white with alkali. He got down about two feet, and stopped to take a breather. "How deep did you dig yours?" he asked.

"Four feet," she said.

"I'm glad you didn't go any farther."

She took the dipper down to the creek and brought back a drink of cold water. In another hour he had the grave four feet deep. He looped one bridle rein under the dead man's neck, the second one under his knees. He took one rein and Catherine the other. They lowered him with the reins, and pulled the reins out. Bart covered his face with an old work coat of Ben's, and shoveled in the dirt.

It was midmorning when they finished, and Bart was wringing wet in the hot sun. He went back to the house with Catherine and had some more pancakes. "We're almost out of bacon," she said.

"These suit me fine." Bart poured sorghum on the cakes. "But I'll get us some meat tomorrow, maybe."

"We could kill a steer—a two-year-old, maybe."

He stared at her in simulated shock. "Catherine, you haven't learned the first rule about Panhandle ranching—or Texan ranching, for that matter."

"What is that?"

"Never eat your own beef."

She said seriously, "I thought that was a joke."

He finished his pancakes. "It's a joke, yes, ma'am, but there's also a lot of truth in it. There was a time when Texas ranchers got pretty careless about that."

"I thought you came from New Mexico," she said suddenly.

He glanced at her. "I was raised in Texas—never said any different."

"I'm sorry."

But he wondered, then, if Ben Lewis's widow had anything in mind—any reason for checking up on him.

It was only nine miles to the home ranch of the JA's—Goodnight's headquarters. He went in through a big gate with the flowing JA burned into a short plank and fastened to the gate with wire. He trotted the black up to the ranch yard. The JA's had a big outfit. The ranch-house was built of wood—regular pine planks that must have been freighted in from Dodge; there were a dozen corrals, two or three sheds and a big barn, a half dozen wagons drawn up in a neat row alongside the big house.

Goodnight came out to meet him, his massive shoulders driving him over the hard-packed ground.

"Come in and sit, young man." He shook hands. "Tony, get coffee! Come on in, Wagner. Glad to see you. Have a cigar?" Goodnight felt in his vest pocket. "Out of cigars again!" he said, exasperated. "Had a bunch of bigwigs in from St. Louis yesterday and they smoked up all my cigars. I'll have to take some of old Myers's weed until my next train comes in from Dodge. Sorry as hell, Wagner."

"It's all right," said Bart. "I came to talk about court Monday."

They sat on stumps under a big cottonwood tree, and Bart rolled a cigarette.

He tossed the sack to Goodnight, who started making his own.

"You got some ideas on Judge Willis's court?" asked Goodnight.

Bart watched three cowhands ride into the yard and dismount. In a pen near the gate there were four buffalo cows and two calves. He struck a match. "The outlaws are hard against it," he said. "They tried to burn out the Lewis place last night. We stood them off, but they did burn the shed."

Goodnight looked at him keenly. "If you don't mind an honest question, are you interested in Miz Lewis or in the place?"

"I'll give you an honest answer," said Bart. "I might be interested in both—or neither. Right at the moment I've got my back up over these outlaws. Xenophon Jones tried to buy me to keep Catherine from shooting at them until they could set fire to the place."

"How much?"

Bart moistened his lips. "A thousand dollars."

"A thousand dollars look pretty good to you?" asked Goodnight.

"Not good enough."

"Who shot the man?"

"It was too dark to tell."

Goodnight considered. "Did Jones himself make you that offer?"

"He said he was Jones."

"What did he look like?"

"Fairly tall man, good-looking, black hat, light brown whiskers."

Goodnight puffed at the cigarette. "Jones, all right. That might be important evidence some day." His keen eyes sought Wagner's. "I take it you aim to be around."

"That depends."

Goodnight nodded. "It usually does."

A man left the corral and came over, his spurs jangling as he walked. Goodnight introduced him. "Lee Jasper, my foreman."

"Pleased to meet you," said Bart.

Jasper glanced at him and grunted, then turned to Goodnight. "We're missing two cows and the Pueblo bull from the hackberry pasture."

"One of your bulls is on the Quarter Circle JB," said Bart.

Jasper grunted again.

Goodnight said to Bart, "I'll send somebody after him next week."

Jasper said, "We'd better get him sooner than that."

Goodnight said, "We'll be busy with court until the end of the week." He chuckled. "We'll give old Ben's cows a treat. He always bought cheap bulls."

Jasper grunted and went back to the corral. The men were harnessing a wagon.

Goodnight looked at Bart. "Now, you got ideas about court?"

Bart picked up a twig and began to draw brands in the dirt. "I'm pretty sure by now that Xenophon Jones and his gang will do everything short of shooting the judge to keep court from being held."

"I'm glad to hear somebody with some sense," Goodnight grumbled. "That thick-headed judge won't believe it until he looks down the wrong end of a Winchester." He looked at Bart. "What decided you?"

"Various things."

"Well, whatever—does the decision over your staying depend on my answer?"

"Partly."

"Hm. All right, what do you think we can do about it and still avoid a slaughter?"

Bart told him.

Goodnight listened attentively, then whistled. "Dangerous business," he said.

Bart drew a Quarter Circle JB Connected. "What isn't?"

"It will take a man who is a professional with six-shooters—and not too old."

Bart nodded briefly.

"Stinkin' outlaws!" Goodnight muttered.

"They mean business. That's why Piggie Benson is coming down from Tascosa with fifty gunmen."

Goodnight studied him. "If we try a thing like that," he said, "you realize the success of it depends on one man standing up against the ringleaders?"

Bart drew a JA in the dust. "I figgered it."

"And those ringleaders will be Xenophon Jones, Stud Murphy, and Piggie Benson."

"Yes."

"And the man to stand up against them is going to be you."

"I can't say I am astonished."

"If it works," Goodnight said slowly, "you've got to shoot down the three of them—and they're all good men with a six-gun."

"Maybe they are. Maybe they are not."

"I only know what I hear," said Goodnight.

Bart studied the design he had drawn. "Good chance to find out for sure."

Goodnight leaned forward. "What makes you think you've got a chance?"

Bart drew a Matador Flying V in the dirt. "I killed the Yagers," he said.

Goodnight's eyes narrowed. "I recollect now. They say you killed a dozen men in El Paso."

"Seven."

"And still alive." He looked curiously at Bart. "What are you doing here?"

"There's sixteen hundred dollars on my head for killing the fourth Yager—and the only way I can clear it up is to find the man who—"

He stopped abruptly, fully realizing for the first time that the man he had been seeking was dead.

But Goodnight was saying with satisfaction, "You finally got them."

"It sounds as if you knew them."

"When I was driving down through Horsehead Crossing and up through New Mexico," Goodnight said, "the Yagers stole their foundation herd by stampeding my cattle." He looked pleased. "I won't say I'm glad you killed them—but it was damn' good riddance."

"The last one was looking for me and I knew it," said Bart, "so I went over to Socorro and set up a gambling game to give him an opening."

"How many times did you shoot?" asked Goodnight.

"He shot twice. I shot once."

"And they put money on your head?"

Bart nodded. "The Yagers married into the Alguilars."

Goodnight nodded.

Bart drew an LJ in the dirt. "Do you think it has a chance to work?"

"If you've got the guts and the skill to go through with it, I'll go along with you, and I can get plenty of help. Tom Harding will appoint you acting deputy, and he can deputize a hundred hands from the big ranches around. I can talk the association into paying the right man a thousand dollars if he pulls it off—a nice gravestone if he doesn't." He paused. "We can put up a good front."

"If we put up the front," said Bart, "and if we get in there at the right second, we'll put it over, because—" He heard a hen cackle, and raised his head. "You got chickens, Mr. Goodnight?"

Goodnight snorted. "I'm one of them damn' fools that thinks a rancher ought to raise something besides cattle. I'm the only one in the Panhandle favors chickens except Miz Lewis."

"You knew about that?"

Goodnight snorted. "I offered to sell her some, but old Ben raised hell. Then I offered to give her some, she was so disappointed, but old Ben suddenly turned out to have more pride than he'd ever had in his life."

"She got them finally, though."

Goodnight nodded. "I hear she laid down the law to him in Clarendon, and he had to give in." His eyes swept the area around the barns. "Sure, I got hundreds of 'em—out behind the big corral. You don't see 'em from here. They scratch in the mesquite, mostly."

"Mrs. Lewis's chickens were all killed by the Jones gang," Bart said slowly, "and she misses them. Maybe sometime—"

"Sure, sure!" Goodnight waved his arm. "Got a settin' hen going into a fever right now. Come over next week and I'll give you the hen and a setting of eggs."

"Thank you," said Bart. "I know she'd appreciate it."

"You were saying you thought we'd win because—"

"Nobody but the leaders will really want to fight," said Bart, "and as soon as the leaders are gone—if it can be done before they all get into it—the rest will leave the country without firing a shot." Bart drew a JB Connected in the dirt.

"You know what that brand is?" asked Goodnight.

"Sure." Bart looked at him questioningly.

"Turn it one quarter clockwise," Goodnight said, "and you have a CB Connected."

Bart tossed away the twig. "Old Ben isn't cold yet," he said.

Goodnight chuckled. "Old Ben was cold before they shot him. Catherine never had anybody to keep her warm in bed."

Bart got up. "Mr. Goodnight—"

Goodnight slapped him on the back with a blow that rocked him. "I been watchin' men and women for a long time, young man. I've seen her look at you."

Bart said slowly, "I don't know if I'd be good for her."

"You stay around there a few more days, and I think she'll make up your mind for you," said Goodnight. "I wish I had those damn' cigars to celebrate."

Bart started for his horse.

"Wait a minute," said Goodnight. "I'll ride a ways with you."

He walked bowlegged out to the corral and saddled a big bay gelding. Up on a hillside, a crew of men was building a branding chute. "We're still trailing cattle west and north," Goodnight said, "so we road-brand 'em."

Goodnight stopped at the house to tell the cook he'd be back after dark. They had coffee and a piece of cornbread with slabs of butter on it.

Goodnight said as they mounted, "We'll visit the Matador headquarters, the Shoe Bar, the Slash K, and the LJ. Out of the five ranches we can get plenty of hands. We can't cover them all today, though. Tell you—we'll drop over to the Slash K and the LJ, and I'll send word out from the Slash K to the others, and tell them to meet at the LJ early Monday morning."

"Time enough," said Bart.

They went to the Slash K and had good success. They had a drink, and the Slash K owner sent runners to the Shoe Bar and the Matador.

They went on to the LJ, and the sun was beginning to drop. Bart said, "The foreman here has got no use for me."

Goodnight chuckled. "Neither has mine."

Bart said, "I thought so."

"You know why?"

Bart listened for a moment to the weird call of a screech owl from a cottonwood somewhere along the creek. "No," he said.

"You look too competent—and foremen don't like for anybody to be competent but them."

"I suppose that's part of it."

"What's the rest of it?" Goodnight was sharp as a fresh-honed razor. "Stella Harding?" he guessed.

Bart looked at him absently. "He's lost his head over her."

"And naturally she won't look at him. That girl wants most, whatever she can't have." He looked keenly at Bart. "I imagine you're in line."

Bart gave no answer.

They rode into the LJ yard a while later. Tom Harding came to meet them. Hector Johnson stayed back at the corral, where they had a horse pulled up in a sling and were cleaning out its intestines the only way they could. Stella was nowhere in sight.

Goodnight told Tom Harding what they planned, and Harding approved with enthusiasm. He looked at Bart. "I figgered you was a good man," he said.

Bart was uncomfortable. "It might save some lives," he said.

Hector Johnson came around the corner, his right arm smeared with grease up to the shoulder. He looked at Bart and Goodnight, and went back.

Harding said, "Raise your right hand."

Bart raised it.

"Do you swear to do your duty as acting deputy sheriff and to uphold the laws of Texas to the best of your knowledge and ability?"

"I do."

"You're a deputy. I haven't got a badge, but you won't need one, I reckon. I never had one myself. Likewise"—he smiled—"I never heard an oath given, but this here one's good enough, I reckon."

"That's official," said Goodnight. "Then we'll meet here Monday morning."

"I'll be ready," said Harding.

"I'll notify Judge Willis."

Bart and Goodnight mounted their horses. "You want somebody to ride with you a ways?" asked Harding.

The sun was getting low, but Goodnight guffawed. "I rode the Palo Duro Canyon when there was still Indians in it. I don't need help now."

He and Bart rode together for two miles; then Goodnight said, "I'm cutting off here. It's shorter, and I can almost reach the ranch by dark. You'll be a little later, though."

"It doesn't bother me," said Bart. He thought to himself, "if they haven't set a watch on the ranch and know I'm away. If they have, it will be bad for Catherine when it gets dark."

Goodnight said, "Sorry I didn't have that cigar, Bart. Next time, maybe."

"There'll be time." Bart kicked the black into a fast trot. It was less than two hours till dark, and he began to worry.

He crossed the creek by a dead cottonwood that stood up stark and bare with leafless branches. The black splashed through the water, and then Stella Harding rode her chestnut out from beside the tree. He pulled up the black. "You do a lot of riding," he said.

She smiled. "The Panhandle is a big place."

He glanced at the sun but stopped the horse. "You'll be late getting home," he said.

"And you'll be late getting back to Catherine."

He said, "That's where my job is."

"There's more attraction there than a job," she said cynically.

He squirmed. "Everybody in the Panhandle is trying to pair me up with Catherine Lewis."

"Including Mrs. Lewis?" asked Stella.

"She has not made any advances," he said.

Stella pushed her horse closer. "But I have?" she asked in her low voice.

"I was not thinking that, but if that's the way you want it—"

"Bart, you've teased me long enough!" she cried.

He raised his eyebrows. "I?"

"Do you mean to imply that I have pursued you?" she demanded.

He sighed. "I imply nothing. I've got a lot of things to think about, and maybe my answers don't make sense."

"You were talking about court Monday. Bart, are you going to draw against the outlaws?"

"We all will, if necessary."

Her eyes shone. "I'd like to see that," she said.

"I don't doubt that you will be there." He spoke abruptly. "Why did you leave Catherine in such a state yesterday?"

She put her white fingers on the back of his bronzed hand. "I did do that rather cleverly, didn't I?"

"You mean you let her think the worst—that I insulted you—deliberately?"

Stella smiled. "She's such an innocent little thing, she's prepared to believe the worst and make the most of it."

"It was a dirty trick to play on her and me," he said.

"It kept you two apart, didn't it?"

He frowned. "I'm tired of insinuations."

"This *is* a primitive country," she said with sarcasm. "There isn't much time for subtleties. Life goes on, and sometimes it goes out. You have to live when you have a chance."

He looked at her, narrow-eyed. He would, if he should be lucky, kill the three outlaws—and then what? The same old story: move on?

"You're no good for her anyway," said Stella. "A man like you brings trouble and violence. You've had three fights since you've known her. Do you think she would like being married to a man like that?"

"How do you know about the fights?" he demanded.

She smiled mysteriously. "I told the truth, didn't I?"

He did not answer.

"Do you think it would be right to subject her to a life of uncertainty?"

He watched the prairie ahead, and she rode along silently, waiting.

At last he said slowly, "Stella, meet me at the livery stable after court adjourns Monday."

She began to smile. "You mean it, Bart?"

"Be there," he said firmly.

"You won't be sorry," she called as he loped on.

The sun had gone down when he turned the last corner and saw the Quarter Circle JB spread out before him. The western Caprock threw the entire canyon into darkness. The tinkling of a bell mare from somewhere a long way off sounded distant but clear in the still air of evening—as if the whole world had stopped to take an easy breath.

He made out a yellow light in the window of the sod house, and let the black slow to a trot. In fifteen minutes he was near the house and saw a dark bay horse ground-tied near the front door. He frowned, but he knew it was not an outlaw's horse, so he took off the black's saddle and threw it over a low limb of the cottonwood tree. The black was sweating hard from the evening's run. He patted its neck and sent it on to graze. Then he walked to the house.

Through the broken glass of the side window he saw a man sitting at the table with a cigar and a cup of coffee. Bart was hungry, and the fragrant smoke of the cigar was tantalizing. He paused to knock, and then opened the back door.

Catherine was standing, with her back to the stove, laughing at something that had been said. The man at the table was thirty or thirty-five years old, small, slender, black-haired, and wore a small black goatee.

Catherine looked at Bart, still laughing, but the sight of him seemed to remind her of something that sobered her instantly. "Bart, this is Captain Arrington of the Texas Rangers."

"Arrington! I—" Even for a veteran lawman, Arrington's name was one to inspire respect. But Bart looked at him and sensed something wrong. He glanced at Catherine and noted her soberness. He turned back to Arrington. "Heard about you," he said.

Catherine's back was turned while she poured coffee.

Arrington took the cigar out of his mouth. "Lot of people have," he said. "Not always pleasantly."

Catherine set the cup across the table from Arrington. "Captain Arrington was telling me stories about the war. He was in—what was it, Captain?"

"Mosby's Guerrillas," said Bart, sitting down.

Arrington studied him with deep, speculative eyes. "You've been around Texas a good deal, Wagner?"

"Yes."

"Is Bart Wagner your real name?"

"Yes," Bart said sharply.

There was silence for a moment. Catherine looked at Bart, puzzled, and then at Arrington. It had been like a short, sharp explosion of gunfire, and now the participants backed away to load their guns.

"Want to tell me who you are?" Arrington asked suddenly.

"*You're* a Ranger," said Bart. "You tell me."

"You wiped out the Yagers."

Bart glanced up at Arrington. "You've been talking to Harding?"

"I have talked to no one. I just rode in from Mobeetie."

Bart said slowly, "Then I know how you found out all this so soon."

Arrington turned the cigar but said nothing. His eyes remained fixed on Bart.

Bart looked at the row of cigars in Arrington's vest pocket, and started rolling a cigarette. "Xenophon Jones passed it on to you," he suggested.

Arrington said quietly, "That's the way I get a lot of information: one outlaw tells on another one."

"I'm not an outlaw," said Bart.

"You have a price on your head."

"That does not make me an outlaw."

"You're running from the law."

Bart looked up. "Do you have a warrant?"

Arrington regarded him over the cigar. "You're a quick man with an answer."

"In El Paso," said Bart, "you wouldn't last more than sixty days if you are slow at anything—as I'm sure you know."

"As a matter of fact," said Arrington, "I'm not here to arrest you for the New Mexican officials. What I'm here on is strictly Texas business."

"I have done nothing in Texas."

"You killed a man."

"I killed seven men as a deputy in El Paso, but there was an inquest on every one, and I got a clear bill."

"It isn't El Paso I have in mind," said Arrington.

Bart started to shake his head.

"How about last night?" asked Arrington.

"Oh." Bart felt relieved. "We shot at them in the dark. We didn't know we'd hit one until this morning."

"Mrs. Lewis tells me they've been trying to burn the house."

"Yes."

"You have any evidence to support that."

"They burned the shed," Bart said.

"Jones says they were just hurrahing you a little, but you had it in for them on account of a fight you had with Murphy in Clarendon—"

"So Murphy was in on the burning," said Bart.

"Sounds like it."

"Hell of a way to hurrah anybody," said Bart.

"Nevertheless, a complaint has been made, and it's my job to be sure."

"Jones wants to keep me away from court Monday."

"Maybe. Maybe not. I've got my job to do—and I know only one way to do it."

"How?"

"Dig up the body."

Bart finished his coffee and shrugged.

"Before we go any further," said Arrington, "who was shooting what?"

Bart said, "I had a pair of .44's."

"And she had the big Sharps?"

Bart hesitated. "I fired the Sharps too," he said.

"But—" Catherine was wide-eyed.

"She had fired it before I came up to the house from the shed, where I was sleeping, but I used it after that," Bart said firmly.

Arrington asked, "Who knocked out the windows?"

"I did, several days ago," said Catherine. "The first time they were here. The lower panes, that is."

"They shot out the upper panes," said Bart.

Arrington got up. He was very slender but very straight and very alert. "If the bullet went in from the front, it will help," he said. "And if it was a Sharps slug, it might have come from either of you. In that case, we might assume it was fired by Mrs. Lewis, because nobody could prove otherwise, and I think a jury would not blame her. But if it was a .44 slug, I'll have to take you along, Bart." He bowed slightly to Catherine. "In spite of the fact that Mrs. Lewis has vouched for you in every possible way."

Bart said in a clipped voice, "You're the law in the Panhandle."

Catherine said passionately, "The law must be blind, to listen to a man like Xenophon Jones against a man like Bart."

"Not blind, ma'am—impartial," said Arrington. "The law works on a long-time basis. A hundred years is nothing in the eyes of the law."

Catherine said firmly, "You are not only blind. You are not acting very smart, Captain Arrington."

He said patiently, "I know how you feel, ma'am, but remember this: while I am apparently acting like a fool, I am also following up a complaint, and that fact will not be lost on a man like Xenophon Jones. I don't expect Wagner to be convicted, but it's my job to take him in if the evidence so indicates—and I'll take him in."

"You—"

"Catherine," said Bart, "it won't pay to argue with the Ranger."

She looked at Bart, started to answer, then subsided.

"I wish you'd hang up that gun belt," said Arrington.

"All right."

"Now it's late, and we can't go anywhere tonight. I say we get some sleep."

They were up at daylight, and Catherine had breakfast ready. Arrington finished, and said to Bart: "I hate to make you dig him up after you worked so hard to bury him."

Bart stopped abruptly. "I'm not digging up one shovelful, Captain Arrington, unless the state of Texas agrees to pay me for it."

"You'll dig if I tell you to," Arrington said softly.

"I'll dig if you agree to pay me."

Arrington said, "What if I tell you to anyway?"

Bart answered, "A dead man doesn't dig anybody up. Besides" —he smiled—"no Ranger will shoot a man like this."

"All right." Arrington's eyes were piercing. "Tell you what I'll do."

"Yes."

"I'll ask you to take turns with me."

Bart took a deep breath and looked at Arrington. "Asking is different."

"I should have known that," Arrington sighed. "I'll flip a quarter to see who starts."

Bart nodded. The quarter came heads, and Bart picked up the shovel and started for the grave. "What was this hombre's name?" he asked.

"Tex-Mex was all the name I ever knew. He used to be down at Fort Concho, but I never knew whether he was Mexican or *anglo*—probably both."

They reached the grave, Catherine behind them.

Bart sank his shovel into the soft dirt. "He isn't going to smell good," he said.

Arrington tightened his nostrils. "He never did," he answered.

CHAPTER XI

CATHERINE MOVED back when they got him uncovered. Bart pulled the coat off the body and climbed out of the grave. Arrington took a deep breath and went down in. He found the place where the bullet had entered Tex-Mex's body, and studied its course. He was there quite a while before he climbed out.

He wiped the blade of a big jackknife on his levis, and put the knife in his pocket. "He was hit in the side," he said, and held a bulbous-looking piece of lead for them to see. "It's no Sharps, Wagner."

Bart looked at his black eyes. "What was its course?"

"It entered from the side, but I can't tell now whether it went forward or backward. The bullet was lying on his front ribs when I found it, but that does not necessarily mean it lodged there, for I turned him over—and his tissues are pretty flimsy by now." He looked straight at Bart. "I'll want you to go into town with me."

Bart was slow answering. "It looks as if it's my word against Xenophon Jones's," he said.

"We're trying to establish law," Arrington said. "We start wherever we can."

Bart said harshly, "And because I voluntarily gave up my guns, you're taking me in."

Arrington's eyes went flat. "We'll go back to the house and I'll give you your six-shooters and an even draw," he said.

Bart said, "I don't like drawing on a Texas Ranger. That's not saying I won't," he added quickly. "But I don't like it."

Arrington's eyes softened a very little. "Then don't say nasty things," he warned.

Bart said acidulously, "Sure. I know you want to clean things up in the Panhandle. Xenophon Jones is a notorious cow thief and killer, and it's him you want—so you start by taking me."

Arrington's eyes did not change. "The law is impartial," he said. "If it isn't, it isn't law. If you are accused of killing, you go up for hearing like anybody else. If I didn't take you, I'd have no right to take an outlaw on the same kind of evidence." He glanced at the bullet. "I don't think you can be held on evidence like this, but that is for the court to say."

"And if the court says I have to stand trial—"

"Then it will be up to a jury. You know that as well as I do."

"Meantime, Jones is running loose."

"Meantime also," said Arrington, "we are showing everybody we mean business, and we are creating respect for the law."

"—while the outlaws are free to leave the country."

"The important thing," said Arrington, "is not to punish but to establish order. If they leave before we get evidence against them, all the better."

"Where will you be Monday?"

"No telling," said Arrington.

Bart said sarcastically, "Maybe you could do better to turn your talents to seeing that court is held properly and without intimidation."

Arrington sighed. "Maybe I could—but I can't take a hand unless the judge asks me, and he isn't going to ask me, because he doesn't believe it's as bad in the Panhandle as everybody tells him."

Bart picked up the shovel. "Let's get him covered up so the wind can blow some fresh air."

Arrington said, "I'll give you your parole."

Bart paused with his foot on the shovel. "I don't want a parole," he said. "I'm making no promises."

Arrington's voice was unmoved. "You fill in half, and you go stand under the cottonwood tree while I fill in the other half."

Bart said brusquely, "I'll finish the job." He had half a notion to say more, but, to tell the truth, he felt a little sorry for Arrington. The captain was known all over the Southwest as a lawman who never admitted he was whipped, and he was in a bad position now through none of his own choosing. Furthermore, he was a man with a quick temper, and too much rawhiding might produce more than just that cold-eyed stare.

It was advisable not to rub Arrington too far the wrong way, for something very important was coming up: the session of court at Clarendon. Bart shoveled in the dirt, and considered the possibilities.

Arrington was known as fearless and competent. However, he would be limited to a certain extent by his position as a Ranger; he was a good shot, but he was not known for being in a hurry to shoot. That meant his usefulness in court, even if he should somehow be drawn into the scheme, would be limited. As a Ranger, he would have to wait for some overt move on the part of Jones—and by that time it would be too late.

The only way to avoid a general gunfight was to shoot the outlaw leaders immediately when trouble started. Two of those actually known to Bart were Xenophon Jones and Stud Murphy, and if Piggie Benson should be siding them, he could be included on the basis of birds-of-a-feather. If those three could be disposed of at once, there was a very good chance that the hired gunmen from Tascosa would be caught flat-footed before they knew what to shoot at, and by the time they figured it out, the fight would be over and the forces of law would be in control. The whole plan, however, hinged on a man very fast with his hardware and very accurate with his head. There might be such men in the Panhandle besides himself, but Bart had not heard of them.

He finished filling the grave and tromped the dirt down to keep it from blowing away. Then he leaned on the shovel to catch his breath.

Arrington was lighting a cigar. "I understand you work for Miz Lewis," he said.

"Have been."

"She can get along without you for a week or two."

Catherine, now red-eyed, said pleadingly, "Don't you think, Captain, that you could let him—"

"Ma'am," said Arrington, shaking his head, "I have to go through with this."

"You'd better come in and eat before you go, then."

"I have to go by the Half Moon to see Ike Logan. Claims he has evidence of Jones's branding work." He puffed on the cigar. "Doubt it very much myself. I've been there before." He dropped the burned-out match to the hard-packed ground. "Have to take a look, though." He turned the cigar thoughtfully in his mouth. "We could make a swing by the Half Moon and stop at the LJ for a place to sleep. Haven't seen Tom Harding in quite a while." He made up his mind, and looked at Catherine with a quick smile. "Do you have any more of that jim-dandy cornbread, ma'am?"

She nodded quickly. "I can stir up some in a couple of minutes."

Something in her voice caused Bart to look at her: a quickness or eagerness that seemed out of place.

Arrington did not notice it. He glanced at Bart. "We'll wait, Wagner," and added to Catherine, "The state will pay for the meal, ma'am."

They washed while Catherine got busy with cornbread, mixing it in the big crock with a huge iron spoon. Bart washed first and moved back while Arrington washed. He did not want any movement of his to be mistaken for an attempt to snatch one of Arrington's six-shooters.

Arrington finished a quick rinse of his face and turned his back to the wall while he dried. By that time, Catherine had a panful of cornbread in the oven and was stoking up the fire.

Arrington said, "Smells mighty good, ma'am."

She turned quickly. "It hasn't started to cook yet."

Arrington grinned. "Cornbread as good as that," he said, "I could smell into the middle of next week."

Bart was still puzzled by the unusual brightness in her eyes.

Arrington sat down at the table as Catherine poured coffee. "Better stoke up," Arrington said to Bart. "Never know how these trips of mine are going to turn out. Sometimes it's a long haul between meals." He picked up his half-smoked cigar and relighted it. Bart started a cigarette. Catherine put the last piece of cedar into the stove, and Bart looked up as she thumped the lid back in place.

"Mind if I go out and get her some wood?" he asked.

Arrington looked at him levelly. "I offered you your parole," he said.

Bart nodded. "All right, I'll take it long enough to bring in the wood."

Arrington nodded.

Bart went out, eyeing his guns hanging on the wall. Something was building up; he did not know what.

He carried in three armloads, and the smell of hot cornbread began to fill his nostrils. He had a respectable pile of wood on the floor at the right side of the stove, and Catherine said, "That's plenty for a couple of weeks. You better sit down and gather your breath."

He sat down. Arrington got up and went to the stove, tossed in the cigar stub, started to reach for another cigar. He noted there was only one in his pocket, and changed his mind. He went back to the table and sat down across from Bart, his back to the curtain that acted as a partition. Catherine put the bear oil in the center of the table. She turned to the stove. Her movements were quick and sure. She used the corner of her apron to open the oven door, and a cloud of warm fragrance poured out. Arrington said, "Smells mighty good, Miz Lewis—and not even you can deny it."

She let the pan sit on the oven door while she used a butcher knife to cut the bread into squares. Then she took the pan to the table and set it in front of Arrington. "Help yourself, Captain."

Arrington picked out a corner piece and put it on his plate. Bart helped himself.

They ate fast and silently, with Catherine sitting at the end of the table.

Presently Bart looked up. "Who's going to keep Xenophon Jones from burning the Quarter Circle JB while I'm gone?" he asked.

Arrington said, "I spoke to Jones about that, and he promised me that he and his men would leave her alone until you had a chance to get back from your preliminary hearing."

Catherine asked indignantly, "Are you taking the word of an outlaw?"

"Ma'am—" Arrington pushed his hat to the back of his head. "Until I get a conviction against Xenophon Jones, I cannot assume he is an outlaw. I hear a lot of things about Jones, and I admit he's probably as much of an outlaw as he is said to be, but in the eyes of the law, either I have to see him in the act or I have to get a legal conviction. When that happens, then I can assume he's as bad as they claim he is. But to start with, all men are innocent as far as the law is concerned. And as for you, Miz Lewis, Jones won't dare to touch you now that he has promised me."

Catherine stared at him. "I still don't think it's right," she said.

Arrington drained his coffee cup.

"I'll get more," said Catherine, jumping up.

She poured coffee out of the big pot. "Sugar's getting low," she noted. "I'll get some."

"Good coffee, ma'am," said Arrington, reaching for his last cigar.

She set the pot back on the stove. Arrington slipped the band from the cigar, crumpled it, and dropped it on the table.

Bart began to make a cigarette.

Catherine went toward the curtain, and Bart wondered idly, for he had not known that she kept sugar in there. A moment later, however, he discovered why she had gone there. As Arrington struck a match, Catherine's voice came from behind him: "Hands up, Captain. Don't reach for your six-shooters or I'll plow a hole through you."

Arrington froze for an instant, then resumed lighting the cigar. "I've never drawn on a lady," he observed, "and it isn't often a lady has held a gun on me. Mind explaining?"

She held the Sharps centered on his back. "I want Bart Wagner turned loose," she said.

Arrington moved his head slowly to take her in: a small, brown-eyed woman with glossy black hair, holding a big buffalo rifle with unmistakable menace. "Get up," she told Bart, "and get your six-shooters. I'll hold him here until you can get away."

Bart got up slowly, pushed his chair back with the calves of his legs.

"Ma'am," said Arrington, "you're making a mistake."

"You made the first one."

"Wagner," said Arrington, "can't you persuade her to put that thing down?"

Bart could not restrain a grin. "She's a very determined woman, as you can see, Captain."

Arrington began to look a little harassed. "Look here, Wagner, you know better than that."

"I know better than to take an innocent man to Clarendon, too."

"Clarendon, hell! You're going to Mobeetie."

Bart, baffled, said, "Why Mobeetie?"

"There's a justice at Mobeetie."

Bart was enjoying it, though he did not know how long Arrington would control his temper. "It doesn't look as if you'll have much to talk to him about."

Arrington's eyes began to smolder.

"Put on your guns, Bart," said Catherine, "and I'll keep him long enough for you to get away."

Bart looked at Arrington and then at Catherine. He had to admire her courage and her resourcefulness. Such a woman old Ben had had! It was a shame he hadn't realized it.

Bart's six-shooters were hanging on the peg near the wash bench. He threw the belt around him and buckled it, then turned. Arrington glowered at him but kept his hands above the table.

"Miz Lewis," said Arrington without turning, "I'm not a fast man on the draw compared to some, but I shoot mighty straight —and I don't forget. This is not Arrington you're holding up, but the Texas Rangers. If anything happens to me, there will be another one here next week."

She did not bat an eye. "Hurry, Bart," she said.

Bart glanced at Arrington, enjoying it. "I better tell you good-bye first," he said to Catherine.

Her brown eyes widened, and he saw the sudden warmth in them. He went around the table, and by that time she had almost forgotten she was holding the rifle. She had not had much affection, and he felt as mean as a rattler in August for what he was about to do.

He put his arms around her, clamping the rifle between the two of them, and kissed her on the lips.

Though he had known she would accept him, he was astonished at the fervor of her response. He held her tight while she stood on tiptoe to reach his lips, and then, when she relaxed the pressure, Arrington's dry voice came from behind her: "All right."

Catherine fought herself free from Bart's arms and struggled with the rifle. But Bart put his big hand on the barrel and turned it away. "You can't do it now," he told her. "You were forcing him to shoot you. He wouldn't want to, but I'm afraid he would if he had to."

Arrington said in a dry voice, "Take the rifle away from her, Wagner."

Bart tried to twist it out of her hands, but she clung to it and fought furiously.

Arrington said, "Ma'am, this has gone far enough. Up to now I'm willing to forget that you held a rifle on a Ranger, but if this doesn't stop pretty quick I'll take you along to Mobeetie with us."

Her efforts slowed gradually, and she finally let Bart have the rifle, and turned toward the curtain, weeping.

"Let's go," said Arrington.

Bart opened the breech and took out the big straight cartridge. He closed the breech and set the rifle in a corner.

"Catherine, I'm sorry," he said, feeling miserable. "Terribly sorry. I couldn't let you do it. If I had gotten out of Arrington's custody, the Texas Rangers would have been after you and me both—and they wouldn't let up till they got us."

She did not answer, and finally Bart looked at the floor. "We'd better go," he said.

He led the way, but forgot, and knocked his hat off on the door frame. He stooped to pick it up.

They got outside, and Bart saddled the black. "I don't feel right about leaving her unprotected," he said.

Arrington answered quietly, "The Rangers' reputation will hold even Jones down for a few days—and after that, the court at Clarendon will be in effect."

"What if the outlaws face down the court and run it out?"

Arrington said thoughtfully, "I'll ask Goodnight to keep an eye on the JB until you get back."

"What makes you think I'm coming back?"

Arrington watched him get into the saddle. "With her waitin' for you," he said, "you'd be crazy not to."

CHAPTER XII

THEY CUT across the east end of the JB pasture. "It's maybe seventy-five mile to Mobeetie," said Arrington. "It would be easier if you would give me your parole."

"All right," said Bart. "But when we get to Mobeetie you'll have to look out for yourself."

Arrington nodded. "I'm used to that."

They pulled up at a small ranch yard filled with yapping dogs in the early afternoon. A long, gawky man with straggling mustaches and a battered, rain-beaten old farmer's hat came up from the corral. " 'Light," he said, "and make yourselves to home. I'll have the girl put some coffee on."

He disappeared inside the poor house.

"Ike Logan," said Arrington. "Hate to drink his coffee. He might not have any more."

Bart shook his head at the run-down sod house. "He said 'the girl,' " he noted.

Arrington dismounted. "Wife died last winter with TB. Left

·126·

him about a dozen kids. The oldest girl runs the place for him. Does the best she can."

Bart dismounted.

"You can ground-tie the black," said Arrington. "We won't be here long."

"It's not much of a spread," said Bart.

"Jonas Myers in Clarendon owns half-interest, so I don't reckon he will let Logan go broke. But this is no place for a man like Logan. He's strictly a share-farmer—come off the cotton land in Louisiana. He doesn't belong out here at all."

Bart shrugged. "Land is cheap. You can't blame a man for trying. Maybe he got tired of farming somebody else's land."

"I don't doubt it—but he isn't equipped to run cattle in the Panhandle. No money, no knowledge of cattle, and now no wife."

They went inside to get out of the hot sun. The house was sparsely furnished, but neat enough except for kids everywhere like chickens at feeding time. Ike's daughter was about fourteen, brown-haired, wild-looking with her hair over her eyes, although she seemed to have washed it recently. She peered at them as if they were completely strange beings, and did not say a word as she poured coffee out of a battered old graniteware pot that was too heavy for her frail arms.

Ike Logan waved Arrington and Bart to the only two chairs, while he sat on the floor and said in a wheedling voice, "I hear you always carry cigars, Cap'n."

"I been out quite a while," said Arrington. "Mine are all gone. I'm sorry."

Bart handed him his tobacco sack, and Logan started to make a cigarette. "Haven't had a cigar in months," he said.

Arrington set down his coffee. "Jonas Myers tells me you missed some calves."

"Sure, sure!" Logan looked up excitedly. "Found the place in the fence where they went through. They were driven, it looks to me."

"Who drove them?"

Logan licked the paper. "Don't rightly know. Didn't see 'em."

Arrington said sharply, "I can't help you unless you know who did it."

"Can't you trail 'em?" asked Logan.

"Where to? New Mexico?"

Logan started to get up to go to the stove for a light, but Bart tossed him a match, and he sat down again.

More children had been coming in, and the room seemed filled with them—ragged, shaggy-haired, but clean. They stood silently around the walls and watched the men with big, staring eyes. The oldest girl stayed near the stove.

Logan said, "Well, now, Cap'n, you're a Texas Ranger, ain't you?"

"Yes."

"I hear a Texas Ranger can do anything."

"Maybe you heard wrong," said Arrington. "No man on earth can track down a half a dozen calves that went west to stampede the beef issue. They'll wind up with six hundred others, and you'd have to go to New Mexico or Colorado to find them, and what good would it do? You know how much cooperation we get from them."

Bart started to take a spoonful of sugar out of a tin cup, but he looked up and saw the girl's eyes on him; he saw all their eyes on him, and it made him uncomfortable, because he guessed they didn't have much sugar. He turned the spoon and let it dribble back into the cup, and drank his coffee the way it was.

Logan obviously was prepared to make a day of it. He probably didn't have company more than once a month, and he was set to make it as big an event as possible. "You'll stay the night," he said to Arrington.

"Sorry," said Arrington. "I've got lots to do. Have to hit Mobeetie tomorrow."

"You're sure welcome to what we got," said Logan.

"I know, Ike—but I've got the whole Panhandle for a territory, and I have to cover as much of it as I can. That's another reason I can't take time out to trail cattle to New Mexico."

"We ought to have more law," said Logan.

"We will have—as soon as we get court established closer to home. You can't do any business when the county seat and the court are two hundred miles away."

"It's still the law, ain't it?"

"Sure it is." Arrington drank his coffee, also without sugar, although he had used it at the JB. "But look at the complications. It's a three- or four-week round trip to Henrietta. A man has to go there to sign a complaint. The sheriff has to come out here to pick up the defendant. Then the complainant and all witnesses have to go to Henrietta for the trial. From a practical standpoint it doesn't work at all. It's easier to rely on your own six-shooter."

"We ain't all got guns," said Logan, eyeing Bart's gun belt.

"Of course not. That's where the outlaws take advantage."

The children were drifting out, one by one, silently, except the oldest girl, who stood by the stove; and Bart, with plenty of his own troubles to think about, could not help wondering what she had to look forward to. He asked, "What's your daughter's name?"

Logan looked up. "Oh, her? Name's Hepzibah. Call her Hep for short. Real good girl, Hep is. Taken her mother's place like a full-grown woman."

Bart thought that all Hepzibah needed to be a full-grown woman was about sixty days of square meals, but he did not say it.

A small child stuck his shaggy head in the door. "Pa, a man's comin'!" he said.

Logan got up from the floor. "Ain't never had company twice the same day before," he said, looking pleased.

Dogs barked outside. "Keep the coffee on, Hep," he said as he went out.

Dogs continued to bark. The girl stayed in her corner. Arrington said, "We better get started."

Bart got up. Then Logan appeared at the door. "Feller here lookin' for Wagner," he said excitedly.

Bart waited until Stud Murphy appeared—brutally handsome, arrogant, swaggering. "I heard you was here, Wagner," he said, looking in the door. "I thought it was time we finished our trade."

"I wouldn't trade horses with you," Bart said, "even if you stomped me."

Murphy grinned and came inside. As his eyes got accustomed to the dimness, he saw Arrington. "Cap'n Arrington himself," he said. "Big haul."

Arrington said coolly, "I don't know what you're up to, but be mighty sure you don't bite off too big a chew."

Murphy grinned and fastened his insolent eyes on Hepzibah. "Never saw nothin' like this around the Panhandle before," he said.

Logan said, "That's my daughter."

Murphy's nod was filled with insinuation. "I'll remember."

"Look, Murphy," said Arrington, "you got into the wrong race. Say your piece and get out."

Murphy raised his eyebrows. "There's nothing you can do to me, Captain. I ain't broken any law. Leastways, you haven't caught me at it."

"You're wrong if you think there's nothing I can do," Arrington said hotly. "I got to be a captain in the Rangers by slapping bad eggs like you."

"Now, Captain, don't get excited." He turned to Logan. "Ike, ain't you goin' to tell her to pour me some coffee?"

Logan moistened his lips and nodded at Hepzibah, who set a full tin cup on the table. Murphy sat down, his eyes on the thin girl, who turned her face the other way. Murphy poured half a cupful of sugar into his coffee and stirred it with the one spoon.

Arrington sat down, and Bart stayed near the door. Arrington said, "Murphy, you got business with Logan?"

Murphy said, "I had business with Wagner, but he got cold feet and started travelin' with the law."

Bart took a deep breath.

Arrington said evenly, "Your insolence may cost you, Murphy."

"I ain't aimin' to do anything—now." Murphy looked sure of himself. "I just come to deliver a warning to Logan."

Logan choked. "A warning?" he asked in a whiny voice.

"I want you to know us men from Tascosa ain't standing by and letting an imitation court and a two-bit judge railroad our men to the penitentiary on the say-so of the Stock Raisers' Association."

"You're in contempt of court," said Arrington.

"Not yet I ain't—because there ain't no court."

"There was a court the moment the law went into effect," said Arrington. "Furthermore, nobody will ever be railroaded by the court at Clarendon."

Murphy nodded. "That's what we're out to stop."

Arrington said coldly, "You're pushin' me, Murphy."

Murphy looked at him for a moment. His manner was insolent, but he did not goad Arrington further. "All right, Ranger." But he turned to Logan. "Just remember what I said, farmer. Mind which side of the fence you pick."

Murphy cast one leering glance at Hepzibah, and went out. They heard him swear, and then there was a solid thump, and a dog ran, yapping hoarsely.

Arrington exhaled a long breath. "It would be worth a month's pay to work over a man like that," he said.

"What am I going to do, Cap'n?" asked Logan.

Arrington tried to hide his contempt for the cringing man. "Keep your nose clean," he said, "and hope that men like him don't get any more hold than they have."

"He might come back."

"I don't think he will—not right away. They are obviously engaged in a campaign to terrorize the small people in the country."

"Hicks Gentry must have gone straight to him from the LJ," Bart said.

Arrington glanced at him. "I heard about that. Some rough treatment they gave him—if I heard the truth."

"Maybe he had it coming," said Bart.

"Maybe he did."

"Whyn't you arrest him for the way he come in here?" asked Logan.

"For what? He didn't do anything except put on a show."

"He tried to intimidate a witness or a juryman," said Bart.

"You can't prove that," Arrington pointed out. "All he did was say he wouldn't stand for his men being railroaded. That's not intimidation. Anybody can say that."

"His manner—"

"Sure, his manner." Arrington sounded disgusted. "Of course it was intended to be threatening—but we haven't got down to fine points like that yet. The first step in the establishment of a court is to take open-and-shut cases that don't hinge on technicalities. Once you establish the existence of law, then you can go into the other things."

"What can I do if he comes back?" asked Logan.

"Not much," said Arrington. "Come on, Wagner, let's move."

Bart glanced at the girl. She was still hiding her face behind her great shock of hair. He got up and went out after Arrington. They made their way through the dogs, and rode off.

"Hell of a thing," said Arrington. "Some of that coffee money would better go for meat and potatoes. That girl's arms are like pipestems."

Bart agreed.

"That's what we're up against right now," said Arrington, "arrogance—the absolute limit they can get by with. They think nothing of giving a warning right in the face of the law. And of course it was intimidation. It wouldn't be with Charlie Goodnight, but it was with Logan. The law doesn't take account of a feller afraid of his own skin, or a man who's got no business out here in the first place. It's not a country where we can take the time and effort to protect the weaklings. A man has to stand on his own feet—and if he does, the law will try to back him up."

"And if he doesn't," said Bart, "he belongs back in Louisiana."

Arrington kicked his horse into a trot. "That's about the size of it."

"But you have to feel sorry for the wives and kids."

"Who doesn't?" Arrington demanded. "I feel sorry for the poor devil himself, but there isn't enough law to stop killin' and thievin', to say nothing of threats and intimidation. Anyway, you been a lawman. You know you can't bring order in twenty-four hours."

"Yes," Bart said, "I know."

CHAPTER XIII

THEY REACHED the LJ before sundown. Tom Harding met them at the front door and invited them in. He was a cityish-looking man, Harding, with his long brown sideburns pretty near to his jawbones. "Headed for Clarendon?" he asked.

"Mobeetie," said Arrington.

"Mobeetie?" Harding stared at Bart. "You—" He looked back at Arrington. "What for?" he asked.

Arrington sensed the impatience in Harding's voice, and was puzzled by it, but he explained.

Harding said, "Hell of a thing, if you ask me."

"It's the way we have to work," said Arrington.

Harding looked at Bart thoughtfully, then back at Arrington. "We're a little short on beds," he said. "We hired some extra hands to cut poles to ship to Fort Elliott, but we got plenty of room in the hayloft, and plenty of buffalo robes and blankets."

"I'd be obliged, Tom," said Arrington.

"Turn your horses over to Hector."

The big, raw-boned man came up, scowled at Bart, and spoke

to Arrington. He took the horses' reins and went toward the corral.

Arrington observed, "You had some trouble with him."

Bart, aware of Harding's presence, said easily, "Words."

Arrington said to Harding, "I heard in Tascosa that Hector has been like a bull on the prod for six months. Why don't he get married?"

Harding said, "There isn't any surplus of women out here, that I heard of."

They went into the long, low-ceilinged front room. It might have been called a parlor in the East, but in the Panhandle it was a "front room." It was built after the fashion of the adobe houses of the *ricos* of New Mexico and Chihuahua, with massively thick walls that kept out the heat in summer and kept in the heat in winter; great hand-hewed beams crosswise of the ceiling, supporting a crosshatching of small boughs, over which were laid brush and cane, covered with mud from the creek. It made a good construction for a country of little rain.

Harding took them to one end and set them down in rawhide chairs. "Supper will be ready in an hour," he said. "How about a drink?"

Arrington said, "Throat gits mighty scratchy out on the road."

Bart also accepted a glass of Cedar Valley and settled back in the deep-seated chair. Arrington was telling Harding about Murphy's activities at the Half Moon.

Harding put the cork back in the bottle and pushed it to one side. "Logan, poor bastard, is ripe meat for a man like Murphy." He took a deep drink. "But that will all be over after Monday."

Harding looked sharply at Bart, and for a moment Bart was puzzled—first, by the sudden alertness and keenness which was foreign to any remittance-man complacency that Bart had previously associated with Harding; second, by the obvious look of warning in his eyes.

Arrington took in this glance with his own perceptiveness, but chose to ignore it.

Bart understood after a moment, however. Whatever the ranchers around Clarendon planned to do to sustain the first session of court in the Panhandle, was not entirely within the wording of the law itself, and so Arrington should not know about it beforehand.

Bart had a glimpse of something else that he had not seen before: in the transition from lawlessness to law, there often came a time, especially in the West, when the forces that wanted law and order had to take things into their own hands and for a brief time exert force of their own to subdue the outlaws and give law a chance to get its feet on the ground. This period would have to be brief and would have to be unselfish, and perhaps it was not always unselfish, but the sooner and more definitely it was taken care of, the more painless would be the transition. That was what they were facing now in the Panhandle.

They went to supper with the hands, and Arrington pitched in and ate beefsteak and hot biscuits as if he were starved.

"For a little man," Harding observed, "you eat a heap, Captain."

"Never get full," said Arrington.

They ate in silence from there on, finished in fifteen minutes, and went back to the end of the front room, where Harding poured more drinks.

"I haven't seen Stella tonight," said Arrington.

Harding answered lightly, "Oh, she's out riding."

But Bart, puzzled, saw the attempt at lightness fade as Harding looked through the narrow window toward the road that led to the gate.

He realized that Harding was worried, and he recalled that Stella had waylaid him several times out on the prairie, seemingly with no fear of danger from the outlaws. He thought about it for a moment, and wondered if there was any significance to her riding alone, and also, where did she go? He realized too that her father was wondering the same thing. But Bart thought about it and decided that he did not care.

He sipped his Cedar Valley. "What I don't understand is how they can have a saloon in Clarendon."

"Jones put one in there."

"The deeds—"

"Just another thing to argue about," said Arrington. "They could go to court, but imagine holding a trial two hundred miles away. By the time they came to trial, Jones would close the doors of the saloon, and there would no longer be a cause of action. At the same time, a lot of money would have been spent by those interested in enforcing the provisions of the deed. The plain fact of the matter is—as I have told you before—we're too far from the seat of justice for it to mean anything."

"We *could* fight over that as well as over a man stealing cattle," said Harding, "but with a saloon, a lot of people would divide according to whether they personally are wet or dry, while with a cattle thief we have 100 per cent of the honest people behind us."

"The thing is," said Arrington, "to get over the first hump we must have a clear-cut case, and preferably a criminal offense that everybody understands."

"Then the case of Three-Finger and Indian George will make a good test case," said Bart.

Again Harding shot a warning glance at him.

"I understand they're trying them for cattle theft because they have good evidence." Arrington finished his drink. "It is important," he said. "If something happens to start the court off wrong, the Panhandle won't work its way out of the dust for years."

It was dark when they walked outside. The night was still for a moment, and the stars overhead seemed to be almost within their touch. A horse squealed in one of the corrals, and for a moment there was thudding as two of the night horses carried on an exploratory fight.

"Been gettin' too much corn," said Harding. "I'll start riding them down during the day, and they won't be so rambunctious."

The sharp yelp of a coyote came from up on the Caprock, and Harding shrugged. "Still no rain," he said. "I wish they'd howl in the daytime once in a while."

From somewhere to the north came the hoarse bass voice of a

lobo wolf, and from the opposite direction, toward the south, sounded the soft cadence of a whippoorwill.

Outside the cowhands' bunkhouse, six men gathered around a man with a mouth organ, and sang *Old Joe Clarke*:

> When I was a little girl,
> I used to play with toys;
> Now I am a bigger girl,
> I'd rather play with boys.

"This is the time that's worth living out here," said Arrington.

Harding grunted. "A night like this helps a man to forget the hot days and the burning winds and the sandstorms—and the outlaws."

They climbed the ladder to the loft and the musty, sweet smell of hay.

"You cut it yourself?" asked Arrington.

"Down along the creek," said Harding. "Forty-five acres of nice meadow down there."

They all walked out on the floor. "I suggest you sleep here next to the window. You'll get a cool wind all night." Harding felt on the floor. "Here are the buffalo robes and plenty of blankets. You'll be comfortable."

"The only thing that would stop me," said Arrington, "would be a good horse race." He yawned.

"See you in the morning." Harding went down the ladder.

There was enough light from the stars to make their beds, and Bart got his blankets spread and took off his boots in silence. They heard the barn door slam.

"What beats me," said Arrington, "is where Stella went to. I think Tom's worried about it too—but why didn't he say so?"

"You know her?" asked Bart.

"Yes."

"Rather well?"

"Enough."

"In Kansas City?"

"St. Louis."

"You had trouble with her?"

He could hear Arrington settling himself on top of the hay. "I went up there to extradite a man for rape," said Arrington, "and found him hiding under Stella's wing." He paused. "She was running a house on Persimmon Hill."

Bart was shocked in spite of himself. "She—her father doesn't know, of course."

Arrington sighed. "Of course not. She was the apple of his eye, and he'd kill the man who even hinted that she is not what she is supposed to be—even though he might suspect it."

"She's in the wrong country, out here," said Bart.

"She would fit better in Mobeetie or Tascosa, but she doesn't dare, because Tom would kill her for sure if he found it out. Meantime, she hangs on out here and raises as much hell as she dares without alienating her father—because she is his sole heir."

"She's led on Hector Johnson."

Arrington snorted. "The way she's teased that poor devil would make a Mexican mule-breeder blush for shame."

"She doesn't sound like the kind to marry."

"It would be hard to imagine," said Arrington. "And God pity the poor devil who got her, thinking to start a family."

Bart began to understand a number of things. He tried to go to sleep but could not. He heard Arrington breathing hard, and crawled slowly to the window to look out.

"I hope you're not going to jump," said Arrington's voice behind him. "There's barbwire down there."

Bart, startled for an instant, chuckled. "If I wanted to jump, I wouldn't be scared of barbwire."

The truth was that Stella was on his mind. She was a mighty seductive woman, and now he knew beyond any doubt that she wasn't fooling. As a wife, no man who knew her would touch her with a ten-foot pole, but as a woman—it was hard to deny that she offered plenty, with every indication that she could and would deliver.

He sat in the window and listened to the cowhands sing their last verse:

Old Joe had a yellow cat,
   She would not sing or pray;
She stuck her head in a buttermilk jar
   And washed her sins away.

Fare you well, Old Joe Clarke,
   Fare you well, I'm gone;
Fare you well, Old Joe Clarke,
   Goodbye, Betsy Brown.

The hands stopped their singing. There was talk for a few minutes, and Bart saw the yellow flare of matches and the glow of cigarettes. There was a low, desultory murmur of voices. Then one man tossed his cigarette to the ground and stepped on it. "Hard day tomorrow," he said. "We're going to ride bog."

"Better take along some extra horses," said another.

"We got our pick. Come on, Shorty. I can't go to sleep without your snorin'."

Shorty answered, "My mother told me I didn't snore."

Somebody chuckled. "You never had a mother!"

"That's right!" said Shorty. "My mother was a cyclone and my daddy was a tarantula. I'm a blue norther gettin' ready to howl."

Somebody slapped him on the back, and there was playful scuffling for a moment; then all quieted down, and they went inside the bunkhouse. For a moment the night was very still, and Bart sat at the window and looked to the southwest and wondered if Catherine was all right. He looked west and remembered the great, wild, haunting eyes of Hepzibah Logan, and recalled with revulsion Stud Murphy's obscene allusions—as much in his facial expressions as anything else. It was particularly repellent to Bart, for he could hardly understand how any man could look at the girl with any thought but to see her get some meat on her bones.

He was about to go back to his blanket when he heard the soft thudding of a horse trotting through grass. In a moment, another horse loped out from behind the cowhands' bunkhouse and went to intercept the first one.

Bart waited. He heard a low greeting and a low answer. Silence for a moment. The horses came closer, slowly. Hector Johnson's voice was low but terribly intense:

"Where have you been? You left before sunup."

Stella answered: "Are you keeping track of me for my father?"

"Of course not. He trusts you."

"But you don't," she said instantly.

"I—" He stopped his horse not far from the barbed wire.

She said impatiently, "I'm of age. It's my business where I go."

But Hector, moved by that terrible impulsion of jealousy, could not help debasing himself. "Stella, I think I have a right—"

"You have no right to me whatsoever," she said aciduously. "I have told you that before."

"But, Stella—"

Bart was glad they were in the shadow, for he sensed that the man was crying. There weren't many men who had not cried over a woman at one time or another, but Bart was glad he couldn't see it.

Her voice had the sting of a thousand yellowjackets. "Take your god-damned hands off of me!"

"Stella!" Hector's voice was full of shocked incredulousness.

"I mean it, you puking cowhand."

"Stella!"

"Unsaddle my horse!" she ordered, and Bart heard her fast steps as she went toward the ranch house.

After a moment, Hector led the two horses to the corral. For a couple of minutes there were sounds of unsaddling. The saddles were thrown over a pole, and the horses were slapped on the rump and sent for grass. Hector Johnson walked across the hard dirt of the yard and went into the bunkhouse.

Arrington's low voice came out of the darkness: "Maybe you have your own opinion now."

"I never argued with you in the first place," said Bart. "But where *has* she been?"

"Tryin' to team up with Xenophon Jones."

Bart thought it over. "Why do you say 'trying'?"

"Figure of speech. To my mind there's no room for a question, but some people are sticklers for proof in things like this."

Bart pulled the blanket over him. "Why doesn't she stay with Jones?"

"It wouldn't be anything new for her. She's had six husbands—but she was married only once."

Bart yawned and hunted for a soft place for his head on the hay, but he was wondering how much Stella knew about the plans for the first day in court; he supposed there was nothing that would keep her from telling Jones all she might know.

"It's a game with her," said Arrington. "I don't make out to understand that kind of a game or the woman who plays it, but I know she's crazy about any man that doesn't want her. That's why she likes Jones. Any woman is dirt to him. And that's what Stella likes—to be treated like dirt. Maybe her daddy was too good to her."

Bart was thinking. Stella was like a steer on a drift fence in a blizzard: he was headed for destruction where he was, but you couldn't drive him away.

"That isn't all." Arrington chuckled. "Stud Murphy wants her as bad as Hector Johnson, and she won't look at him for sour apples."

CHAPTER XIV

THEY WERE up early the next morning. "We'll hit Mobeetie by dark if we keep moving," said Arrington. "It's only forty miles."

"I'll be glad to get it over," said Bart.

They had breakfast with Harding and the hands, and Arrington said, "Tell Stella I'm sorry not to have seen her."

"I'll do that," said Tom Harding.

"We'll get going, Bart."

"I expect to be back Monday morning," Bart told Harding.

"I'll look for you," said Harding.

Arrington glanced sharply at them, but said nothing. Arrington was a smart lawman.

They set out. Arrington seemed to know the way, and both horses appeared strong. The early-morning stars were still bright in the purple sky.

Bart rode in silence for a while, getting his eyes open. The sky began to lighten, and they rode steadily over the rolling prairies to the northeast.

Bart asked him, "What do you know about old Ben?"

"Ben Lewis?"

"Only Ben I know."

Arrington said, "A nasty old man—the kind that would cringe before Xenophon Jones and then take it out on somebody like Catherine."

"I figured that," said Bart. "Was he an outlaw?"

"Sort of semi. He didn't have courage enough to go all the way. He must have known Jones somewhere—maybe back in Missouri—and he had been a sort of go-between or messenger boy for Jones. Then he straightened up, decided to break away and go out for himself. He went to Texas to visit a cousin, and it was then he met Catherine. He was about sixty then. They got married and came up here. Whether it was planned that way with Jones, I don't know. Anyway, soon after Lewis bought his grass, Jones moved in, and they started working together."

"Old Ben might have come out here to go straight."

"It sounds reasonable. His trouble was that he was not strong enough to stick with it."

"His ranch is well located," said Bart, "adjoining the JA and the LJ and not far from the Half Moon."

"It could be an accident," said Arrington. "You got any more tobacco?"

"Sure." Bart handed over the sack.

"I think they used the Quarter Circle JB land as a holding ground." Arrington struck a match. "I don't know whether Catherine ever knew that or not."

The fragrance of tobacco smoke drifted back to Bart. Arrington handed him the sack, and he rolled one himself.

Then Bart got back to his former theme. "With all these thieves and killers running loose, it still looks like some kind of ironic justice to take me in to Mobeetie."

"There's several reasons," said Arrington. "One is: it has the only real jail in the Panhandle. Another is that you can get a quick preliminary hearing."

Bart started to answer, but changed his mind.

Arrington went on: "This is a country ruled by powder and lead, but for any permanent establishment of order we have to have public opinion behind us, and that has to start with the outlaws. The decent people have already got it, but once we get the outlaws thinking they will get an even break from the law, the battle is half over."

He kept wondering about Catherine. He remembered how nice she had felt in his arms, and he wondered if she had known much about old Ben's activities.

Toward noon they pulled off the trail up a dry creek bed. "Feller runs a whisky place here, sells food on the side," said Arrington. "Used to be for buffalo hunters, but now it's outlaws."

Bart asked, "How can you come in here among known outlaws?"

"Why not? I don't bother them unless I've got a specific complaint and a warrant. They know that and they're careful. If any of their men gets tangled up in something and is seen, they skip the country for a while. Meantime, I come and go, and pick up information. Matter of fact, I expect to meet Xenophon Jones here and show I mean business by taking you in."

Bart said, "I hope you know what you're doing. If you don't, you're leading me to a slaughter."

"I know exactly what I'm doing," said Arrington. "I stop here all the time."

They pulled up in front of a sod house set down in the mesquite. It had a sod roof, and flies arose in a cloudlike swarm as the two horses went up to the rail.

A potbellied man came out in front while Arrington was reading the brands on horses tied along the rail.

"I see Jones is here," said Arrington.

The potbellied man watched Arrington with beady eyes. "You looking for him?"

"Just want to talk."

The potbellied man nodded.

"What's to eat?" asked Arrington.

"Buffalo. Dollar a plate."

"Set it out," said Arrington. "We're going on."

They dropped their horses' reins over the hitch rail and dismounted.

A man ducked under the low door frame and came out into the sunlight. He was tall and big; wore a big hat; had cold blue eyes, a big brown mustache and brown whiskers. "I heard you was lookin' for me, Captain."

Arrington stepped into the open. "Howdy, Jones. I thought you'd like to know I got the man you signed a complaint against. You better be on hand in the morning."

Xenophon Jones stared at Bart for a moment, and a cold smile touched his lips and went away. "I can't be there in the morning, Captain."

"He'll be up for preliminary hearing in the morning."

"I can't be in Mobeetie until next Tuesday morning."

Arrington said, "That's too long, Jones. I can't hold a man three or four days on a complaint."

"You saw he killed Tex-Mex."

"Tex-Mex is dead, but there's no proof Wagner killed him."

"You got the bullet, didn't you?"

"I got the bullet," Arrington said sharply, "but I don't know for sure who fired it, and I don't know what Tex-Mex was doing on the JB that night."

Jones frowned. "You mean you're going to turn him loose?"

"I think the J.P. will. Even with whatever you can say against him, this is mighty flimsy evidence."

"You know he killed three men in El P—"

"He won't be tried for what happened in El Paso," Arrington said coldly.

Jones hesitated. A little of his assurance left him.

"Furthermore," said Arrington, "one of your men picked up the wrong horse. That bay down there is a JA brand."

"That's mighty careless of him," said Jones. "Are you sure?"

"Positive. Call him out," said Arrington.

Jones looked truculent for a moment, and Bart began to tighten up. Then Jones said, "All right," and went to the door. "Gentry!" he bawled.

The familiar whiskered face of Hicks Gentry appeared. He blinked in the sunlight and appeared about half asleep, half drunk. His neck was covered with purple and blue bruises.

"Where'd you get that JA horse?" asked Arrington.

"I bought it in Tascosa," said Gentry.

"Let me see your bill of sale."

Gentry fumbled in his pants pockets, looked down at his shirt, the same one he had worn before, and now extremely soiled. He said finally, "I lost it."

Arrington said, "You know better than to ride a JA horse without a bill of sale."

"I forgot," said Gentry.

"You ride into Mobeetie with me and see if you can remember."

Gentry looked at Jones, but the big outlaw shrugged. "You better go along. I'll try to get this straightened out for you." Jones looked at Bart. "This here fellow is going in with you. He was a lawman down in El Paso. You see how it is: everybody has to mind the law."

Gentry stared at Bart, but if he remembered Bart in the LJ yard, he made no sign.

Arrington stepped close to him. "I'll take your guns," he said.

Gentry hesitated, and by that time Arrington had both of his six-shooters. He had done it very smoothly and unobtrusively, and for a moment Gentry hardly realized what had happened. He looked at Arrington and licked his thick lips, then at Jones.

"Go in peaceful," said Jones. "I'll see you get a lawyer."

"He'd better have a bill of sale signed by Charlie Goodnight," said Arrington.

"Meat's ready," said the potbellied man.

They went inside. A bottle of whisky was at their table. Arrington tasted it, and threw it into a corner. "I told you last time I'd pay for no more homemade rotgut."

"It's the only kind there is," said the potbellied man.

"You trot out the Cedar Valley or I'll tell you what that stuff really tastes like," said Arrington.

A moment later a bottle of Cedar Valley was before them. "That's better," said Arrington.

They ate their meal. Bart said, "This is pretty late for buffalo, isn't it? Buffalo were out of circulation two years ago."

"As a matter of fact," said Arrington, eating voraciously, "the ranchers have been eating buffalo up until the last couple of months—from strays. But this isn't buffalo; it's beef."

"Can't you trace it?"

"Not without scouring the prairie. They butcher somewhere within three or four miles and bury the hide. I'll catch them some day when I get time. Meanwhile, it's more important to catch a man like Jones who drives off twenty-five or thirty head at a time."

Bart might have made another sarcastic remark, but he had had several things proved to him: that the arrest of a non-outlaw made an impression on the outlaws; that no matter how justifiable his resentment at being taken in, the law had an answer for everything; and lastly, that the little captain was not scared of anything. He would have charged hell with a bucket of warm water, and Bart resolved, after seeing him walk into this thieves' den and arrest a man for riding a JA horse, to make no more remarks.

Arrington got up and went over to Jones, who was drinking. "You better be in Mobeetie tomorrow if you want to testify."

Jones looked up from under half-lowered eyelids. "Will you be there, Captain?"

"I've got to go up to Fort Elliott to get a prisoner, so I won't be back until late Sunday—but that doesn't make any difference."

Jones grinned.

"All right." Arrington looked around. "Gentry, you can ride that horse in with us."

"I ain't in no condition to ride," said Gentry.

Arrington barely glanced at him. "You want to be tied on?"

Gentry shook his head against the sunlight. "I'll try to ride," he said.

"Unless you want to walk."

Gentry had trouble getting into the saddle of the bay, but Arrington waited. Gentry pulled up his reins and turned the horse. Arrington said, "Wagner, you ride behind."

"My six-shooters are unloaded. I can't do much if he tries to get away," said Bart.

"He won't try. I know him. He won't sober up for two days—and he'd rather be hanged than left on foot on the prairie."

They rode out across the prairie, and an hour later Bart saw dust off to their left against the sun. He spoke to Arrington, who studied it.

"Somebody's making tracks for Mobeetie," Arrington said.

"Trying to waylay us?"

"I don't think so." But Arrington was puzzled. "I don't know, though. They must have come from the place we just left."

They pulled into Mobeetie about dark. The one dusty main street was lined with saloons, and already the oil lamps were lighted and the player pianos were pounding out bright and impersonal versions of "St. James Infirmary" and the lilting "Somebody's Coming When the Dewdrops Fall" or the melancholy "Shall Our Parting Be Forever?" There was no singing yet, and Bart guessed that the dancehall women were hardly sobered up from the night before. Arrington turned off at a hotel and into a street unlighted even by the faint yellow glimmer of a saloon lamp, and pounded on a door in a small building.

"Sheriff in?" asked Arrington.

"He went up to Dodge yesterday to see Charlie Bassett."

"You won't have any trouble with these men," said Arrington. "Watch the ugly one. The other will be out in a few days."

"What do you mean by 'a few days'?" Bart demanded.

Arrington said slowly, "I don't really know that I meant anything."

"I want a lawyer," said Bart.

"How about money?"

Bart said, "I've got my six-shooters."

Arrington considered. "Won't be necessary. I know a young

· 149 ·

fellow who will take you on credit. And I will leave your hardware with the jailer here; name is Taylor."

"Have they eaten?" asked Taylor.

"Not too long ago. The ugly one won't be ready to eat for a while anyway. Hungry, Wagner?"

"Not too."

"I'll send young Allen around to see you. He read law up in Ellsworth; knows what he's doing."

"Thanks."

He was locked into a tiny iron-barred cell next to Gentry, who lay on the floor and went to sleep, snoring raucously.

Half an hour later Taylor came back with his lantern, leading Allen, a youngish man trying to grow a red mustache.

"How soon can I get out of here?" Bart demanded.

Allen shook his head. "If what Arrington says is right, we'll probably get you out as soon as we can get a hearing. I wouldn't count on it altogether, because law is in pretty much of a turmoil up here, but I don't think the J.P. will have you held. It's more a matter of form than anything else, according to Arrington."

"All right," Bart said impatiently. "When can we have a hearing—in the morning?"

Allen shook his head. "Arrington was willing. He said he would stay over long enough to testify in the morning; he didn't think Jones would be here, although he told him to appear. But we can't find the justice."

"Why?"

"Somebody rode in about a half hour ago and offered him twenty dollars to ride out somewhere and perform a wedding tonight."

"Then he should be back in the morning."

Allen shook his head. "He sent word he'd be back Tuesday."

Bart snorted. That was the explanation of the dust cloud they had seen to the west. "Listen," said Bart. "It's against the law to hold me in here. I want out!"

Allen shook his head. "Mister, I'm giving you the best advice I've got. I have no key to the jail."

Bart shouted, "Get me a habeas corpus!"

"I'm sorry," Allen said, "there's no possibility of any legal action of any sort until we can get hold of a judge."

"So a man can stay in jail for months—"

"We hope that after next Monday—"

"Next Monday, hell!" said Bart. "If I'm not out of here tomorrow, there won't *be* any court next Monday."

Allen began to back away. "I'll do what I can," he said.

Bart knew that Allen thought he was touched, and Bart let him go without further trouble. Obviously he had to figure another way out.

He lay on the blanket on the dirt floor and listened for a while to Gentry's snoring. Then, tired from the long ride, he went to sleep.

CHAPTER XV

IT WAS dark inside the jail, and he awoke late the next morning. Taylor was pounding on the bars of the door. "Lady to see you! Lady to see you!"

Bart was up, rubbing the black whiskers on his chin. "I want to wash first," he said.

"I'll bring some water."

Stella, Bart supposed, and wondered what she was up to.

He called Taylor and said he was ready, but then he opened his eyes wide, for it was Catherine who came in! Her head was bare and her black hair gleaming in the early sun until the jailer closed the outer door. "Bart!" she said softly. She reached through the bars and hugged his arm. "Bart, I brought you cornbread and fresh coffee. I made it this morning."

He felt her shoulders. "How did you get here?" he asked.

"I rode. I started as soon as you left."

"Aren't you afraid they'll burn your place?"

"Mr. Goodnight said he didn't think they would do it now. There has been too much fuss. They'll talk for the next few days—but any violence would only make trouble for them."

"Who do you mean by 'them'?"

"The outlaws, of course."

"You were on the road two nights?" he asked.

"One. I stayed at the JA the first night."

"And last night?"

"I camped on the prairie about twelve miles southwest of Mobeetie."

He shuddered. Her camping place could not have been far from the squalid place where Arrington had arrested Gentry. He looked at Gentry; the man was still snoring.

"Why didn't you come on to Mobeetie last night?" he asked. She shook her head. "Ben didn't have horses like your black."

He felt horrified over what might have happened. "You should not have done it," he said to Catherine. "The country between Clarendon and Mobeetie is infested with outlaws. It's worse than when the Comanches were on the warpath."

She was there within his touch, and he couldn't keep from remembering how she had felt in his arms, and for the moment he would ask no further questions. "Open the pail," he said. "I'm hungry."

She pulled a clean cloth torn from a bed sheet out of the pail and revealed a heap of squares of yellow, fragrant cornbread.

"It's warm!" he said. "How on earth—"

"I brought the things with me, and made it out on the prairie this morning."

"Coffee too?"

She nodded.

"You astound me every time you turn around," he said. "I never quite know whether you're helpless or lucky, or just what."

"I told you I was raised on the frontier."

"So you did." He lifted out a warm piece of cornbread and bit into it with relish. Catherine made the best cornbread he had ever eaten anywhere—and he had eaten it in many places.

"Bart," she said in a low voice, "I'm not angry with you for taking the rifle away from me."

He looked at her; he had almost forgotten.

"I know you had to do it," she said.

"I wouldn't have—otherwise."

The jailer opened the outer door, and Bart motioned him to come in. He spoke through a mouthful of cornbread. "It's warm. Have a piece."

The jailer brightened. "Don't mind if I do." He came up, glanced into the pail, took a piece of cornbread and bit into it. "Mighty good," he said a moment later.

"Have another while you're at it."

"Don't mind if I do." He took a second piece. "I'll just leave you folks," he said. "Holler when you're ready to go, miss."

"In a little while," said Bart.

"Take your time." The jailer went out and closed the door.

Bart studied Catherine. "I had the feeling that you were holding your breath while he was here."

"Did you?"

He said thoughtfully, "It seems to me that Xenophon Jones acts strange around you, Catherine. He could smash you with a swing of his arm, but instead of all that, he started in trying to terrify you by killing your chickens. He could have burned your place any time he wanted to, but he acted like a coyote worrying a rattlesnake."

She looked at Gentry, who was still snoring, and spoke in a low voice. "When he came to the door that day and said Ben had been shot—"

Bart, taking out another piece of cornbread, looked at her. "You told me they just dragged the body into the yard and left it. You never said anything about him talking to you."

She hesitated an instant. "You never asked me," she said.

He stared at her. "That's usually a good answer—but not between you and me."

She looked at his eyes. "Are we different?"

"Maybe," he said, as caution recurred to him. "Maybe—and maybe not."

"You heard me tell about it to Mr. Goodnight and Judge Willis."

"Partly, I suppose."

He finished his cornbread in silence, thinking. She poured him a cup of coffee with sugar in it. He took it through the bars, avoiding her eyes. There were a lot of things unexplained about this girl, he realized.

She said brightly, "There's a surprise under the bottom napkin."

He glanced at her, then reached again through the bars and lifted the torn square of bed sheet that had been on the bottom. He stared in the dimness at a .38 Colt, and dropped the cloth back hastily. "Do you know what you're up to?" he demanded.

"Of course. Mr. Goodnight said they were getting rid of you until after court was held Monday, and I decided to spend some of my money for this six-shooter and a sack of tobacco." She looked at him. "Don't you want it, Bart?"

He drew a deep breath. "Right now it's about the only way I can get to Clarendon by Monday." He reached through the bars and took the six-shooter from under the cloth.

"It's loaded," she said, "and here are seven extra shells." She put them in his hand; her fingers were warm and pleasant to his touch. "It was all Mr. Myers had."

"It's enough." He put the six-shooter inside his shirt, and the shells in the lower left pocket of his vest.

"How did the jailer come to overlook this stuff?" he asked.

"He just glanced in the basket and said all right. I guess he doesn't know much about things like this."

"This jail wasn't made for much except to sober up the drunks."

She whispered, "You be careful with that, Bart."

He nodded. "I'll be careful."

Gentry quit snoring abruptly and turned, and Bart said, "You'd better leave. He may be ugly when he wakes up."

"When will I see you?"

"Not before Monday. I'll have to hide out until then, or Arrington or Jones will be down on me."

"Jones?"

"He wants me out of the way a lot more than Arrington wants me in jail."

"How will you get back, Bart?"

"That will be easy," he said. "But you—please do not ride back alone. Find some honest person with whom you can travel."

"All right, Bart." She put her hand through the bars and squeezed his fingers. "Be careful, Bart. Don't let that gun lead you into trouble."

He grinned. "I couldn't get into much more trouble than I got into when I rode up to your place looking for a meal," he said dryly.

"Are you sorry, Bart?"

He looked at her fondly. "No, ma'am, I can't say I am—even if it wasn't what I bargained for."

"I'm glad," she said. "And Bart—do be careful."

"Yes, ma'am, I aim to be."

He watched her leave, heard her speak pleasantly to the jailer, heard the jailer compliment her cornbread—and then the outer door closed and he was left to wonder why it was that the first thing she had thought of was bringing him a six-shooter. Was it the instinctive reaction of an outlaw woman? Was it something she had been put up to by Xenophon Jones to lead him into a trap? Or was it the action of a woman who naturally rushed to protect and help a man in whatever way she knew?

He realized he was suspicious of her because her actions were too good to be true. Stella Harding had not fooled him. Was it Catherine who had pulled the wool over his eyes?

As yet he was too close to be sure. There were some things that bothered him even more. He thought she had more facts concerning the death of old Ben. Why had she not told him the entire story at once? This speculation led to others. Were she and Jones actually using him as a tool in this whole affair? A man hated to be made a fool, especially by a woman he liked.

This latter possibility was supported to a certain extent by Jones's actions regarding Catherine. Here was an admittedly murderous outlaw who seemingly balked at violence to a woman who was hardly more than a girl. Could it be—was it possible that she had been his mistress, perhaps? This might explain a lot of things, except that Catherine certainly seemed innocent. But how many innocent women had he known at Catherine's age?

"Is old Ben's widow gone?" asked a voice from the next cell.

Bart started, then looked at Gentry. The man's eyes were hardly open, but he must have heard them.

"You should have opened your mouth earlier," Bart said, "and you could have had something to eat."

Gentry delivered an uncouth belch. "I never want to eat as long as I live."

"What do you expect from drinking that stuff they sell on the prairie?"

"Listen," said Gentry, sitting up. "I know you got the gun, and I'll keep my trap shut if you don't go off and leave me in here."

Bart made up his mind fast. "I won't," he promised, "if you'll tell me what you were doing there at the supply post."

Gentry's voice was still thick. "I was with Jones."

"You weren't," said Bart. "He would not have let you ride that JA horse along with him."

"Got a drink?" asked Gentry.

"No," said Bart.

"She'd bring you a six-shooter but no whisky. Lemme see the gun."

"I'll keep the gun," said Bart. "If you want out of here—talk."

"I was headed for Mobeetie to tell Jones that Arrington had been at the JB."

Obviously Gentry did not know that Jones himself had sent Arrington to the JB.

"I saw his horse and stopped for a drink. It's damn' dusty out there on the prairie."

"And Jones turned you over to Arrington, and now he is letting you rot in jail."

"He-ell, yes!" Gentry fell flat, then got up on his hands and knees, shaking his head like a buffalo bull hit in the lights with a 500-grain Sharps. Bart watched him through the bars until Gentry turned over and sat up, bracing himself with his arms behind him. "Wouldn't Jones give plenty to know what I know about that woman now?" he muttered.

"What about her?" asked Bart.

"Jones is aiming to call on her tonight at the ranch—and here she is in Mobeetie." Gentry made a noise that was intended as a chuckle, but which came from deep in his throat and sounded like nothing more than an assortment of strange noises.

"You mean he's going to burn the place tonight?" asked Bart.

Gentry stared at him, bleary-eyed. "He never intended to burn it. He was tryin' to scare her. He wants the woman!"

Bart grew cold as he thought about the implications. Whether or not Catherine had ever given Jones any reason to think she would be receptive to him—and Bart doubted that—it was plain that Jones planned to force his attentions on her.

He shuddered as he considered the full possibilities of the situation. Outlaws were not noted for their kindness toward women, and since Jones had publicized his plans, it was apparent that he had given up winning Catherine by fair means and was determined to vent his passion on her in the most spectacular way possible—since it had reached the point where his egotism and not his passion had taken over. That could be a very gruesome thing for a girl like Catherine.

Bart considered the expected results. A crime against women in the Panhandle was worse than murder; on the rare occasions when it occurred, men were treated to some revolting deaths by men who ordinarily were law-abiding. That arose from the fact that on the frontier there were few women, and those who lived there were never half-good or even questionable; they were all good or all bad. And the security of the good ones had to be preserved.

What did Jones have in mind, then? He didn't even dare to kill her and leave her body, for a crime of that nature would call forth the greatest manhunt ever held in Texas—unless he had provided somebody else to take the blame. In that case, the logical suspect would be Bart Wagner.

CHAPTER XVI

BART SAT up straight when he reached that point. He had been around the ranch with Catherine, and nobody there to chaperone them. A public accusation by Xenophon Jones, outlaw though he was, backed up by a word or two from Stella Harding or Hector Johnson or both—Bart felt cold chills down his spine.

He looked again at Gentry. "Do you want to get out of here?" he asked.

"I want to get a drink."

"Listen. When the jailer comes in next time, get him close to your door so I can go to work."

Gentry looked at him. "If you leave me here, I'll gun you down if I have to find you in hell," he growled.

"Do what I said—and keep your mouth shut."

Bart had little stomach for making a deal with a man like Gentry, but far less for what he thought Jones was aiming at. So he sat on his blanket on the floor and tried to make plans.

Within half an hour the jailer opened the outer door. "All right in there?"

"I'm all right," said Bart, "but this hombre next door is having fits."

"D.T.'s," the jailer said.

"He sounded sober to me."

Gentry came to the iron-barred door. "There's a big hole in the floor and a den of snakes under it!" he shouted. "It's murder if you leave me in here!"

The jailer looked at the whiskered face of Gentry, and started to back out. "You're drunk," he said.

Gentry put on a good act. "I may be drunk, but I never see snakes. This here's a real one!" He suddenly seized the bars and shook them with all his strength, and gave a scream that sounded like the dying gurgle of a panther.

The jailer came back in the door with a six-shooter in his hand. "I'll look—but no tricks," he warned. "I'll shoot." He looked through the barred door. "I don't see nothin'."

Bart pointed with his left hand through the bars. "Over there."

The jailer pressed against the bars, and Bart lifted the .38 out of his shirt and pushed it against the jailer's ribs. "Drop the iron," he said softly, "and don't move fast."

The jailer thought about it for a second or two. He could not shoot at Bart from where he was, and he could not turn very fast. The pistol thudded on the dirt, and Gentry snatched it.

"The keys," Bart said. "Open up."

The jailer licked his lips.

"Hurry," Bart said. "I don't want to kill you, but this other hombre might not care."

The jailer unlocked the doors and stepped back. "I wish you wouldn't take my .44," he said. "I paid for it myself."

Bart said, "We'll leave it in the office. Mind you don't start hollering until we get out of gunshot or we might be back."

"I won't say a word," the jailer promised.

They closed the outer door behind them.

"I'm not leavin' mine," said Gentry.

"You're leavin' yours," said Bart evenly.

Gentry looked at him. "What am I gonna use?"

Bart started to give him the .38 but changed his mind. If Catherine had spent her scanty funds to buy the gun for him, he would not turn it over to a man like Gentry. He didn't even want Gentry to touch it. He looked around the office and saw his gun belt on the wall. He buckled it on and gave one of the big six-shooters to Gentry. "Drop the jailer's iron on the desk," he said.

Gentry laid it down unwillingly. "How about horses?"

"They'll be at the livery. Know where that is?"

"Around the corner."

They walked out into the bright sunlight. It was too early for the town of Mobeetie to be awake; there was not even a horse on the street, and the saloons were quiet. No lights burned in them, and only a crippled swamper with a pail and a mop shuffled through a pair of blue swinging doors. Gentry started after him.

"Wait!" said Bart. "You can get a drink after we get the horses."

Gentry grumbled but came back.

Bart had spotted the livery stable, and now led the way. "Have you got money?" he asked Gentry.

The man fumbled in his pocket and came up with a tarnished five-dollar gold piece.

Bart said, "Loan it to me," and picked it from between the man's dirty thumb and forefinger.

They walked inside the livery and climbed over the gate. Bart hammered on the door, and a man with uncombed hair came yawning. "Does everybody in Mobeetie get up at the crack of dawn?" he demanded.

"Who else has?"

"Three people—woman and a man, and another woman— young, pretty."

"What kind of horse did the young one have?"

"Big sorrel plowhorse, like."

"Where were they going?"

"Clarendon. Where you fellers headin'?"

"Tascosa—and we want our horses."

"It used to be that anybody got up in Mobeetie before noon was likely to be shot," the livery man grumbled, "but now that people like Frog Legs Liz and Maggie the Mumps are gone to Tascosa, people are getting up at all sorts of indecent hours." He came down the steps and stared at them. "What horses did ye say?"

"A black," said Bart, "with a dog-iron brand on the lower right hip, and a bay with a JA burned on—"

"Hey, you fellers been in jail! Cap Arrington brung them horses in."

"We're out now," said Bart.

"The black I can let go, but the bay—"

Gentry had the .44 in his hand. "You want to argue about it?"

The livery man turned toward Bart, but Bart was looking at the gate.

"I'll let you have it," the livery man said to Gentry, "because I haven't got no choice. But this is stealin'."

"Never mind," said Gentry. "Get the horse."

Within five minutes the horses were saddled, and the livery man was leading them to the gate. Bart gave him the five-dollar gold piece, and he counted out change in silver dollars. "It's bad business, ridin' a JA horse without a bill of sale," the man said.

Bart answered pleasantly, "I'm glad I'm not doing it," and took the change.

They mounted and rode out. Bart gave the change to Gentry, and began to wonder how to get rid of the man. He would not be very pleasant to travel with, and Bart would not trust his loyalty or his intelligence. The man had moments of shrewdness, but his success as an outlaw must have been due more to Xenophon Jones's direction than to any native resourcefulness.

They rode past the saloon where they had seen the swamper, and Gentry slid off the saddle and almost fell in the dirt. He got up and ran to the doors. Bart got off the black and followed him.

Gentry was arguing with the crippled swamper. "I said I want a bottle of whisky."

He was flourishing the six-shooter, and the swamper was obviously scared. "I said I can't sell it to you, mister. I can't stop you if you take it, but I can't sell it to you."

Gentry aimed his gun at the swamper, but Bart knocked his arm down. "If you want to take the whisky, get it yourself—and leave the money. Don't drag this hombre into it."

"I ordered him to bring me a bottle."

"I told you to get it yourself."

Gentry stared at him, and his mouth worked for a moment. Then he grunted and went behind the bar. He snatched at a bottle, pulled the cork, and took a long swig. He jammed the cork back in and started out.

"Leave the money," said Bart.

Gentry growled but tossed a dollar on the floor.

Bart put the dollar on the bar and followed him out.

Gentry was smacking his lips. "Wanta pull?" he asked.

"Not yet," said Bart.

They rode for two hours, with Gentry steadily pulling at the bottle until he hit the bottom. Then he gave a yell and threw the bottle as far as he could, then spurred the bay into a gallop. He fell off a moment later, rolled over and over and across a patch of prickly pear, and finally came to a stop flat on his back, laughing like a man in a minstrel show.

Bart rode up beside him. The bay had stopped and was grazing a quarter of a mile away. Bart said, "Can you get on your feet?"

Gentry went into another spasm of laughing, and Bart was thoroughly disgusted. He caught up the bay and led it back to where Gentry sat under a tumbleweed.

Gentry was still pretending to laugh, and Bart began to sense something wrong. "What's funny?" he demanded.

"Jones wanted you to escape," said Gentry, suddenly sobering. "He told me to tell you that story about Miz Lewis so you would break jail."

Bart considered. It looked as if, to tell the truth, he was in a bad situation no matter what he did. The fact was that Jones had taken the initiative as far as Bart was concerned, and had done it very smartly.

"Then Jones had no plans about Catherine at all," said Bart.

Gentry laughed again. "Xenophon Jones is out to breed every woman he ever saw except the Harding woman," he said. "He's tired of her."

"Why?"

"She's too bossy."

Gentry was standing. His dirty shirt front was full of prickly pear thorns, and one hand rested on the butt of the six-shooter, which he had stuck into his waistband.

What Bart had originally figured, then, about Jones and his designs on Catherine, was still correct. Bart said, "You broke jail too."

"No jail can hold me," said Gentry, "because there's no law in the Panhandle, no court."

"And you were supposed to get me to break jail so I would leave the Panhandle and get the blame for whatever he does?"

"You already broke jail," said Gentry, "and you're ready to be blamed."

Bart suddenly hated Gentry's whiskered face. "You pimp!" he shouted. "You low-down, coyote-suckin', yellow-livered son-of-a-bitch!"

It was the first time in years he had really lost his temper, and afterward he was sorry he had lost it with Gentry, for Gentry was nothing but a hired man. The only thing was, Gentry was so thoroughly obnoxious in looks, sounds, and smell, that Bart saw the smug look of triumph on his face and forgot himself.

He saw Gentry pull the six-shooter from his waistband, and shouted, "Don't do it!" and dodged at the same time.

Gentry's shot went wild.

Bart shouted, "Stop!" but Gentry shot again.

"I ain't scared of you!" Gentry shouted.

The bullet kicked up dust in Bart's face as he moved. He drew his big six-shooter and fired one shot through Gentry's heart. The man pulled the trigger a third time as he fell, and that bullet jerked at Bart's buckskin vest.

Bart watched him for a moment, saw his fingers relax and the six-shooter drop into the dirt. Bart felt for a pulse but did not find one. He looked at the man's eyes, struck a match and held it close. The pupils did not contract. Gentry was dead.

Bart had no shovel and no time. He picked up the six-shooter, turned the man over on his face, and left him. He tied the bay's reins to a ring on his own saddle, and started off at a lope. The bay led well; it knew enough to run to one side to keep away from the black's heels.

Bart rode west to get away from the trail and the outlaw post. After a while he turned back south. Late in the afternoon he ran into some Half Moon cattle, and knew where he was.

He stopped at the run-down ranch house. Ike Logan was sitting in the shade of a rickety wagon, whittling. "Nice day fer a ride," he said, shading his eyes. "I heard you was in Mobeetie."

"You can hear anything," said Bart, "if you listen long enough. Can a man get a cup of coffee?"

He was starved, but he would not eat at the Half Moon because he knew Logan would not accept payment, and he was unwilling to take anything away from Logan's children. He was impatient to get on to the Quarter Circle JB, but the black had to have a breather.

Logan shooed away the dogs and bawled at the back door, "Put on the coffee, Hep. We got comp'ny."

Bart loosened the saddle girth.

"Funny thing," said Logan, still whittling. "Never had no comp'ny in years until day before yesterday, and ever since there's been a reg'lar stream. You got the makin's?"

Bart handed him the tobacco sack. "Who?" he asked.

"That feller Murphy—he come back about an hour ago."

"For what?" asked Bart.

Logan spoke in a grotesque whisper. "He come to spark Hepzibah. I told her to have nothin' to do with him; his intentions was no good, and I ordered him off the place and threatened to shoot his guts out if he come near her again, but he laughed at me. I'll do it, though. I swear I will."

"How did your daughter take it?"

"The youngun has got more spunk than I give her credit for.

She ain't never had no man sparkin' her, Wagner, and she fell for him like a walnut rollin' off a wagon seat on a rough road."

Bart heard a swish, and looked up in time to see Hepzibah throwing dishwater from the back door. She was pitifully thin, and the only way Bart could understand Murphy's pursuit of her was that he had had so many attractive women that he was tired of them; this seemed to be a distortion of the usual situation, but, thinking back on his experiences with Murphy, Bart realized that it did not seem out of place.

It was easy, of course, to understand the girl. Stuck there on a poor ranch, without clothes, without time even to think of taking care of her looks, she was nevertheless old enough to feel the urge of a woman, and even a casual look from a splendid physical specimen like Murphy was enough to send her blood pressure up—if she had any blood pressure at all.

He sat there in the sun, listening to Logan ramble on but not hearing what he said. He was tired of running in circles around Xenophon Jones. It seemed to him that it was time to take matters in his own hands. A shoot-out with Jones might possibly settle the question of court and save Catherine from whatever Jones had in store for her. If Stud Murphy could be included in the shooting, it would save Hepzibah from something bound to be unpleasant if not tragic. And Bart could not see that he himself had much to lose.

Once again he was back at the point where he had been many times before: it was time to shoot and move on.

He said, "You mentioned Murphy was here today. Know where he came from?"

"They was camped over in old Ben's north pasture. I seen them go in there about noon."

"You see everything," said Bart.

"I like to know what my neighbors is up to."

"Is Mrs. Lewis home?"

"Can't say she is."

He thought more about it as he sipped the hot coffee. Catherine could hardly be expected back before dark, even if she came straight back from Mobeetie. If Jones had any plans for her, he must realize that things were beginning to boil in the Panhandle, and he would not have long. Besides that, sometime this afternoon Jones would hear from Mobeetie that Bart had escaped and Gentry had been killed. He'd be bound to try whatever he had in mind as soon as possible.

Bart realized that he could not possibly ride into Jones's camp and get away alive. There were too many men in Jones's gang who would not worry a minute over shooting a man in the back.

"I'm going to take a nap down by the creek," he said. "Will you let me know when Mrs. Lewis comes home?"

"Sure will. I'll send the younguns to watch the road, and I'll keep an eye on the north."

"I'll bring you a handful of cigars next time I come from town," said Bart.

Logan brightened. "Sure. You bet."

And Bart added under his breath, "And some dress material for Hepzibah." The poor girl had not seen a new dress all her life, most likely, for she had made over her mother's things. He glanced at her and saw her big eyes on him, and saw her turn away suddenly, awkwardly, and almost wondered that such a seeming nonentity as Hepzibah could be moved by normal human urges, and could in turn stir them in men. She seemed colorless except for the deep eyes peering from behind the shaggy hair. And yet, he realized, every human being was entitled to feelings, and poverty did not necessarily change that.

He thanked her, but she said no word. She did not even nod, but her eyes seemed to get bigger as she looked at him, and it came to him that Hepzibah had changed since he had seen her before. It made him pause for a moment when he realized that the mere fact of a man's wanting to spark her—no matter who the man was—had already done something for her, had started a development of maturity.

"Can't figger out that girl," Logan said when they were alone. "Been tongue-tied all her life—but she sure blessed me out this afternoon."

"It's a natural thing," said Bart. "Happens to every girl. She grows until she's no longer a little girl, and then some day a man looks at her and she grows up completely—and there's nothing you can do about it."

"I reckon you're right," said Logan. "You musta been raised in a big family yourself."

"I was the oldest of seven."

"Now me —"

Bart broke in. "What day is today?"

"Saturday."

"Day after tomorrow is Monday. Listen, why don't you go up on the hill there and keep an eye to the north for Mrs. Lewis."

Logan nodded, and Bart walked off. He knew the black wouldn't go very far, as tired as it was.

He lay down, pulling his hat over his eyes. For a moment or two he heard the children playing around the corrals, and Logan's customary meaningless fussing at them as he went by.

Bart could intercept Catherine and send her to the JA or the LJ until after court, or he could lie in wait for Xenophon Jones and Stud Murphy. But lying in wait would prove nothing, and the lawman's instinct was strong in him: he wanted some evidence besides a lot of vague talk.

He went to sleep under the hot sun. Perhaps it was all imagination. Probably Catherine would not get back at all that night. . . .

CHAPTER XVII

HE AWOKE out of a sound sleep to hear Logan saying, "Wagner! Bart Wagner!" and Bart tried to force his eyes open. Logan finally touched his shoulder, and Bart awoke and swung to a sitting position. "At least you know how to wake a man up," he said.

"I got shot at once in a cow camp by touchin' a man first. That was down near San Antone when I was ridin' watch on a trail herd. I went over to this fellow and I didn't know his name yet and I—"

"Did Mrs. Lewis come home?" asked Bart.

"Rode through about ten minutes ago."

"Did you speak to her?"

"Yeah. Said she traded horses somewheres up on the plains so she could get home tonight. Said she was expectin' you."

Bart pulled on his hat. "You told her I was here?"

"Well, no," said Logan. "You didn't say I should, and I—"

"Good." Bart stood up. "Have you seen the black lately?"

Logan squinted and scratched his ear. "No, sir, can't say that I have, right now. I'll send the kids lookin', though."

"Never mind. You know where Jones's camp is?"

"Yes, sir. You got the makin's?"

Bart gave him the sack of tobacco. "You go up to where you can keep an eye on Jones. If a party leaves his camp and heads toward the JB, come and tell me immediately—*pronto!*"

"Yes, sir."

"If you do your part, I'll see you get a whole box of cigars. If you don't, I'll wring your neck."

"Yes, sir. Yes, *sir.*" He handed back the sack.

"Get that cigarette rolled and get up there where you can watch."

Logan lit the cigarette, tossed the match away, and shuffled off to the northwest.

Bart found his saddle and the feedbag on it. He poured a handful of dry corn into the hard leather of the nosebag and rattled it a few times. He heard no trotting hooves, no answering whicker, and he walked in a semicircle around the house, rattling the corn.

Hepzibah looked out the door at him. It was almost dark, and her big eyes were luminous against the dark background of her hair. "Sorry to disturb you," he said. "I'm looking for my horse."

"I saw the black goin' south," she said, "soon after you went to sleep."

It was the first time he had heard her speak, and she had an unexpectedly soft and pleasant voice.

South? That was the direction of the JB, and he realized then that the black must have come to think of the JB as its home pasture.

Two small children watched him from behind Hepzibah, and he heard others playing Run, Sheep, Run in the front yard to the accompaniment of barking from innumerable dogs. Then Logan's voice came from behind him, breathless. "Five men," he said, "saddled up and went south at a lope."

Bart swung on him. "The black is gone! Have you got a horse?"

"Sort of an old plowhorse," said Logan. "You want I should send fer him?"

"God almighty, yes!" Bart shouted.

"Tommy! Tommy! Get old Sampson!"

Bart checked the loads in his six-shooters. The .38 was in his shirt.

"Looks like you was aimin' fer trouble," said Logan.

"Not aiming—just getting ready."

"You got the makin's?"

Bart said, "Here. Keep the sack."

"Thanks, Mr. Wagner."

Bart groaned when Sampson plodded up. He was so old his hair was turning gray.

"I haven't got no saddle," said Logan.

"I'll use mine."

He got out on the road. Sampson's greatest virtue was his size. He could not be kicked into a lope or a gallop, but he fell into a rough trot that covered a fair amount of ground, and he kept it up for almost two hours without stopping. Then Bart saw the light in the window of the JB, and slowed down. He didn't think they would have a guard, for they all would want to see whatever Jones intended.

He got off of Sampson and tied the horse to a limb near old Ben's grave. He settled his gun belt on his hips and walked quietly around the house at a distance. He heard loud laughter, but kept a tight rein on himself. At the back he counted, against the starry sky, five saddle horses tied to the corral. He pulled in slowly, got close to the door, and listened.

"I think she'd look better standing on the table," said Stud Murphy's voice, and Bart recognized the heat in his taut voice.

There was a slight scuffle. Bart started in, but controlled himself once more. If he had it figured right, there would soon be a much better time for him to enter.

He heard Catherine expostulate, but he guessed that Jones had picked her up and stood her in the middle of the table, for he heard a thump.

Jones's voice, filled with something more than mere lust, and sounding strange and almost cracked, said: "I figger she'd look better with her dress off."

One man guffawed. Another said, "You reckon it'll say 'Hornsby's Steamed Wheat' on the back of her drawers?"

Jones's high, strained voice answered: "I'm not interested in the back of her drawers."

Bart held himself.

He heard a rip of cloth, a shriek by Catherine, and an instant of silence. At that moment he hit the door with his foot and his shoulder, charged in with a six-shooter in each hand.

He held one .44 on Jones, the other in the general direction of Stud Murphy.

Catherine stood barefooted on the table, naked from toe to head, her torn clothing on the floor, while she tried frantically but ineffectively to cover herself with her hands. Her face was as white as a bleached bed sheet, and she stared at Bart, first unbelieving and incredulous, then abruptly hopeful, then grateful.

Bart said softly, "Step down from the table, Catherine."

Jones's voice was hoarse, almost choked. "This is none of your business, Wagner!"

Bart kept one .44 lined up on Jones's breastbone. "It is now."

Catherine fled behind the curtain. At that moment Stud Murphy drew his six-shooter to cover Bart, but did not fire, and Bart kept his one .44 aimed at Jones. "Tell him to drop it," he said.

Some hope flickered in Jones's eyes—a hope that his consuming desires might not be frustrated after all. He said, "He can pull the trigger as quick as you can."

Bart smiled tightly. "But not quick enough. Before I die, I'll pull mine. And you'll die too. Tell him to put it up."

Jones's mouth worked, and Bart guessed he was having quite a battle with himself.

"Hurry," said Bart. "I'm getting nervous."

"Murphy has a gun on your back."

"I figured he would have. He could put five bullets in me, but I'd still be able to pull the trigger."

"I'm willing to bet you can't."

"That bet is easy to call," said Bart. "I'm raising you—your own life. It's up to you."

Jones moistened his lips, and Bart knew from his uncertain eyes that Jones was backing down.

"Tell your men to drop their hardware on the table and go out one at a time," Bart said.

Jones began to get angry. "Wagner, you won't get by with this."

Bart said, "You've got more cards, but I've got the best one—a bead on your wishbone. Tell them to get going."

Jones stared at him for a long time. He looked into the black hole of the .44 pointing at his heart. He looked at Bart's eyes. His glance darted toward the curtain where Catherine had disappeared, and he licked his dry lips.

"It makes no difference," Bart said steadily, "how many times you get the drop on me. No matter what you do, there's only one way for you to walk out of this house alive. Tell your men to drop their hardware on the table as they go out."

Jones swallowed hard.

"Tell Murphy to drop his first," said Bart.

Jones hesitated, but in the end his fear for his life overcame his mammoth egotism and his mania—of whatever form it might take—for the woman. He broke. "All right, Murphy. Do what he says." And having made the first move, he glanced again at that big black hole aimed at his heart, and became anxious. "Don't make any wrong move," he said. "He's crazy but he'll do it. I see it in his eyes. Drop your gun and go outside."

Murphy's face turned dark in the light of the coal-oil lamp. The cords knotted in his thick neck; obviously Murphy had had his own ideas about the woman. "The next time I meet you," he said harshly, "it'll be on different terms."

"Yes," said Bart. "They might be even, for a change."

Murphy stepped forward slowly.

"Don't make a mistake and bump me as you go out," said Bart. "You can get me—but I'll get him."

The sweat stood out on Jones's forehead. "Do what he says," he begged. "Don't make a false move."

Murphy's eyes were filled with the rage of frustrated lust—but he was not the one who had the .44 aimed at his heart. He dropped both of his six-shooters on the table, and Bart permitted himself a full breath. He was standing with his back to the door, and actually he had a good chance to get two or three of them, but that was not enough. If shooting started, he was bound to die. And there would still be Catherine and two or three men left, and these were like the hostile Indians of the Great Plains, whose energies after a battle inevitably turned to sexual frenzy. He kept his back to the door as Murphy went out, then moved to one side.

"One at a time," said Bart, holding his .44's motionless, both pointed at Jones.

Jones nodded, almost hastily. Another man dropped his guns on the table and went out. A third. The fourth.

Only Jones was left.

Bart breathed a little more easily. "All right, Jones. You have almost got a reprieve from a bullet. If you make a move now, it's far too late."

"You'll get paid back for stickin' your nose into this," said Jones harshly.

"Drop the guns," said Bart. "I'm getting nervous."

Jones tossed his guns to the table, and Bart began to feel weak inside. One wrong move—one man who might suddenly have decided it was a good chance to get rid of Jones—and for a few seconds fire would blaze until the cabin would be as light as day; lead would smash its way into every corner; and afterward the acrid smoke would fill the room and for a few brief moments hide the holocaust of blood and death. But Jones went outside, and it was all over for the time being.

Bart blew out the lamp behind him. "Get some clothes on," he told Catherine in a low voice. "We have got to ride."

He heard her gasp and fall on the floor. He leaped to the curtain and found her fainted. He picked her up and laid her on the buffalo robe. Then he tiptoed back to the water bucket.

He crouched in the open door for a second and saw two men walking toward the horses. The moon was coming up. He got a dipperful of water and went back to Catherine. He heard her faint voice: "Bart?"

"Yes. Don't worry. Get on some clothes of some kind and we'll head out for the JA until this is over."

"Isn't it over now?"

"It's just started," he told her.

She was up, and he gave her water in the darkness. "Mr. Goodnight and Captain Arrington said they would not try anything until after court," she said.

"They were figuring on normal men. These men are abnormal. The things they do cannot be figured the same as those of other men."

He heard her shiver. "This is what they dare to do now, under the shadow of the court," Bart said. "It is nothing to what they will do if they back down the court Monday."

She took a drink of the water. "I was terribly frightened," she said.

"I don't blame you."

He stepped back, and heard her fumbling for a dress.

"Do you think they will try to stop the court now?" she asked.

"They have no choice. They are confronted with an attempted rape, and that's a hanging charge. They've *got* to wipe out the court or leave the country."

"Maybe they will leave."

"With their insolence and arrogance and their hate for me because I interfered between you and them, they won't move a step until they're forced. They will be in Clarendon Monday with Piggie Benson and his men, and they'll be loaded for bear. Besides that, I'm a witness against them now."

"You would be a witness against them for what—for tonight?" she said.

He nodded in the dark. "So would you."

She gasped. "Bart, I could never repeat all the awful things they said to me before you got here—what they were going to do."

"Maybe you won't have to. There were five men, and I would know them all—but if Murphy and Jones are disposed of, the others will run. Maybe the others won't even show up in Clarendon after that. I don't know. But I do know we've got more fighting ahead before there will be law in the Panhandle."

CHAPTER XVIII

HE WENT outside cautiously, and stayed against the house until he saw them riding far down the valley in the moonlight. Then he called the black, and got another horse for Catherine. The black had been grazing across the creek, and came promptly.

They reached the JA ranch about midnight, and the foreman, Lee Jasper, got out of bed to listen to Bart's story. He called Goodnight, who was furious when he heard about it.

"Every single one of them will be blasted into hell," he said, "whether with hot lead or a tight rope."

Bart told him about being in jail at Mobeetie, and Goodnight laughed. "Just keep out of his sight. Arrington is ace-high. If he knew what we're planning, he would buck like an eight-year-old steer with a heelfly under his tail, but after it's all over, he'll say, well, he couldn't very well help it since he didn't know anything about it, and inasmuch as it turned out all right—"

"Do you think it will—without a general shoot-out, that is?"

"It's your idea, isn't it?" asked Goodnight.

"Yes—but now I'm beginning to wonder. The arrogance and defiance of these men is hard to believe."

"It doesn't go very deep," said Goodnight. "They haven't the tradition behind them that makes them stick together as a unit and back one another till the last dog is hung."

"I hope you're right. I'd hate to see a lot of people killed."

Goodnight sighed. "They'll run like a bunch of mangy yellow coyotes. The thing is—oh hell, where's my tobacco?"

"Here's some. No, I guess I gave it to Ike Logan."

"Good for nothin'," muttered Goodnight. "Come on in and I'll get us some tobacco."

Catherine had been taken inside by Mrs. Goodnight. Bart followed Charlie into the house, into the fragrant smell of cedar. He stepped on a bearskin rug and stopped. Goodnight scratched a match on his trousers, and a yellow flame broke out. He put the chimney back on the lamp. His massive frame threw shadows over half the room.

"Sit down, sit down." He pulled two sacks of Bull Durham out of a desk drawer and tossed one to Bart. "Light up," he said, "and I'll get us a drink. You've had some hard days recently."

"It seems like quite a while," Bart said, "since I've passed a peaceful night *and* day."

Goodnight poured whisky in two glasses and pushed one across the big cottonwood table. He sat in a huge homemade chair covered with cowhide filled with brands—mainly the JA.

Bart got his cigarette going. He sank back on the rawhide strips, dangling the cigarette in fingers suddenly weary and devoid of strength. He swallowed a good-sized slug of bourbon and relaxed.

"You better ride over to the LJ in the morning," Goodnight said. "Since you're the key man, you'll want to be sure everything is going off the way it should."

"I'll do that." Bart took another swallow. "I wonder if they'll burn the JB tomorrow."

"I don't think so—but don't worry about it. Believe me, their gall has been somewhat shaken by what happened tonight, and I don't think they'll go back to the same place. But I think by

Monday they'll be ready to fight it out in Clarendon. Jones is a stubborn-minded man, and he's set on running things in the Panhandle."

"He picked a hard way to go about it."

"If outlaws ran things the way we run a big ranch, the rest of us wouldn't have a chance."

Bart finished his whisky and slid the glass back across the table.

"Another one?" Goodnight reached for the bottle.

"Not for me. I'm ready to go to sleep."

Goodnight got up and put the cork in the bottle. "I'll put you up in the next room."

He was awake the next morning for breakfast. Since it was Sunday, they did not get up as early as usual. He sat at the table with the family and some of the hands, and filled himself with ham and eggs, hot biscuits with butter and peach preserves, pancakes, and watermelon. Catherine and Mrs. Goodnight would eat later.

When he finished, it was hard to get up. He had a cigarette and went outside and squatted by the well, and watched some of the hands pitch horseshoes. They would not have the entire day off, but unless it was roundup time or special work was needed, they would have a short workday. Two of them had made the long trip into Clarendon on horseback before daylight to go to church.

"Got my doubts about it," said Goodnight. "I suspect there's some girls in the case—except I know there's no girls in Clarendon."

Bart went presently to saddle up, and he was riding the black slowly through the yard when he saw Catherine come outside. She looked clean and fresh and unhurt from the night before.

"Mr. Goodnight will be responsible for you until Tuesday at least," he told her. "And if they burn down your house, the ranchers will pitch in and put you up another one."

"People are mighty nice," she said. "But you are the nicest of all."

His face felt warm. "It isn't much," he said.

She walked close to his stirrup. "You risked your life last night, Bart."

"It wasn't much," he repeated.

"It was a terrible risk. Jones and Murphy were crazy."

He looked away. "Well, it worked," he said.

"I can never forget it, Bart. You are a very brave man."

He looked down at her. "Catherine," he said, "I want to know one thing. Everybody mixed up in this—especially those on the other side—keep insisting you know more about old Ben's death than you told." He looked down at her. "Is that so?"

Her brown eyes were open and frank. "Yes, I do. I've tried to tell you, but you have turned it into something else."

He was afraid to ask the next question, but he asked it anyway. "What about it?"

She looked at the ground for a moment, and then back up, and he felt terrible because of the shame he had brought to her face.

"Ben sold me to Xenophon Jones," she said.

He stared at her, shocked by what she had said, reproachful of himself for having made her say it. Then he nodded slowly, although she was staring at the ground.

"Ben never wanted to touch me," she said in a low voice, "and Xenophon Jones came along and knew something was wrong. When he found it out, he—he was like a wild man. He was after me from the day he came to hide out at our place. When I wouldn't have anything to do with him, he started working on Ben, and finally Ben made a deal with him."

"For money?" Bart asked, incredulous.

"As far as I know."

"That isn't human," Bart said slowly. "You can't sell human beings these days—certainly not a wife."

"I heard them talking one day about a thousand dollars, and I always thought that was the price, but I never knew. I didn't remember it until later when I found out he had made the deal."

"How did Ben tell you about it."

"He started out by saying Jones was younger than he was, and more suitable as a husband. But I told him he was all right. There were a lot of things a person would not like about Ben, but I married him and I intended to stick to him. He suggested I live with Jones for a month, and I got pretty mad. Finally he said he had promised, but I told him it made no difference: he had no right to promise a thing like that." She looked up at Bart, asking him to understand. "This all happened over several days, and he would see Jones in between times and talk it over."

"And the day Ben got killed—"

"Ben had insisted I had to go meet Jones up at the spring, but I had refused. He said then that he had already taken the money and he had to do something about it, and I shamed him. Finally he broke down and confessed it was a terrible thing to do, and he said he'd go up to the spring and have it out with Jones. He would not let me go with him, but I walked up the creek bed and heard them arguing. And finally Ben said no, he absolutely wouldn't try to force me; he'd pay the money back, but he wasn't turning me over to them. And Jones and Murphy both shot him together. Then they drug him to the house and left him in the back yard." Her voice broke. "It was probably the only real good thing Ben ever did, and that's why I buried him so carefully."

She was crying in silence, her face turned upward, and Bart touched her briefly, then moved the horse slowly toward the gate, while she walked along, holding to the stirrup.

"I know, Bart, that he caused trouble for you. Old Ben caused trouble for a lot of people, and many didn't like him. He was a man it was easy to not like, because he wasn't very nice, and he was weak—weak in many ways. But that one time in his life he was a man, and I was proud of him"—tears were streaming down her face—"and I made a promise not to tell the world that he had sold me, for I thought he had redeemed himself when he died."

Bart leaned down and squeezed her hand. "Catherine," he said, "you did exactly right, and I am sorry I made you tell. I will never repeat it."

"They might put Jones and Murphy on trial, though. What will we do then?"

He said harshly, "I don't think either one will ever go on trial."

But he saw where the series of events was taking him irrevocably. Ben Lewis was dead and could not testify for him. Bart was in the position of defending Ben's widow, who alone could give, as far as he knew, any testimony about the mirror-shining. Her evidence would not be firsthand, but, since Ben was dead, it would have some weight. But he could not ask her to testify to that in court, for a clever lawyer would insist on bringing out the entire situation on the ranch when Bart had come on the scene, and Catherine's shame would be revealed. It began to seem that he would have to keep on moving of necessity, even though he was beginning to think it could be extremely pleasant to stay. He heard the chickens' clucking and raised his head. "I'll have to be going," he said.

She smiled through her tears. "Whatever happens, Bart, I'll be waiting."

They had passed a clump of willow trees and were out of sight of the house. He slid out of the saddle and kissed her hard, thinking it might be the last time. She kissed him back, not knowing, he realized, what was in his mind.

He hugged her fiercely and then got into the saddle. "So long, Catherine."

"So long, Bart."

As long as he could look back, he could see her, a tiny dot of white against the green of the trees and the dusty gray of the grass. And he knew she stood there longer than that, for a black horse could be seen a long way across the prairie. . . .

It was fourteen miles to the LJ without going around by the Quarter Circle JB, and he decided to take the short cut. He was jogging along, only an hour from the LJ, when he saw dust on the prairie to his left front, and stopped long enough to identify Stella Harding's chestnut gelding, traveling in the general direction of Xenophon Jones's camp of the night before. She would cross Half Moon range and reach Jones in a couple of hours. He sat the black for a moment, thinking over the lay of the land, and then backtrailed, but instead of returning to the JA, he forked off and went to the Half Moon.

He put the black into a gallop as soon as he got a little distance away from his stopping point, and now he began to use his spurs.

The black was a big horse, fast and with plenty of bottom, and he had no doubt it could outrun the chestnut by considerable over a stretch. However, he had taken the long way around, and he had now to cut in ahead of her.

He went through the bottom along Hackberry Creek, skirted Logan's place, and rode up onto the slope over which Stella must ride if she had not done so already. He noted that old Sampson had returned home, just as the black had returned to the JB. He reached the top of the slope and looked east and north. He saw the chestnut come up out of a ravine, and Stella lined the horse out west.

Bart cut her off with the black in ten minutes of hard riding. He rode up alongside and grabbed the chestnut's cheek strap and brought it down to a halt.

Stella was furious. "What do you think you're doing? Who gave you a right to stop me?"

"I took the right," he said. "Where you going?"

Her black eyes were defiant. "For a ride."

"Ride back to the ranch with me."

"I don't want to ride with you."

He said, "You wanted me to go to Kansas City with you."

She stormed. "Bart Wagner, you infuriate me!"

"I have infuriated others," he said. "Most of them are dead."

"Is that a threat?"

He grinned. "You wouldn't be any fun dead."

"If it is—" She held a six-shooter in her hand.

He smiled. "It's not in position to shoot," he told her, and in one smooth motion seized the barrel. He turned the cylinder and pushed out the cartridges, then gave it back to her. "Remember to load it the next time you go somewhere, in case you want to shoot a snake."

She was coldly furious because he had thwarted her in something she had wanted to do, as she had been furious with Hector Johnson for trying to interfere belatedly the night Bart and Arrington had spent on the LJ. "I'm not going with you under any circumstances," she said.

"It will do you no good to try to go anywhere else," he said. "The black can outrun the chestnut all day long."

She was so angry she was speechless.

"Tell me why you want to see Xenophon Jones."

"Because he is a man."

"There are men on the LJ."

"Not like him."

Bart studied her, and she looked away.

"I've heard," he said. "It seems to be all over the Panhandle. Everybody knows but your father."

She gave a look of exaggerated impatience. "He doesn't know any more than the day he was born."

"He always struck me as a mighty solid hombre," said Bart.

"Solid and stupid."

"Your kind has contempt for anybody who doesn't see through you, doesn't it?"

She sighed heavily.

"Stud Murphy wants you."

She looked at Bart. "I'd take him if I couldn't get Xenophon Jones—but there's something wrong with him. It's in his eyes. I've seen it before."

"When you were a whore on Persimmon Hill?"

She glared at him, open-mouthed. Then her red lips formed into a thin line. "You dirty skunk! You yellow-livered bastard! You maggoty, piss-drenched son-of-a-bitch!"

He said quietly, "I thought you would verify it."

She struck at him with the empty six-shooter. He dodged, and the gun hit the cantle, and the front sight slashed a furrow in the leather covering.

The black jumped forward, but Bart turned it and circled in behind her. "Stella," he said, "I hope you get control of your temper before we reach the LJ."

She rode for a while in sullen silence.

"I don't think," he said, "that Stud Murphy is good for you. He wants the girl on the Half Moon."

Instantly he regretted having said it. He was trying to goad her into telling him something, but he had not meant to drag Hepzibah into it.

"Oh, that—" She did not finish. "If he would turn me down for a slut like that, I'd kill him."

He wanted to defend Hepzibah, but he didn't want to turn Stella's wrath against her. "I think what you said about him is right. He acts strange around women."

He asked presently, "Want to change your mind about me and go to Kansas City?"

She looked at him sharply, her thoughts turning instantly to something else. "I hear you can handle a keno deck."

"I can deal cards," he said.

"A good team can make money in Kansas City. All the cattle money in Texas and New Mexico and the Nations goes into that town."

He said, "A team?"

She raised her eyebrows. "There are other ways to make money besides over a deck of cards."

He nodded slowly.

Her look was calculating. "Still thinking about it, then?"

"Still thinking." He did not tell her about Ben Lewis and the fact that Catherine was the only one who knew what Ben had done in El Paso, nor did he tell her that he was trying to console himself with the thought that by going to Kansas City with her he would be removing her from a position where she could upset the lives of persons like Hepzibah and Catherine.

"What can I do to persuade you?" she asked.

"Nothing now." He stared at her as a sudden fear struck him. "I hope," he said, "that you have not told them what we are planning." At the same time, he wondered just how much she knew of the plans.

She scoffed. "Why should I? Do you expect a bunch of farmers to beat men like Xenophon Jones and Stud Murphy and Piggie Benson?" She looked at him with new fire in her eyes. "Those men are killers!"

He smiled wryly. She thought it was as simple as a stand-up and shoot-down fight. "They have yellow in them too."

"Not if they know what they're going up against."

"And you were going to tell them tonight," he observed.

She swung back, again furious. "You tricked me!"

He said, "Ma'am, you're a tricky one to deal with."

"I had no thought of telling them," she declared.

He saw the LJ ranch gate appear over the top of the next slope. "I for one do not believe a word of it," he said.

She did not answer.

Bart, however, was counting up the deadly results of the information she had intended to give them. If they should know definitely that the ranchers were depending on Bart Wagner, their course would be simple: to converge their fire on Bart and take him out of the fight immediately. In such a case, Bart would never know the outcome, for he would be dead beyond any question.

They rode in silence for a hundred yards. "What are you going to tell them at the ranch?" she asked.

"What would you have told them?"

"That I went for a ride," she said.

"I'll tell them you were lost and I found you."

"They will know better."

He shrugged. "They probably know you're not out riding aimlessly, too. Hector knew where you were the other night."

Her face contorted. "You s—"

He held up a hand to quiet her. "No more profanity, please. We are nearing civilization."

But he was soberly considering the possibilities of her intention to talk to Jones, and he saw only one way of forestalling that: an appeal to her selfishness. As they rode toward the barn, he said: "Remember, you are to meet me after the thing is settled."

She looked at him and nodded. Her black eyes were unreadable.

He met Tom Harding after Stella disappeared in the house. "Have a drink, Bart?"

"I'm a little dry," Bart admitted.

They had the drink inside. "No liquor allowed on the place as far as the hands are concerned," said Harding. "I keep it here and I use it, like all the other ranchers in the Panhandle, but there's no drinking and no gambling among the help. Saves a lot of trouble."

Bart sat for a while, gathering strength.

"We could go outside where it's cool," said Harding. "Hot day up here on the plains. Wish we had Charlie Goodnight's creek."

They went out toward the barn and sat down on a bale of hay.

Bart asked, "What do you look for tomorrow?"

Harding drew a cigar out of his pocket, sniffed it, and lit it slowly, carefully, then puffed the fragrant smoke into the still air. He looked suddenly at Bart. "Sorry. I didn't think to bring you one, Bart. I'll get you a couple when we go back to the house."

"Never mind," said Bart, and pulled out his tobacco sack. He made a cigarette, and when he put the sack away, he became aware of the .38 bullets still in his vest pocket, and decided to leave them there for luck.

"I don't think it will be easy," Harding said at last. "No man who has been in the Panhandle any length of time thinks that. It's been said before—but these outlaws, from Dutch Henry and Goodanuff on down, are the most arrogant bastards on earth, or at least in the United States. They aren't worried too much. They can always go up into the Public Land Strip if the Texas Rangers get after them. Right now, though, I'd say they got everything in their favor."

"You heard any more about Piggie Benson's crew?"

"I sent a man up to Tascosa day before yesterday. He got back this morning," Harding said heavily. "He says Benson has signed up fifty-two men to ride down here this afternoon and be ready to move in on Clarendon in the morning."

"Do you believe it?"

"Knowing Benson—yes."

"What have you heard from the other ranchers?"

"They'll be here in the morning. We'll move the chuck wagons in early. Goodnight is furnishing three; I'm putting up one."

Bart leaned back against the barn, watching the house, his hands locked behind his head. "You better keep an eye on Stella. It won't be too good for her to go out today, with that gang coming down from Tascosa. They will all be liquored up and wild—and they might figure she knows something and try to get it out of her."

"You're right," said Harding. "I'll speak to Hector."

Bart said easily, "She might resent Hector because he's your foreman. You better pick somebody else she won't notice."

Harding sighed. "She's a high-spirited girl. I don't know how I'll ever make her satisfied, out here on the ranch."

Bart paused. "It will work out," he said.

"She was always a little willful."

"Things like that are hard to get over," said Bart.

"I thought it would settle her down to live on the ranch, but I guess it hasn't helped."

They smoked in silence for a while. Harding called a young fellow and spoke to him in a low voice; the boy went to the corral and saddled a horse and led it into the shade in the barn.

Hector Johnson was thoughtfully braiding a *mecate* out of black and white horsehair; an older man was cutting up a big cottonwood log with a bucksaw. Everywhere the ranch was peaceful and quiet and gave no indication of the events building for the next day.

He saw Stella late in the afternoon when she came out in the yard. She was dressed to kill, and smelled of fancy perfume like a skunk upwind in a narrow creek bottom on a warm day— except she smelled good.

He wandered over slowly, so as not to be noticed. "You look nice," he said.

Her red lips curved. "I'm thinking about tomorrow."

He hesitated. He had been trying to reconcile himself to the idea without success.

Her eyes narrowed instantly. "You and I will be better for each other than you and Catherine Lewis."

He said, "One thing that bothers me is that you will cut my throat the minute somebody else comes along—and I'm a man who doesn't look good in a cut throat."

She said with scorn, "You're afraid of me."

"Maybe I am." And maybe he was—but not in the way she was thinking.

"You're having me watched," she said.

"I thought it might save you some trouble—and us a lot of trouble."

"Who do you mean by 'us'?"

"Your dad and me."

"Dad!" she said scornfully. "A hopeless old—" For a moment she had trouble finding a word to express her contempt without exhibiting shocking irreverence.

"—thumb-twiddler." She added, "That's the kindest thing I could ever say about him."

He looked at her steadily. "Your dad built himself a pretty good ranch out here."

"Sitting at a desk, signing checks, giving orders. *He* doesn't get out there and do the hard work."

"Maybe he doesn't have to. Maybe he can't."

"Of course he can't. He had a bad case of heart disease."

"Heart disease?" Bart stared at her. "I didn't know that."

She curled her lip superciliously. "There still are a few things you don't know."

"Maybe you're right."

He thought about Stella as he watched her go toward the barn. He didn't think she would ride in her ordinary clothes, but he would not have bet on it. Apparently his doubt was shared by the young fellow assigned to watch her, for he got up from his whittling and went into the barn.

Stella was a strange one. She had contempt for a great many things, even for her father and the money he had made, which would all be hers. She was a restless woman. Whatever the status quo happened to be at any given moment, that was what she did not like and could not endure. It was the wrong attitude for the Panhandle, where you played whatever hand was dealt you, and tried to make it stick.

If you couldn't play it, you moved on.

CHAPTER XIX

THEY BEGAN to arrive at three o'clock in the morning, when sixteen men from the Slash K rode up, all armed with six-shooters, rifles, and knives, and announced grimly that they were ready for action.

Harding roused the cook, and he built a fire in the range and put on a big pot of coffee.

"We'll have breakfast about five," Harding said.

The cook was an old, grizzled man with hands that must have given him pain, for the joints were swollen and caused difficulty in his movements. "You're takin' me, Colonel?" he asked with a deep-South drawl.

"I'm certainly not taking you," said Harding. "Hell, you were too old to fight the War of 1812. What do you want to start now for?"

The cook turned from the coffee grinder and dumped a trayful of coffee into the pot. "Fever's gittin' into my blood, Colonel. I was raised on tobacco juice an' powder smoke."

"So is every other man who's coming this morning. So are

Benson and Murphy and Jones. Now look, Smitty. Good cooks are scarce. You stay out of this, for if any of us are left over, we'll be hungry."

Smitty did not answer. He put another piece of wood in the stove. "I'd sure like to see it."

But Harding had moved on to stop the argument.

The Slash K men, commanded by a tall, clean-shaved young fellow who talked with a West Texas twang, settled down to smoking and low-voiced talk, filling the big Harding kitchen comfortably without getting in Smitty's way. Some slouched in chairs, still half asleep; some lay on the floor, propped up on their elbows. One stood in the doorway, chewing vigorously, and occasionally spitting into the dark.

Harding came back from the barn. "I want every man to be sure about one thing," said Harding. "Absolutely no shells under the triggers. We want no accidental shot going off to start a slaughter."

The big-hatted man in the doorway said, "We come to fight, Colonel."

"You came to *win* a fight," said Harding, "and it's just as good won by a loaded six-shooter as if won by a smoking barrel—and a lot less graves to dig when it's over."

Hector Johnson appeared in the doorway and looked wildly for Harding, saw him, and beckoned. Harding got up, nodded to Bart, and went outside past the man in the doorway. Bart followed him, and they met Johnson around the corner.

Johnson glared at Bart and said, "This is private business, Colonel."

Harding, unperturbed, said, "This is no time for private business. Anyway, Wagner knows all about this. Spill it out."

Bart could see Johnson's face in the yellow light from the kitchen window. He looked at Bart and frowned, then addressed Harding. "Stella just left the ranch, Colonel."

Harding was instantly alert. "I told Beans to keep an eye on her."

"He went to sleep, Colonel—but she didn't."

"How do you know she's gone for sure?"

"The chestnut isn't in its stall."

"How long ago?"

"Quarter of an hour, maybe. The droppings are still warm."

"Well—" Harding hesitated. "Damn it, she's old enough to know what she's doing. Leave her be. We've got more important things right now. Anyway, she'll show up later."

Bart said thoughtfully, "It might be, Colonel, that she has a mistaken idea of warning Jones and his men to save them from getting killed—and that would tip our hand. Of course I'm not saying she would tell them what we're up to—but it would be just like a woman."

His tactic was successful. Harding sighed heavily. "It *would* be like a woman. All right, Hector, you better go see what she's up to. Take the sorrel. You'll need a good horse to head the chestnut. You say she went west?"

"Yes."

Johnson had not said it, so apparently Harding knew more about Stella's activities than they had supposed. "You know the way?" he asked.

"It goes right by the Half Moon place."

"You been there lately?"

"Two or three times."

Somehow Hector's answer was too fast, but Harding did not notice. "Try to get back in time." He looked up as the sound of hooves came from the direction of the gate. "We'll need all the help we can get."

Hector glanced at him, and for a second Hector's face was clearly outlined and strongly shadowed by the lamplight. "I'll be back in time."

Harding watched him run to the barn. "Hector's got his mind set on Stella," he said. "I wish she would change her way toward him."

Bart did not answer. In that glimpse of Hector's face he had seen something that puzzled him: not concern for Stella, but something Bart could not identify, as if Hector's mind had been somewhere else.

"Come to think of it," said Harding, "I reckon it's a good thing you wanted me to send him after her. Men like these here outlaws go crazy at a time like this, and it sure is no place for a woman to be. I was in an outlaw camp once—deputy sheriff on a posse, and they captured me and held me as a hostage—when they brought in a woman they had taken from a ranch." He shook his head. "I'll never forget her screams to my dying day."

Bart was looking into the darkness, trying to anticipate what might happen out there to the west.

The creaking of wagons came loud in the night air, and Charlie Goodnight loped forward on his big horse. "I told them not to show a light," he said. "There's no sense advertising this meeting."

"Get down and go in the kitchen for coffee," said Harding. "We'll take care of the horses."

The big chuck wagons—Charles Goodnight's own invention of a few years before—lumbered by, pulled by four mules each, and thirty-three riders followed them.

Bart went inside. The cook had on three pots of coffee and was stirring up pancake batter. The kitchen now was buzzing with talk as men greeted one another. Many of them knew many others by sight, but the Panhandle was so vast and ranch work so demanding that they hardly saw one another except at the calf roundup in the spring or the beef roundup in the fall.

Harding and Goodnight clumped off to the library, and a moment later Harding looked out and called Bart. "Want a drink?" he asked when they sat down.

"Not now," said Bart.

"Hell," Goodnight said indignantly, "I'm not making a ride like this so early in the morning for nothing."

Harding opened the bottle. "How many we got lined up altogether?" he asked.

Goodnight poured a medium-sized drink. "Close to ninety."

"Lot of men," said Bart, making a cigarette.

Harding pulled out a box of cigars and held it to Goodnight, who took one. "I'd offer you one," said Harding to Bart, "but I guess you like your cigarettes better."

Goodnight looked up quickly, about to speak, but Bart kept his eyes on his work.

"I figure," said Harding, putting the box back on his desk, "we'll pull out of here about five. That should throw the wagons into Clarendon around seven. Court opens at eight, and I don't figure the outlaws will get there much before eight."

Goodnight, lighting his cigar, nodded. For some reason, his eyes, over the cigar, were on Bart. "Ought to come about right."

"We'll have to leave the saddle horses here and take the wagons in loaded, to keep from tipping our hand."

Goodnight nodded. "I talked to Judge Willis yesterday. He's still scared, but he's game. He said remember one thing: the court can have no official part of any violence, and we will have to be careful not to overdo it."

Bart put the tobacco sack in his vest pocket. "I know that," he said.

Goodnight took a swallow of whisky, then looked up. "More coming," he said.

They went outside. It was around four o'clock, and the sky would soon be lightening in the east. Twelve men jogged in from the distant Matadors, and were followed by fifteen from smaller spreads in the area. Goodnight chewed on his cigar and walked back and forth, his massive shoulders restless under the vigorous drive of his powerful body. "Ninety-four men," he announced finally, "counting yours."

"I admit I was a little scared," Harding said, "that some might back out at the last minute."

Goodnight glared at him. "No man who had the guts to stay in the Panhandle more than two years would back out of a thing like this," he said.

The hands were lined up at the door with plates, getting pancakes and going back into the yard to eat, hunkered around in small groups.

"You seen Hector yet?" Harding asked Bart.

"Not yet. It's early, though," said Bart. He had figured an hour each way for Hector, but with Stella in the play, it was hard to know.

He had reached the point where he was not worried about either Hector or Stella, but he was calculating every possible move at the showdown, going over and over them in his mind, and he realized that a great deal of tension was building up within him. . . .

A half hour later, as the last cowboy came out of the kitchen with a plate, he stopped in the doorway and looked to the west. "I heard a shot," he said.

Bart glanced at Harding. Every man in the yard was instantly on his feet, straining his eyes across the prairie, which was light enough to show horses and cattle at a distance.

Goodnight said, "I heard it too."

"A .44, maybe—or a big Sharps. Hard to tell at this distance."

"It was a .44," said the foreman from the Slash K.

"Was there another one?" asked Harding.

"Only one," said the tall foreman.

"Maybe a drunk outlaw. They're probably getting ready to ride out, up there in Jones's camp."

Goodnight looked at the lightening sky in the east. "In that case, we'd better move," he said.

The cook appeared in the door. "Everybody et?" he bawled.

Nobody said otherwise, and Harding answered, "All et, Smitty."

"I'm throwin' what's left to the hogs," Smitty announced.

Goodnight arose. "Let's go," he said quietly. . . .

They made a strange cavalcade a little later, with four canvas-covered chuck wagons strung out on the road, and five men—Bart, Harding, Goodnight, Lee Jasper, and the Slash K foreman—on horseback. Bart had suggested it would look better that way. The wagons were crowded inside, but it was not very far to Clarendon.

They pulled into town at ten minutes to seven, and Goodnight had them run the wagons into a large semicircle confronting the place where Willis would put his desk to be used as a bench. An area was left about twice as big as a large public hall. A few curious citizens ventured out to see what was going on, and Goodnight enlisted their help at unharnessing the teams. The canvas was puckered tight at each end of each wagon. Jonas Myers said, "I don't see the sense of lining up a bunch of empty chuck wagons in front of the judge's bench."

Goodnight's answer was a sharp rebuke. "You don't expect the judge to talk to an open prairie, do you?"

It did not, as logic, carry much weight, but Goodnight's manner did, as always. Myers shut up and went back into his store.

Judge Willis came out to the ground and talked with Goodnight in low tones, and they called Harding and Bart and the other two.

"I'm trying to impress on Charlie," said Judge Willis, "the absolute necessity of taking no untoward step. Whatever is done must be to uphold the law and not in any sense to intimidate it."

"Judge," said Bart, "I don't think there's a man with us who has any desire to do anything more than see the regular procedure of your court upheld."

"Good." Willis's voice was unusually low and musical that morning. "Court will be called at eight o'clock."

"Meantime," said Goodnight, "why don't you go have a drink with me?"

Judge Willis looked at Goodnight. The judge obviously was apprehensive, but he murmured, "Charlie, you said something," and they went off toward the saloon.

An old desk was brought from Myers's store and set on the ground facing the wagons. A rawhide-bottom chair from the saloon was put behind the desk. There were no seats for spectators, but the townspeople began to drift in and squat in the dirt before the desk, curious to see if such a phenomenon as a court was actually to operate in the lawless Panhandle. Temple Houston, a young man with long, flowing, tawny hair and bangs over his eyes, came up the street from the direction of the post office in big hat and high-heeled boots. He was the son of old Sam, and known as a brilliant lawyer when he wanted to be. He was just the kind of district attorney for a case like this, thought Bart.

J. N. Browning, who had been district attorney, arrived with a case full of papers, and Bart guessed he would defend the accused. Al Wheeler, the sheriff from Mobeetie, came in with his prisoners, Three-Finger Halvorson and Indian George. Halvorson was big, stolid, unemotional; he had pale blue eyes that seemed to watch nothing. Indian George was smaller, thin in the body, dark of face, with black hair, and black eyes that darted everywhere.

At ten minutes to eight, Judge Willis, seeming very small and slender beside so many big men, strode up to his desk and thumped down a copy of the statutes. He looked at his watch. He opened a long, canvas-bound book that said "Day Ledger" on the cover, and laid the statutes on it to keep it open. He produced a bottle of ink and a steel pen, and sat in the chair for a few moments, writing the heading for his notes on the top of a blank page. He sat back and looked at the brilliant blue sky. The sun was already hot, and a big horsefly buzzed around his desk. Willis said something to the sheriff, who gave him a folded copy of the *Ford County Globe*, and Willis took a swipe at the fly but missed, and the fly buzzed away with renewed vigor.

Willis looked again at his watch, and Bart was finding it hard to breathe. The area within the wagons was fairly well filled, mostly with men squatting on their doubled legs and balanced on their toes. A few women in sunbonnets and gingham dresses stood in a close group on the east edge of the crowd, between two of Goodnight's wagons. All the wagons faced Willis's desk broadside on, but there was no sign of life about them except that on each of them two men sat in the wagon seat. A few Goodnight men or LJ men or Slash K men sat on the doubletrees or lounged near the end gates.

A low hum of talk arose while Willis was looking at the sky, and the pleasant odor of burning tobacco drifted over the area. Bart, dressed in his striped California pants and his beaded white buckskin vest, stood with one foot on a wagon-wheel hub, and, without moving, watched Xenophon Jones and Stud Murphy walk into the area between the two wagons on the circle across from the women, and take up a stand about forty feet from Willis's desk.

The talking stopped abruptly. Men drifted in silently from all around the wagons, to form, Bart saw, a complete semicircle inside the wagons.

Bart caught Goodnight's eye. Goodnight looked apprehensive too, and Bart did not blame him. Bart himself was thoroughly worried. There were at least seventy outlaws in the area of the court—twenty more than they had anticipated—and the situation was made for mass slaughter on the slightest miscalculation.

Bart's throat was tight. He did not move immediately, but watched Judge Willis. If Willis knew what this development meant—and he must have suspected it from the cessation of talk before him—he did not reveal it, but continued to study the blue sky over the tops of the wagons.

Harding was not in sight. Neither was Hector Johnson—and it did not help their plans. Bart was stationed between two wagons in the center of the semicircle, and Harding, Johnson, and Goodnight were to be spaced at intervals so as to face Jones, Murphy, and Benson. But at the moment, the only open support Bart had was that of Goodnight, who had moved a little apart from the group of women. He held no weapon, but Bart assumed that he had a rifle handy in the wagon behind him.

Perhaps, thought Bart, Stella had turned her talents to Hector Johnson to detain him until after the showdown—in which case it was understandable that he would not take his scheduled place.

Bart studied the handsome, arrogant Jones, and tried to decide whether Jones knew what was in the wagons, but he could not decide. Unconsciously he felt for the butts of his six-shooters, and then tried to relax as Willis looked at his watch. Willis tapped the table with a closed jackknife and said, "Sheriff, will you announce the court?"

Wheeler, standing, sang out: "O yes, O yes, the district court for the Thirty-fifth Judicial District of the State of Texas, holding its first session in Clarendon, is now open."

Willis picked up his pen and dipped it in the ink. "The first case is the State of Texas versus Indian George—no surname known—and a man known as Three-Finger Halvorson, charged with unlawful alteration of cattle brands." He looked at the defendants. "How do you plead?"

Browning, squatting in the dirt, with some papers on his lap, looked up. "Not guilty, your honor."

Willis wrote in his book, and said to Wheeler, "Proceed with the jury."

Wheeler took a folded and worn sheaf of papers from his vest pocket. There were half a dozen sheets about three by four inches, which appeared to have been torn from a small notebook such as those furnished surveyors by manufacturers of engineering supplies. Names had been written on the sheets with a lead pencil. Wheeler carefully unfolded the sheets and began to look for the first page. He got them arranged to his satisfaction and straightened them out. He examined the first page and raised his head. "Stub Miller," he called in a loud voice.

CHAPTER XX

A SHORT, bow-legged man with long mustaches stood up in the crowd. "I'm him," he said.

"Come up here," said Wheeler.

Temple Houston, his hat off and his tawny hair gleaming in the sun, asked:

"Where do you work, Mr. Miller?"

"Any place where the pay is fair and the food is good."

There was a snicker from Stud Murphy, whose heavy black mustache gave him an appearance of menace. Evidently Murphy knew something about courts, thought Bart, who was watching him and studying the overriding animal force that was always noticeable about Murphy.

Houston asked smoothly, "Mr. Miller, are you working on a ranch at the present time?"

"I'm ridin' line up on the Caprock for the Double Rafter."

"What county is that in?"

"Lubbock."

"You're a long way from home, Mr. Miller."

"It's in this district. That's what Mr. Goodnight said."

Again Murphy snickered, but Judge Willis ignored it. Bart glanced at Xenophon Jones, beside Murphy. Jones was the really magnificent one in appearance. As tall as Murphy or Bart himself; big in the shoulders, tapered to the ground; his chin covered with light brown whiskers, his eyes cold and blue, his face shaded by a black hat—his mouth now held a faint sneer of derision.

"You don't know of your own knowledge?"

"No, sir, that ain't my business. I can dose a cow with piles or I can shovel out a horse with the founders, but—"

"If his honor says your county is in this district, you would accept that, would you not?"

"If who?"

"The judge." Houston inclined his head toward Willis, who was writing in his ledger and did not look up.

"Yes, your honor. Sure I would."

"How long have you been with the Double Rafter?"

"Seven months."

"Do you know what is required of a juryman?"

"Sure. You say whether a man is guilty or not."

"Do you believe in corporal punishment—hanging?"

"Sure. If he's guilty of murder or stealin' a horse, string 'im up."

Houston looked absently at the audience. "The factor of capital punishment is not, however, pertinent in this case."

"Thank you, counsel," murmured Browning.

"I merely mentioned it to establish the fact that the witness has some knowledge of court procedure and an idea of justice." Houston turned to Miller. "Are you willing to weigh the evidence according to the rules his honor will give you?"

"Do my best."

Houston bowed ceremoniously to Browning. Houston's tawny hair swayed forward and back with the movement. "Your panelman, Mr. Browning."

Browning stood up, clutching his various papers in both hands. "Mr. Miller, how long have you been in Texas?"

"All my life. I was borned at Nacogdoches."

"Have you ever been in another state?"

"Never had time. Anyways, Texas is big enough for me."

A cynical smile hovered about the mouth of Xenophon Jones, and Bart felt satisfied that he did not know what was coming.

"You are aware," said Browning, "that in Texas only a property owner can sit on a jury."

"Yes, sir. That is—real estate, you mean?"

"Exactly," said Browning with some sarcasm. "Are you a property owner, Mr. Miller?"

"Yes, sir."

Miller must have been coached, for he was playing his answers close to his vest.

Browning asked loudly and with a fine air of imposed patience, "Of what property are you possessed, Mr. Miller?"

The panelman slapped the judge's bench with a folded paper. "I own lot No. 10, block 6, Goodnight's First Subdivision, Clarendon Outlots."

Bart could not restrain a smile. The man had memorized his answer perfectly, even to the legal description.

Bart looked around. Murphy's mouth was open, revealing for the first time his unusually thick lips. Jones was staring at Miller in cold fury, realizing that he had been beaten in the first phase.

Browning glanced at the paper, stalling for time. He looked at the signature on the deed. "Mr. Miller, when did you buy this piece of property?"

"Last Friday."

"For what purpose?"

"So's I could sit on the jury to try them two cow thieves!"

Browning straightened and turned to Willis. "Your honor, this panelman admits prejudice."

Willis said quietly, "Not altogether, Mr. Browning. He has said also that he will judge the evidence by the court's instruction. Unless you can show further indication—"

Browning wheeled to Miller. "How much, Mr. Miller, did you pay for this—this little kingdom?"

"One dollar," Miller said promptly.

"One dollar! Do you call that a proper consideration for this—this—" He stopped from seeming indignation.

"Yes, sir," said Miller. "For that piece I do. Have you seen it?"

Browning restrained himself. "I even doubt that such a lot exists," he said with a display of great skepticism.

Temple Houston said courteously, "Does counsel wish to call Charles Goodnight, who had the outlots surveyed, and have him sworn?"

Browning glared at Houston. "For a nickel I would," he said under his breath.

Houston ostentatiously took his hand from his vest pocket and held out a coin.

Browning recovered himself. "Your honor, I am of course aware of Mr. Goodnight's great personal reputation in the Panhandle and in all of Texas—I might say in all of the West. If his signature appears on the deed, I will not question that fact further."

Temple Houston asked, "Does counsel know Mr. Goodnight's signature?"

Browning drew himself up. "I will advise counsel that Mr. Goodnight was without legal existence in the State of Texas until I was able to decipher his signature."

Houston smiled at that sally, for Goodnight's almost illegible script was well known. "Then it will not be necessary for us to call him to the stand."

Browning snapped, "Of course not!" He turned back to the panelman. "Mr. Miller, it is a well known fact of ranch life that cowhands are usually paid on the first of the month, is it not?"

"I never been paid any other time except on a trail drive."

"That custom exists also on the Double Rafter, I take it."

"Yes, sir."

"Now, then, this is the twenty-second. Do you mean to tell the court that you had money left over from the first of June?"

"No, sir. I drew the dollar to pay for the lot."

Browning nodded wisely. "So then the money did not come out of your pocket at all?"

"It came out of my wages."

"Do you maintain that this lot actually cost you one dollar in money?"

"Well, not exactly. Everybody who bought a lot gets a one-dollar raise this month."

Browning turned quickly to the judge. "Your honor!" he cried dramatically.

Willis's deep, musical voice reverberated over the crowd. "Yes, Mr. Browning?"

"Your honor, of all the bald-faced, outrageous, unmitigated—"

Willis broke in gently. "Counsel is using a great many adjectives," he admonished.

"But, your honor, this patent, unblushing conspiracy to interfere with justice—"

"Mr. Miller," said Judge Willis, "have you been advised as to how long this one-dollar pay raise will be in effect?"

"For keeps," said Miller. "They told us it was permanent."

Willis said gently, "Well, Mr. Browning?"

Browning compressed his lips.

Bart glanced at Jones and Murphy. Both showed incredulity and indignation. But Bart saw something that turned him cold, for a new man stood beside them—Piggie Benson from Tascosa. He had small, bulbous, piggy eyes. He was known from Brownsville to Great Falls as a hired killer, and he did not look like a man to be fooled with unless a person was the kind to take a smoke sitting on a prairie-dog hole full of rattlesnakes. Benson was tall, slender, hollow-chested, bent over—with two guns at his thighs and those bulbous eyes that looked everywhere. He might not be very fast or very straight in his shots, and again he might be—but certainly he was a man who would start drawing and keep shooting until something loosened up.

Bart had almost hoped for a while that the outlaws were bluffing, but now he knew better. The three most deadly men in the Panhandle were ready for a showdown. They had hoped to win on the property-owner technicality, but they had not relied on it.

Bart looked at Goodnight. He could not see Harding in the crowd, but Goodnight was using a toothpick to cover his smile with his hand. Goodnight had indeed picked well for the first panelman. Whether Miller was a lot smarter than he looked, or whether Goodnight had gambled that Miller would make a fine first panelman, did not matter. Miller was frank enough to appear completely honest, and yet clever enough or naïve enough to make Browning appear ridiculous in the eyes of the crowd and of prospective jurymen. The first part of the fight had been won.

Browning, to gain time, said to Miller, "Mr. Miller, tell me how it feels to be a property owner in this glorious part of the world?"

Fine sarcasm.

But Miller said with great and unexpected dignity: "Mr. Browning, I mighta thought it was a joke when I bought this here lot, but I don't think so no more. I never owned no land before, and I got to say it makes me feel real proud to say I bought a piece of real estate in Clarendon, real proud to own a little bitty piece of Texas land. If I'd of known how I was gonna feel, I'd of been willing to pay a lot more for it." He said sincerely, "Yes, sir, I'm real proud."

A very effective statement. Bart, studying the crowd, had not moved. He was near the center of the perimeter, where he could see everything in the area of the "courtroom," but not where he was noticeable. There had not been a sound from inside the wagons.

"Your honor." Browning turned to Willis in desperation. "Your honor," he said in a lower voice, which he controlled with apparent effort, "it is obvious that we have here a plain case of intent. This man—"

"Intent to what, Mr. Browning?"

"Intent to defeat the law."

Willis sat forward and put his elbows on the table, brought his fingertips together. "The court is inclined to agree with counsel that there is evidence of intent, but intent alone is not prohibited by law. The court came to Clarendon with the intent of establishing order and justice. There can hardly be a case made of intent, Mr. Browning, unless counsel can show evidence of fraudulent intent or of intent to subvert the ends of justice."

The horsefly buzzed around Willis's head, and he picked up the *Globe*.

"This so-called real estate purchase is a joke, your honor."

"I do not think," said Willis, eyeing the horsefly, "that there is any joke about a transaction that gives a man faith in his own dignity, as the sale of this lot has done to this panelman." He swung at the horsefly, but missed. He laid down the paper and wrote in his ledger. "If there is no further objection," he said, "the court will order the panelman to take his place as the first member of the jury."

Bart looked at the three outlaws standing together: Jones, with his wavy brown whiskers; Murphy, with his glossy black mustache; Benson, with his bulbous, piggy eyes. Murphy's look darted from Willis to Browning to Miller and then to Goodnight; he was plainly outraged. Jones's lips were grim; he was well aware that things were going badly for him. Only Benson was unmoved. He had been hired to kill, and he was unconcerned with the technicalities.

The three of them presented a problem for Bart. He thought he could get two of them in a showdown—but which two should he try for? Tentatively he thought he should concentrate on Murphy and Jones, partly because, if somebody had to die, their deaths would relieve a number of personal problems in the area, and partly because those two were nearer him, while Benson was on the far side and might be covered by one of them at the moment of the showdown.

The second panelman came up, was questioned and accepted. He too had a deed to a lot, and Browning did not try to break him down. He was accepted in a matter of minutes, and so it went with the next nine.

As the last panelman was called, Bart heard pounding hooves on the road from the LJ. From where he was, he was unable to see, and he did not want to move, but there were at least three horses, perhaps more. They pulled up beyond the crowd on the other side of the wagons, for the crowd had unaccountably grown and spread beyond the wagons. Bart turned his attention back to the trial.

The twelfth man was seated on his haunches at one end of the judge's bench, biting off a fresh chew. There were no chairs for the jury.

Willis made a note in his ledger, and said, "Call the first witness."

Temple Houston said in a far-carrying voice: "The first witness is Hector Johnson."

There was a flurry as Hector broke through the ring and went forward. Bart's eyes narrowed, for Hector was dusty and sweating hard, and obviously had just returned from trailing Stella, and had followed them into Clarendon as fast as possible. There was a little stir among the spectators.

"Will you swear the witness?" Willis said to Wheeler.

Wheeler said, "Hold up your right hand. Do you swear to tell the truth, the whole truth, and nothing but the truth, so help you God?"

Hector, white-faced and breathless, said, "I do."

Temple Houston stepped up with a great flourish, his tawny hair golden in the sunlight. "Your name?"

"Hector Johnson."

"Address?"

"Clarendon."

"Your occupation?"

"Foreman at the LJ ranch."

"How long, Mr. Johnson, have you held this job?"

"About four months."

"When did you come to the Panhandle?"

"Two years ago."

"You're satisfied with your job?"

Hector squirmed a little. He couldn't see where all that was leading. "It's a good job," he said, "but I'd like to have a ranch of my own."

"In other words, you are not bound to the LJ by any permanent bond?"

"I don't know what you mean."

"If they failed to pay you on the first of the month, you'd go somewhere else. Is that right?"

"Yes, sir."

"Where were you born, Mr. Johnson?"

"Near Macon, Georgia."

"You don't talk like a Georgian."

"I went to Boston when my pa died, and then—"

"You fought in the Union army?" Houston asked quickly.

"Sir, I went to New Orleans to join the Confederate army."

"Then you are familiar with the problems of this part of the country?"

"I think so."

Houston swung and pointed a finger dramatically at Halvorson and Indian George. "Do you know these men?"

"By sight."

"Tell me when you last saw them."

Willis was busy making notes in his ledger, and the scratch of his pen was loud in the brief silences between questions and answers, but the horsefly buzzed back, and he looked up, annoyed.

Hector was studying his fingernails. "That was on Wednesday last week."

"Where?"

"In a ravine on the hackberry pasture at the LJ."

"This ravine—is it wooded or brushy?"

"It's hidden on both banks by mesquite and some kind of bushes—plum bushes, I guess."

"Then it is not visible at a distance?"

"Not any farther than a stone's throw."

"Is it large enough for men to hide in?"

"Plenty. Several men could hide in it, and nobody would ever know unless they rode up on them."

"And these two men were in the ravine that day?"

"Them and another man—Hicks Gentry."

"How did you come to know they were there?"

"They had built a branding fire and—"

"Your honor," said Browning, "I object. A conclusion unsupported by the evidence."

"Sustained," said Willis quietly, without looking up.

The ring of outlaws snickered as they grasped the significance of the ruling. Willis frowned but did not look up.

Temple Houston looked around dramatically at the snickerers, and then said grandly to Hector: "You may say they had built a fire; you may not at this time say what for."

"But I know what it was for!" Hector said.

Houston said with an air of great patience: "As far as the judge is concerned, it has not been shown. The rules of evidence require that you do not assume any fact not supported by the evidence."

Hector got his back up. "Nobody in his right mind would build a fire on a hot day in a place like that unless they were getting ready to burn some hides."

Houston said kindly, "Mr. Johnson, I observed you ride in at a gallop barely in time to take your place in the witness chair, and I perceive that you are still breathing hard and that you exhibit all the indications of a person laboring under great emotional stress."

"Yes, sir."

"Do you mind telling us what it is?"

Browning said, "Objection! Not pertinent to the issue!"

But Temple Houston for the moment had become obsessed with that mystical quality which his enemies said leagued him with the devil. He peered narrow-eyed at Hector Johnson, and some impulsion drove him to fight for the point. "Your honor," he said quietly, "I don't know what this man is laboring under, but I do perceive that he is under great stress. I am willing to be bound by his evidence, but if counsel objects after hearing it, I will consent to its being stricken from the record."

For any lawyer to make such a proposition—to himself be bound by the evidence while giving his opponent the choice of acceptance or rejection—was a quick way to judicial suicide, but Houston was gambling on blind intuition, and he was a man who had done that many times and had made it pay off.

Willis studied him and then looked at Hector. Bart leaned forward. Hector's underjaw was quivering.

"You may answer," said Willis.

Hector said, "I just came from the Half Moon ranch. Stud Murphy shot Stella Harding and killed her! I brung the body back to the LJ!"

There was a dead and terrible silence for a moment. Then the horsefly buzzed over the area in a circle and headed back toward the blacksmith shop.

Bart looked at the three outlaws. Murphy's eyes were distended, and he must have moved forward or started to draw his six-shooter, for all the spectators between him and the judge's bench were flattened against the ground—but Jones had a hand on his forearm, and held him back.

Hector stared stonily at the ground, struggling with his own tragic knowledge.

Willis watched Hector for a moment. Then he took a deep breath and looked at his book. "The court is of the opinion, counsel, that that remark should be stricken from the minutes."

Temple Houston said with innate dignity, "Yes, your honor. Counsel agrees."

But he had made a tremendous point. For Stud Murphy stood among them branded as a murderer. Some sort of shoot-out was inevitable, Bart knew now. Under no conceivable circumstances could this first session of court end peacefully, for its very ending probably meant the rope for Murphy. Bart loosened his .44's for the hundredth time. He could only speculate on what had happened at the Half Moon. Had Stella, at the last, tried to keep them from coming, knowing that her father might be in the line of fire? It was impossible to say. Only Hector Johnson knew the answers—unless there were other witnesses—and it came to Bart with a shock that he still did not know where Harding was, unless he perhaps had ridden up with Hector.

Temple Houston lowered his voice. "I hope you will forgive me, Mr. Johnson, in the face of this tragedy which understandably has upset you a great deal, but as you know, this is a very vital case for the entire Panhandle. Do you feel like going on?"

Hector said, as if in great pain, "Go on."

"Tell us in your own words about the discovery of these two men in the ravine."

Hector exhaled a long breath and pulled himself together. "I was riding the draw on Hackberry Creek looking for steers back in those ravines. We had found one the week before with a broken leg, and Tom thought there might be more in there. I smelled the smoke of cedar wood, and I knew there must be a fire there. I got down on the ground and located the smoke against the sky. It was about a quarter of a mile away. Then I took two hands with me and snuck up the draw until we found the ravine. I sent one man up on top, and me and the other one went up the ravine on foot, and we all threw down on the three men together."

"Can you tell us what you found?"

"They had a fire going and a cinch-ring in the fire. We took their guns and started them—"

"Were there any cattle in the vicinity?"

"About a hundred yards upstream there were three two-year-olds in a smaller ravine, held back by brush piled across a narrow place."

"Were those three steers branded?"

"They were all branded LJ."

"Mr. Johnson, can you suggest how that brand might be altered?"

"Yes, sir. We had two hides sent back a month ago from Dodge City with the brands tailored."

"What was the LJ changed to?"

"E Flower de Luce Hook."

Houston smiled gently. "Mr. Johnson, for the benefit of those of us who have not lived in South Texas, will you describe that brand?"

"Well, two bars made the L into a E, and a couple of hooks at the top of the J make a Flower de Luce."

"What was that last phrase?" asked Willis.

"It's cattle-land for Fleur de Lis, your honor," said Houston.

Willis glanced at Browning, saw no objection, and said, "Thank you, counsel."

Houston went on. "What did you do with the three men, Mr. Johnson?"

"We brought 'em to the LJ and put two of 'em—these here two—into the barn with their hands and feet tied. Then we tried to persuade the other one, Hicks Gentry, to testify against them."

"Was your persuasion successful?"

"Not exactly."

"What kind of persuasion did you use?"

Hector looked uncomfortable. "We—that is, we propped up a wagon tongue and sort of—pulled him up by a rope until his feet were off the ground."

"Did Mr. Gentry like that treatment?"

Hector said, "No, sir, I don't think he did."

Temple Houston raised his eyebrows and shrugged. "It doesn't sound like treatment that a man might take particular exception to."

Hector frowned. "No, sir, maybe not, but—you see—well, he —damn it, we had the rope tied around his neck!"

Only Judge Willis remained grave and seemingly unmoved by that statement. Houston permitted himself a brief, dramatic smile.

Bart could see no point to that particular testimony except that Houston was showing off to win the crowd.

Bart started to glance again at the three men on the opposite side of the circle, but he saw a movement closer to the judge's bench, and caught his breath.

Captain Arrington of the Texas Rangers had just arrived in court!

Bart held his breath. What would happen if Arrington chose to arrest him for breaking jail?

But at the moment, Arrington was quietly watching the witness.

Houston asked, "What happened to Mr. Gentry?"

"We turned him loose finally, and told him to go back and tell Xenophon Jones we meant business!"

Houston's eyes widened dramatically. "Have you heard from this gentleman since?"

"I heard he was found this side of Mobeetie with a bullet in him."

"Do you know who killed him?"

Hector shook his head.

Houston observed conversationally, "I heard he had fired three shots from his six-shooter. Can you explain that?"

"It sounds to me like he was a hell of a poor shot."

Judge Willis said coldly, "Counsel will confine himself to the issue."

Houston bowed deeply. "Counsel apologizes to the court."

Willis did not look up.

Houston turned. "Your witness, Mr. Browning."

Browning seemed to be at a loss. His questions were largely repetitious; he tried to show that it was a completely normal thing for three men to build a fire in the ravine, but Hector Johnson refused to concede it.

"Not on a day when it's over a hundred in the shade," he said.

"I'm afraid," said Willis, tiring of Browning's repeated attempts, "that unless new evidence is introduced, counsel may have to concede the question of normality in this aspect of the case."

"Yes, your honor."

"Do you have any further questions, Mr. Houston?"

Houston bowed. Again his tawny hair gleamed in the brilliant sun. "No, your honor."

"Call your next witness."

"We rest our case on this witness, your honor."

Bart smiled at the audacity of Houston's maneuver. Houston had removed Johnson from the stand with no further possibility of Browning's shaking his testimony; it was unlikely that Browning would try to introduce a perjured witness, for about the only defense now was an alibi—and that would be difficult to sustain in the face of three witnesses. So rather than take a chance on one of the two other hands' being broken by Browning, who was, after all, a very shrewd and competent lawyer, Houston had effectively stopped all testimony unless one of the two defendants should take the stand.

Hector Johnson moved slowly through the spectators and took his stand by the first wagon. Bart observed the sun beating down on the canvas, with no ventilation from either end, and wondered how hot it was inside the wagons.

Browning stepped forward. "Three-Finger Halvorson will testify in his own behalf."

Judge Willis looked up sharply. Obviously he was puzzled by the move, but after a moment he must have decided it was a desperation try, for he turned to his book and began to write. But Bart suddenly got the feeling that it was not a desperation try in a legal sense: this was the prelude to the showdown. He took a deep breath and again checked the positions of the three outlaws.

Browning established Halvorson's identity and got him to say that they had built the fire to cook a jack rabbit they had shot, and that he did not realize they were on LJ land. It was an utter accident that the cinch-ring had been in the fire; he had not known it himself; they had built the fire on the remains of an old fire, and the ring must have been there, unnoticed by them until Hector Johnson pulled it out of the ashes.

Houston took the witness for cross-examination. "Mr. Halvorson," he said in a friendly manner, "how old are you?"

Halvorson's voice was guttural. "Twenty-seven."

"Born where?"

"Kansas."

"How long have you been in the Panhandle?"

"One year."

"Where are you employed?"

Halvorson glared at him.

Houston said genially, "I said where are you employed?"

Halvorson was silent.

Houston turned to Willis. "Your honor, this is surely according to the rules of evidence. I am merely inquiring into his occupation."

"I did not touch upon his occupation," said Browning.

"Of course not, counsel," said Houston. "However, you introduced the witness, and it is an inherent right of any counsel to inquire briefly into the witness's background, at least as to his age, origin, residence, and occupation."

"Your honor," said Browning, "I object!"

Willis said without looking up, "The court is of the opinion that counsel will concede that the prosecutor has a point. Overruled."

"I asked you," said Houston, suddenly sharp, and no longer friendly, "where you are employed!"

Bart knew then that his feeling was correct. The air was charged with high tension; the explosion was not far off. He leaned away from the wagon wheel to keep his hands clear. He heard a sound from behind him, but did not turn; probably it was somebody getting in better position to see—or out of the line of fire. Trouble could start at any instant. He glanced across at the group of women, and then looked for Arrington. But the Ranger had disappeared; nor was Harding yet in sight.

"Again I ask you," said Houston, "where you are employed."

"Your honor!" shouted Stud Murphy. "We object!"

Bart brought his foot down slowly from the wheel hub.

Judge Willis looked up and waited what seemed like a long time. Then his musical bass voice rolled out over the spectators: "Will you give your name, please, if you are appearing in behalf of the defendants?"

Murphy's eyes narrowed. He did not answer.

Willis looked at Houston. "I think you'd better proceed, counsel."

Houston repeated, "I asked you, Halvorson, where you are employed."

"He doesn't have to answer that," Xenophon Jones said loudly.

Bart moved forward to the wagon tongue.

Judge Willis looked up. He knew that murder was in the air, but he appeared as calm and unruffled as a cow chewing beargrass blooms in the shade. "Your name, please," he said.

Jones's blue eyes were cold. He did not answer.

Houston said to Halvorson, "You know that you are subject to a fine for contempt if you do not answer?"

Browning shouted, "Objection!"

"Overruled," Willis said gently.

"He is admonishing the witness," said Browning.

"He is advising him as to his liability. Only the court admonishes, Mr. Browning."

"What is the answer, Mr. Halvorson?" Houston demanded.

Piggie Benson spoke for the first time: "We say he don't answer that question."

Bart stepped across the wagon tongue. All three of the principals had committed themselves. Two men at the edge of the crowd near the outlaw trio got up and moved hurriedly back through the wagons to get out of the line of fire.

Willis murmured, unperturbed: "You seem to have three associates in counsel, Mr. Browning. Would you care to identify them?"

Browning said, "They can speak for themselves, your honor."

Houston's voice sounded with astonishing thunder: "The answer, Mr. Halvorson!"

All three of the outlaws spoke at once. "He doesn't have to answer." "Tell him to go to hell!" "Get out of that witness box!"

Judge Willis frowned and drew a deep breath. The horsefly buzzed around his head, and Willis struck at it with the paper, but missed again. Then he said to the spectators, "A legal trial cannot be held under such circumstances of interference. I find you three gentlemen each guilty of contempt of court, and I sentence each of you to pay a fine of one hundred dollars." He turned to Wheeler. "The court will have to be cleared, sheriff, until order is resumed."

Wheeler looked at the three outlaws, swallowed, and said, "This county is not in my jurisdiction, Your Honor."

"The answer!" Houston demanded again of Halvorson.

Across the way, near the women, the blacksmith Holt pushed to the front of the standing spectators with a rifle in his hands.

Willis spoke in a low voice to Wheeler, and then wrote in his book. "The court has just entered the names of Xenophon Jones, Stud Murphy, and Piggie Benson as appearing in behalf of defendant. The minutes will also show that these three men have been adjudged guilty of contempt. The court also notes, off the record, that this session must be postponed *sine die* unless order is restored."

Stud Murphy stepped forward two paces. "Get out of there, Halvorson!" he shouted. "You're a free man!"

"Wait a minute!" Bart said in a loud voice.

He moved forward. He was dimly aware that suddenly the inner area was clear of spectators. Judge Willis, the sheriff, the lawyers, the defendants, and the jury remained in place, but in the semicircle of men immediately within the wagons were only Charles Goodnight, Bart Wagner, and the seventy outlaws.

Bart's arms hung slightly bent as he moved to put himself in line with both Murphy and Jones. Benson, he saw, moved to one side.

"These two men," Bart said to Jones across the open space, "are prisoners of the law. They will be tried according to the law, and sentenced if found guilty."

Jones moved out a little from the other two. "Who's talkin'?" he asked.

"I'm talking," said Bart. "With lead if necessary."

"If I draw on you, you'll die," said Jones.

Bart smiled as he walked a little farther into the open. "If I draw on you, all three of you will die. You are surrounded—all of you." He looked around the entire semicircle. "These chuck wagons are filled with rifles—and men behind them. If you open fire, you and your men will be shot down like dogs!" He pointed to the wagon behind the tree.

Jones did not move his head, but Murphy looked, and snarled something unintelligible.

All around the semicircle, the men of Jones's gang and the hired guns of Benson's hardcase crew looked at the wagon. From both ends of it, rifle barrels protruded, and along the wagon box, through slits in the canvas, were half a dozen more—all aimed at the outlaws.

Jones's cold eyes darted to the opposite side of the semicircle, and Bart knew from the hardness in his eyes that he had seen the same thing there—a hundred rifles and six-shooters held on him and his men.

"You are all completely surrounded," Bart said in a loud voice, "and the first man to draw a gun will die."

He saw the eyes of the hired gunmen alongside the three leaders swing around the arc, and for a moment he thought the contest would be won without a gunfight, but he kept his eyes on Jones.

Jones drew suddenly with blinding speed from both holsters.

Bart moved too fast for any eye to see. His .44's sprang forward, one spouting fire and lead at Jones, the other at Murphy.

The area that had constituted the courtroom erupted in flame and thunder and hot lead. He knew that Murphy shot at him, for he felt the heat from the muzzle blast. Jones fired once or twice. Then Murphy lurched, but kept shooting. Jones threw up his hands and went over backward, his guns throwing flame into the blue sky.

Two big six-shooters fired from behind Bart, but he did not turn. He moved his aim toward Benson, but the man was on the ground. Bart felt warm blood running down his side, and then a cloud of white smoke rolled over everything.

After that brief but incredibly violent burst of gunfire, there was no sound but for the ringing of the shots in his ears, but he stood motionless until the smoke began to thin and lift.

The three outlaws were limp in the dirt. Arrington stood between the wagons, looking down at them. Up near the front, Hector Johnson stood with six-shooters in his hands. On the far side, Charlie Goodnight had a rifle.

Bart stood across from Arrington and looked down at the dead outlaws: Xenophon Jones with his wavy brown whiskers—a man with a strange twist in his character; Stud Murphy with his big black mustache—nothing strange about him except that he was true to his nickname; and Piggie Benson, hollow-chested even in death, his bulbous eyes wide open at the sky but now beginning to glaze over.

Bart put his six-shooters away. Wheeler corraled some men to help him examine the bodies and carry them out. The outlaws who had been brought in as hired gunmen had disappeared, and Charles Goodnight was plugging up the hole in Bart's side. "Too low for lungs; too far to one side for stomach; too high for guts," he announced. "Maybe you'll carry that one for a while."

Bart nodded.

"How do you feel?" asked Goodnight.

"I could use a drink," said Bart.

"Drinks will be provided," said Goodnight. "Damn' soon."

Bart saw Harding come up. "You got Benson?" he asked.

Harding shrugged. "You were watching the other two. I sort of concentrated on Benson."

"Where'd you learn?" Bart demanded.

"El Paso—same place you did. I was a cousin of John Selman. My name was Bill."

"Bill Selman?" asked Bart.

"I changed it to keep strangers from shooting at me." Harding chuckled. "Figure I saved half a dozen lives the day I did that."

Bart said, "Why did you stand where the lead was bound to come?"

Harding said, "You picked the best spot."

Judge Willis, still seated behind the desk, looked calmly over the spectators, now composed primarily of the hundred men who had poured out of the chuck wagons, glad to get some fresh air. "The court believes," Willis said quietly, "that the proceedings may be resumed very shortly."

Goodnight went up to the desk. "It seems to me, Judge, that the immediate interests of justice might best be served if you recessed court for a few minutes so everybody could have a drink."

The horsefly buzzed loudly across the area. "If the court properly recalls," said Judge Willis, "counsel for the prosecution was interrogating the witness as to his occupation." He watched the bodies removed, then picked up his pen. "The minutes of the court will show," he said to Houston, "that the defendants have been unexpectedly deprived of the services of three voluntary pleaders."

The horsefly alighted on his desk. Quietly the judge picked up the rolled paper and took careful aim. He brought it down and blasted the fly devastatingly, then used the paper to brush its squashed body to the ground. Then he looked up. "Did the court hear a motion for a fifteen-minute recess."

"Yes, your honor," said Goodnight. "I suggested—"

Judge Willis arose. "Charlie," he said, "you really said something."

CHAPTER XXI

BACK AT the LJ that afternoon, Stella's body was laid out in the front room, and people sat around in the semidarkness and talked in low tones. To Bart's astonishment, Ike Logan and Hepzibah were there with Ike's many children, all gotten up in pathetic Sunday clothes. Ike's face was skinned up and bruised, and he looked as if he had been run through a meat grinder, but he cornered Goodnight's foreman, who was there representing the JA, and borrowed his tobacco, while Hepzibah sat in a corner, saying nothing, but watching everything from her almost-hidden eyes.

Bart went out and had a drink. He had been dry for years, it seemed; that always happened to him after a gunfight. He said thoughtfully to Harding, "You were a gunfighter—but you settled down."

"I figured that I had less chance of meeting up with a would-be killer by staying in one place than if I went on the road."

"Maybe you're right."

Bart saw Hector Johnson leave the front room, and got up to meet him outside. "Thanks," he said, "for helping."

"I never even fired," said Hector.

"The most dangerous gun," said Bart, "is one that has not been fired." He began to make a cigarette.

Hector said, "I know you're wonderin' what happened this morning, Mr. Wagner."

"I certainly am," said Bart.

"Mr. Harding sent me after Stella. I followed her to the Half Moon ranch. I wasn't far behind. When I got there, a hell of a fight was going on inside. Stud Murphy had come to force his attentions on Hepzibah, and old man Logan got his back up at last and started fightin' Murphy. Murphy was already crazy, and he begun to cut the old man down piece by piece. Hepzibah got the kids outside, and come back to help her pa. About that time Stella came and saw what had happened, and started fightin' Murphy too. Jealous, I reckon. Murphy laughed, and shot her just as I got to the door. She fell against me, and Murphy finally turned tail and ran." He hesitated. "We brought the body here."

"It must have been a blow to you," said Bart, licking the cigarette paper.

Hector looked up. "I guess not too much. I was wrought up the way Murphy had backed Hepzibah up in a corner and tried to make her undress, and when I got to Clarendon, all I wanted to do was settle things with him."

Bart said, puzzled, "You wanted to marry Stella, didn't you?"

Hector looked at him. "I give that up several days ago. I wasn't wrought up for him killing Stella. She had it coming. But what he intended to do with Hepzibah, and what he was doing to the old man, cutting him down piece by piece." Hector broke off. "He's dead," he said harshly. "I'm glad he's dead. If I had got my hands on him, he'd have died a lot slower."

"Is Hepzibah all right now?"

"She was powerful scared, but not hurt. She's all right. She's been through so much in her life, she bounces right back."

Bart nodded.

"I'm going to court her as soon as this is over."

"Court—Hepzibah?" asked Bart.

"Yes. I decided several days ago that Stella wasn't my kind."

Bart shook hands. "You're using good judgment."

"I got a little piece of land between the LJ and the Half Moon.

We could build there, I guess, and run a few cows—at least until the next girl gets the hang of running the family."

"I like that," said Bart. "I like Hepzibah. She hasn't had much. Maybe you can give her a few things a woman is entitled to."

"I'll sure try if she'll let me," said Hector. . . .

It was midafternoon when Bart reached the JA. "Miz Lewis here?" he asked Goodnight.

"You mean Catherine?" Goodnight boomed.

Bart nodded.

Goodnight shook hands with him. "Some of the nicest gunwork I ever saw. You and Tom had all three on the ground before I got my rifle up. You did a great thing for the Panhandle today, Bart."

Bart shrugged.

Goodnight looked at him. "I'd like to know something. Stella Harding was telling it around that you had arranged to leave Clarendon with her after the fight for Kansas City. Anything to it?"

Bart looked up, thoughtful. "There was considerable to it. I never thought, in the first place, I could settle anywhere. I never was crazy about Stella, but—she was a woman, and for a man on the scout, one woman is as good as another. He doesn't want to get tangled up with a good woman anyway—I mean—"

"I know what you mean. I know all about Stella. Some of my hands run into her in St. Louis. But you was going away with her?"

"I saw she was going to cause her father nothing but grief, and I thought as long as she wanted to go, I could do him a good turn at the same time."

"But now Stella is dead—"

Bart said, "That had nothing to do with it. Even after I heard Hector say that, I still thought I would head out of town as soon as it was over."

"Because you was too good for a girl like Catherine?"

"Because I wasn't good enough."

"What changed your mind?"

"Old Tom Harding, standing behind me, drawing his six-shooters to side me. I thought if he could do it for me, maybe I could do it for somebody else some day. And on top of all that, when the smoke drifted away I realized that there was, sure enough, a time for violence, and we had used it, and maybe we had done some good, because it looks to me as if Judge Willis and Temple Houston and the rest have done what you set out to do. So maybe I didn't need to keep moving after all; maybe I had filled my place—and maybe I had found a new place."

Goodnight said, "She told me you come here hunting Ben."

"I did," said Bart. "But I don't feel it's as important now as it was. With law in the Panhandle, I just realized this morning that it will be a protection for me too, and maybe I can settle down like anybody else. Tom Harding did."

Goodnight nodded, smiling. "I told you wrong about Catherine being here. I wanted to find out first how you felt."

"Satisfied now?" asked Bart.

Goodnight nodded. "Catherine left here about an hour ago," said Goodnight. "She said if you asked, to tell you she's gone back to the Quarter Circle JB Connected."

"Mr. Goodnight, there's one thing you could do for me."

"I'll do a lot of things for you before you're a year older," said Goodnight. "What is it right this minute?"

"You said you had a setting of eggs and a hen for Catherine. I'd kinda like to take 'em with me. Her chickens kept Catherine company."

Goodnight nodded wisely. "Shows you what a judge of character I am. I figured your answers would be satisfactory, and I figured you would ask for the chickens." He pointed to a box. "I've got them all ready. Tie the box on behind your saddle."

Bart smiled broadly. "Thank you, Mr. Goodnight. I—"

"Oh, hell," said Goodnight, embarrassed. "Here's a box of cigars to go with it. You haven't had a decent smoke since you hit the Panhandle."

"That's sure—"

"All right," Goodnight said impatiently. "Now get going. She's waitin'."

Bart got up on the black. He suddenly felt as if he were floating. He rode across country until he saw the cottonwood, and heard carpenter work somewhere ahead. He thought at first that

Goodnight had a crew rebuilding the shed, but there was no activity back there. He rode to the cottonwood and took off the chickens and set down the box. He unsaddled the black and turned it loose. He tucked the still-unopened box of cigars under his arm. Then two riders came over the hill—Arrington and Judge Willis. Bart waited.

Judge Willis said, "Charlie sent me over here. Said you wanted to see me."

"Well, I—"

"I never saw Charlie that wrong," said Arrington.

"Captain," said Bart, "how do I stand with you?"

Arrington shrugged. "What can I do? No complaining witnesses —not even for Gentry."

Bart grinned. The carpentry sounds continued. He said, "I'll see if Catherine is of the same mind."

He went around to the back. Catherine was on a chair, sawing out the door frame at the top.

"What in hell are you doing?" he demanded.

She blushed deep red. "I thought—you might be—oh, Bart!"

She fell from the chair into his arms. She cried for a moment, while he fingered the tight, half-dollar-size curl on her neck. Then she raised her star-bright eyes to his, and only then did he realize that she had not been confident, but only hoping. "You—you're staying!" she said, and began to cry again.

He heard Willis's voice. "It looks as if you two are getting practiced up for after the ceremony. If you can compose yourselves, I'll say the words."

Catherine smiled through her tears. Bart looked down at her and felt a tenderness he had never known before.

Willis went through the words, and pronounced them man and wife. Bart opened the box of cigars and passed them to the men. "If you wait a while," he said, "maybe my wife will mix up some cornbread."

Willis looked at them gravely. "There's a time for fighting," he said, "and a time for loving. There's also a time for riding on."

They rode over the hill, but Bart and Catherine were not watching. They were in each other's arms.